The Actor

BY

NIVEN BUSCH

Simon and Schuster, New York

1955

LIBRARY OF CONGRESS CATALOG CARD NUMBER: 55–6956
MANUFACTURED IN THE UNITED STATES OF AMERICA
BY H. WOLFF BOOK MFG. CO., INC., NEW YORK, N. Y.

To Carmencita

The Actor

1

Let people deny a woman's intuition. She wouldn't argue with them, she could only speak for herself. She always knew! Little things would fall together, what he'd done, the way he'd looked, how much money (most important) he'd in his pocket: she might be as happy as a clam, not giving him a thought, then suddenly the brightest day would turn black, misery would squeeze her heart, her breath stop. God! She would know, she would take her oath on her hope of heaven that Dan was out catting and she would always be right, she hadn't been wrong yet.

She quickened her pace, half-run, half-walk, dragging behind her the little cart she'd made herself out of a Sunkist crate and two wheels off a coaster wagon. She'd found the wheels in the garage after they'd moved back into the house on Lefferts Drive: the rest of the wagon (bright red it had been with golden letters on the side) was long gone and Harold himself, to whom she and Dan had given it one Christmas or birthday, now a grown man. But she liked things put to use. It had been only a few whacks with the hammer to knock on the axle and a handle with a strong crosspiece to hold to.

"Now I don't have to shop at Bond's, that robber," she'd told Dan, her small face gleaming with the pride of craftsmanship. "With this I can go over to the Farmers' Market.

They have such things there, but carrying the damn big paper sacks will break your back. With this I can pop down there in a minute and no weight at all. It will be as good as having another car almost, when you're away. See what I mean? You see?" she demanded, poking her big husband with a stubby, none-too-clean forefinger. It was always good to stir him up with such pokes when she wanted his opinion on some new project.

He had looked down at the crate on wheels from his great height and said slowly and practically, "It's a mile and a quarter each way minimum to Farmers'; it's only a block to Bond's."

"It's my feet and it's my wagon," Jill had said sharply. "What are you crabbing about? You'll eat the food if I tote it home, won't you?"

She looked up at him with her keen birdlike eyes, her head on one side and her nerves jumping with love and irritation.

"Sure, Ma, I'll eat it. I'll eat it all right," Dan said, and went slowly back into the house. Just like him, to crab about the stinking wagon instead of telling her that she'd been smart to use the wheels. She felt what was in his mind: he didn't want the neighbors to see his wife running to the market with a crate on wheels when she'd once let the servants do the shopping and sat back, when she went out, in a custom-built European car with a pair of steer's horns as long as your arm on the radiator. Who cared? Living in the past wouldn't get the bills paid.

The coaster bounced off a curb: Jill crossed Laurel Drive, then carefully pulled up the loaded wagon on the opposite sidewalk: the pang of pain that gripped her had made her forget where she was going. Why, why had he picked today, when she was so happy bringing home the things he liked: the

(4)

tiny, glistening Olympia oysters from Puget Sound, ice cold in their gray juice, locked up in a fresh paper carton, the jelly doughnuts, the fresh-ground hamburger, the French bread and the rest: today of all days when she had been planning a feast, celebrating the turn in their fortunes! He had been working at Columbia Studio—and the check would be a big one: just how much he had refused to say—nor would she spoil his pleasure by demanding to know.

The check! Like the second phase of a cerebral stroke, a new realization came to her: beyond doubt he had picked it up, falsehearted devil that he was, without saying a word to her. He'd picked it up, then gone to blow the whole of it on some floozie. Oh, Sacred Heart of Jesus Who died on the Cross! The shame of it! The uselessness of it, to have a husband like that! Why had the dear Lord in His mercy cursed her with a fickle-hearted thing who would go down the line for any dandiprat who wiggled her butt at him?

The stretches of trotting in Jill's walk had now become longer: sweat trickled out of the bandanna she had wrapped around her hair, a few red strands of which poked damply down above her penciled eyebrows; the legs of her silk slacks flapped around her ankles and her sandals beat a refrain on the sidewalk: clickety-clack. She was a small woman, delicately and yet fiercely made, wiry and strong. She was at this time forty-eight years old and could look thirty-five or ninety, depending on her mood, the way she was dressed, and the slant of the light. Her body had not lost its shape: her breasts were round and tough, her flanks hard and her teeth the same that nature gave her: only in her small, quick, gray-brown eyes, so full of giving, were the anger, the strain of the years, the yearning and the bafflement. She was a fighter. Her face at certain times—as when she had caught Dan in some trans-

(5)

gression—was a fighter's face, formidable, unconquerable, in spite of its fragility, its femininity: a squarish pugface of the sort usually described as Irish (as indeed she was) although such faces are not necessarily Irish at all. Her skin was lightly freckled. In addition to the slacks, bandanna, and low shoes, she wore a silk blouse with green dolphins on it and a gold wrist watch which Dan had given her ten years earlier, on the occasion of their nineteenth anniversary. God damn him, she thought, as the watch, its band now much too big for her, kept sliding down over the hand that dragged the cart. I'll take it off and hock it, then I'll buy a ticket and I'll go away somewhere. I will for sure.

She had now crossed Crescent and Havenhurst, reached Lefferts Drive: she turned north, slowing down somewhat. Here the houses were set back on small dabs of lawn, some shoddy, but most neatly kept. The warm spring day was cooling into evening. Sprinklers sent rainbows of water spinning into the still air and a boy on a bicycle, riding "no hands," threw folded copies of the *Hollywood Citizen-News* into porches, patios, and doorways—and also, alas! into hedges and raingutters. This was her street. Because of the keenness of her perceptions—like the perpetual radar contact with Dan—she would have known it was her street without looking, known by the smells and busy sounds, by the pulse and the hum of it. The street belonged to her and she to it: she would have fitted so well nowhere else on earth. It was a street largely inhabited by workers in the studios located round about: people whose knowledge of certain handicrafts made possible the immense illusion of motion pictures. The citizens of Crescent, Laurel, Havenhurst, Fairfax, Orange, Snell and other nearby streets made pictures with their hands. They were stage carpenters, grips, juicers, musical arrangers,

(6)

draftsmen, greensmen, first and second assistants, extras, camera operators, animators and heaven knows what all: some masqueraders, some plain Sunday stay-at-homers, family raisers, TV lookers. There was a deaf man who had spent his days for twenty years drawing eyelashes on a mouse; there was a comedian whose granite, deadpale features stamped with the image of mankind's mournful and abused innocence had convulsed the whole world and earned him large sums of money and who had put all such foolishness behind him and settled down to live contentedly on charity; there was an acrobat who had taken to drugs and a retired studio librarian who fed a lame quail on her front porch twice a day, also some beautiful young women who went out on call, and other artisans too numerous to mention. Fantasy lived in the flesh of Lefferts Drive, but like all streets it was a place of struggle. Each house, whether neat or dowdy, was the outpost of a secret war: in the perpetual deceptive California summer the same things happened as in streets of far-off cities where the wind howled and the snow piled in drifts: there were sirens, yells in the night, payments missed, wives missed; the meter-reader came, the doctor came, the years went up and down the street with a dusty broom. In only two respects was fantasy supreme, namely the architecture and the clothing—two manifestations of the human spirit which, as scholars would have it, are closely connected. For just as the inhabitants of the street assumed fancy dress each morning, their choice of costume prescribed not by the uses of a craft or by convention but solely by their own dreams, so the bungalows of the street echoed the architectural traditions of the world's romantic places: the Casbah, the Côte d'Azur, and Stratford-on-Avon, cheek to cheek: in one block you might see a Moorish castle, a Normandy chateau, and a villa designed to overlook a South Sea

(7)

lagoon, all constructed in miniature of materials so flimsy it seemed impossible they could have lasted six months let alone the twenty-five or thirty years that some of them had brazened out.

For instance, take the house occupied by Mr. and Mrs. Dan Prader. The windows were all high and pointed, the doors narrow; the roof rolled down in a candy-like curve like the roof of the gingerbread house in *Hansel and Gretel*. Its material was stucco, its color buffalo-chip brindle, its tradition what one wag described as Early Nothing. The only excuse anyone could possibly find for living in such a house would be that he had picked it up at a bank auction, at a colossal saving—yet the incredible fact was that Dan and Jill had built the bungalow to their order, going to special expense to obtain its unique effects, all this in the late twenties, when building costs were high!

Jill ran the cart up the bumpy concrete driveway. The garage, of course, was empty, though by this time (almost six) Dan should have been home for at least an hour. Dumping her groceries on the porch she ran into the kitchen as if to perform some decisive act, but unable to think what act this was to be, she sat down at the table. She put her arms on the table and lowered her face onto them. All the vitality that had sustained her on the trip home from the market had drained away; her will seemed dead, her mind clouded.

"Lord, Lord," she moaned, turning her head from side to side, grinding her forehead against her arms. She doubted her own intuition; she tried hopelessly to escape from its conviction.

"Maybe I'm wrong," she thought. "Maybe he'll be home yet . . . What's the sense of getting all riled up?"

But even as this thought brushed through her she knew

better, felt again the pull of her knowledge of Dan.

"No, no, he's at it. He's out on the town!"

She raised her head. Her eyes were wet. These were no tears of love or softness but simply a fluid squeezed out of her by the tension she was suffering.

"Out on the town!" she cried aloud in the small dim room.

Conscious that it was getting dark, she switched the lights on. She walked to the stove and back, twisting her head to watch the telephone even when her back was turned to it. Where to call, to check on him? He subscribed to a phone exchange run by a woman named Bobbi; everyone in pictures had to have an exchange number if he didn't have a house with servants or the use of a hotel switchboard. But Jill couldn't bear to call Bobbi: the minute she said "has Dan checked?" Bobbi would know her shame. Bobbi would sympathize and make a show of trying to locate him—(hopeless, of course, since he never checked with Bobbi when out on a tear). If she could get a car she might go out and look for him in The Corral, Coyote's, Bellyful of Blues, or other bars frequented by him and his cronies: that might be best. But who would lend the car? Markis Dakropolis, a kindly, middle-aged Greek who lived on Lefferts not too far away might help her out: he was a friend of Dan's, came over sometimes with the boys to play red-dog or poker, losing gladly and invariably for the sake of being with picture people, his idols. But Markis . . . no, she couldn't explain to Markis either, couldn't expose herself: by a freakish contradiction of logic she felt as if to do so would be letting Dan down, betraying her loyalty to him.

There was one chance left. Firmly now, confident as an assistant director passing on an order, she dialed the number of a drugstore on the corner of Gower and Sunset.

"Harry, this is Jill."

"Harry's in the back," the clerk said. "Who is calling?"

"Mrs. Dan Prader. Who is this?"

"It's Melvyn, Mrs. Prader."

"Have you seen Dan, Melvyn? I'm expecting him home and . . . there's an important message for him."

"He's not here, Mrs. Prader. I haven't seen him all day."

"I see. Well, look, Melvyn, would you do me a great favor? Just take a look out front—see if he's out there talking to somebody. He might just be standing there and—"

The drugstore, in an area known as Gower Gulch, was a favorite with Dan and his friends: it occupied the site once adorned by a saddle store and though the latter establishment had been gone for some years its tradition remained vivid: cowhands fresh from the range and others whose only contacts with a horse were booked through Central Casting used the soda fountain and the sidewalk outside as a combined club and job exchange. At almost any hour of the day or evening a few hard-bitten refugees from distant frontiers could be seen there rocking gently on heeled boots, apparently deriving the same reassurance from window displays of douches, vitamins, and heating pads that they had formerly found in guns and tooled leather and a glimpse, through the plateglass, of a saddlemaker working at his bench.

Jill could tell from the cessation of offstage noises at the other end, horns of cars going past and voices in the store, that Melvyn had put his hand over the mouthpiece.

"He's not here, Mrs. Prader," he reported. "Shotgun Emmet's sitting at the counter now having some coffee. He ain't seen him either. I got to go, Mrs. Prader . . ." Melvyn added in a tone of some impatience, as Jill showed no sign of getting off the line, "I got to wait on the customers . . ."

"All right, damn you," Jill said, her rage breaking. "But

(10)

don't expect any more trade from me if you can't even walk as far as the door to look for a . . ."

Realizing she was talking into a dead instrument she slowly hung up and resumed her pacing of the floor.

There was only one thing to do.

Jill opened the grocery sack. She jammed a few sweets in her mouth, then put the oysters, milk and eggs in the icebox. She turned out the kitchen lights, locked up the house and hurried down the street to Mrs. Arden's.

"Dan's loose," she said.

Mrs. Arden was watering her flowerbed.

"What if he is?" she demanded unfeelingly. "He'll come home."

"He went to Columbia to get his check. I've got to get to him before he spends it. He'll be in one of those bars out Melrose or Western, there's only a few he'll go to."

Mrs. Arden nodded. She turned off the hose-bib and began to coil the hose with powerful flexing motions of her large sunburned arms.

"You better come in and have a cup of tea," she said more warmly.

"To hell with tea," Jill said. "I haven't got much time."

Mrs. Arden laughed—not in a derisive but a sympathetic fashion as if Jill's rudeness had revealed for the first time the true nature of the emergency. She now led the way into the house—a miniature Swiss chalet in extremely bad repair—her large body, one undented pour of flesh from thighs to neck, wobbling in a manner which expressed cooperation.

"Jake's dinner is on the stove, potroast," she said. "When he gets here I'll give it to him, then we'll take the car. We'll get the son of a bitch together."

2

At six forty-five P.M. Mr. Jacob Arden, a mill foreman at
Paramount, returned to his home; having been supplied with a
plate of food and an explanation of the current emergency he
consented to the use of his automobile by his wife and Jill
Prader. At the same time, give or take ten minutes, Dan
Prader was standing with his silver belt buckle clamped
against the bar of The Cinch, an establishment on Western
Avenue, drinking his third Orange Crush and looking with
enjoyment at the reflection in the big bar mirror of a young
woman seated, with a female companion, at a corner table.

Dan loved bars. He loved the murk of them, the pungent
liquor smells, the lights which were always slightly dimmed,
the softness of people's movements, the shadowiness of words
and thoughts. He loved the glint of things in bars, of women's
eyes, the slant of faces, the shine of glasses and the colored
glow of bottles, and the feeling of remoteness, the mysterious
authority which set the bar apart, removing it from the coarse
sounds and happenings of the outside world. Strangely
enough, his devotion to the environment of bars was an ab-
straction, an ideal; he himself neither drank nor smoked, regarding both these practices without aversion but with the
conviction that they were not for him. They were all right for
those who understood them; for his part he didn't and had

never, beyond the usual cursory and in his case none-too-happy investigations of a normal boyhood, been prompted to find out more. Once, in the era of his popularity in motion pictures, he had permitted an article entitled "Why I Abstain from Alcohol and Tobacco" to be ghosted over his signature and syndicated through the land and even in foreign countries, a literary effort which did much to confirm the conspicuous position he then held as an idol of the young and, as one highbrow critic expressed it, a genuine American folk-type. Advertisers of breakfast foods, gymnastic equipment, cathartics, bread and other commodities designed for juvenile consumption over Dan's paid endorsement were reassured by his emancipation from the habits which enslaved weaker characters; they knew he would not get them into trouble. It had been taken as gospel by millions of small fry (and taken rightly) that when Dan said in a signed advertisement I EAT CRACKLIES he ate them, and no question about it, just as he performed his own stunts in the pictures which had made him famous. Once a writer for an advertising agency, working on Dan's weekly though rather short-lived radio show, had invented the "Triple-C's" slogan ("Clean Living, Clean Thinking, Clean Teeth") from which had sprung the nationwide Dan-Prader-Triple-C-Clubs, opening up a whole new market for Prader-endorsed products; Triple-C buttons (confirming club membership) were manufactured for Dan personally in large lots and distributed to all who wrote in enclosing twenty-five cents and a dentifrice top. Unfortunately some complication in his studio contract had made it impossible to copyright the Triple-C idea in Dan's name; when he later left this studio, the whole project was taken over intact and conducted from then on with even greater profit by his successor.

It was now more than fifteen years since Dan had starred in

a motion picture but the change in his fortunes, gradual at first, had not altered his personal habits. He still didn't drink or use tobacco because he just didn't like them; he had sometimes wished he liked them better because he saw clearly that, though not praiseworthy in themselves, especially for a man who kept in condition, their use was one of those companionable links which bound people together. He liked people. This, outside of the atmosphere and the freedom from problems, was what he enjoyed most of all in bars: he would stand sipping his soda pop and soaking up the friendliness of people, which he frequently abetted by standing treat, until his own well-being overflowed and he would exhibit the same quick talent for affection and intolerance of opposition as one who was intoxicated by beverages instead of sheer conviviality.

At the moment when he spied the young woman at the corner table he was rapidly reaching this point. He had had an interesting day. He had been here and there. He had talked to friends, received and spent money, and in short, partaken once more of the full life which for some time and particularly in past months, due to poverty, had been mostly denied him. Even the orange pop had begun to taste marvelous. He took another swig of it. He smiled at the girl's image in the mirror and at life in general. All his life he had smiled that way, delighting in the world of men and women and things happening and in his part in it all. He had been awake less than ten hours yet in that period he had already crammed more activity than he had known in the previous eight months of routine living.

The strong and good and happy day had begun for him an hour before noon when the fingers of the payclerk at Columbia Studio picked his check out of a box of other checks and with a quick twinkle like an acrobat's legs folding and unfolding flipped it to him under the grilled window. Dan had thought of going home; he had promised Jill he would—and he had meant to keep his promise—but as he picked up the check and nodded to the twinkle-fingered cashier as if he could pick up a check like this any old morning, a better thought had come to him.

Fifteen minutes later he had parked his car in the driveway of the Lakeview Golf Club.

He had chosen a place well away from the row of gleaming and expensive cars parked closer to the club: he was ashamed of his own vehicle, an ancient Buick, but he locked it carefully before proceeding up the gravel path toward the grillroom entrance. He was an immense man, six foot four, broadly and harmoniously built, slightly more than fifty years old. His heavy-boned, big-featured face showed few signs of age: lines a little deep, maybe, especially two harsh straight ones running like gutters from pits under his broad cheekbones to each side of his mouth: gray hair at the temples in need of a trim. But a good-looking man: that much you could certainly say. Facially, his nose was his best feature—large even for his size, well shaped, with a slight bulge near its tip. His eyes were reddish, deep set, slightly too close together: his brows were shaggy, his mouth generous though a little mean at the corners, his skull broad, almost kingly. His thighs, in the tight levis, bulged with powerful muscles; his large, broad hands were held slightly away from his sides as if pulled out thus by the pressure of the broad shoulders above them. Except for the levis and an old, stained Stetson, his clothes were the height of western fashion, a costume highly decorative even though not entirely in keeping with the décor of a golf club.

As he passed the hedge dividing the path from the caddie

yard, the caddies waiting for loops looked up from their dice and acey-deucy games and studied him with interest. The caddies were the club's unofficial welcome committee, schooled in social niceties as subtle as the conventions of a palace. Recognition from them was accorded only to great names: a cheerful "Hello, King" when Gable strolled past; a subdued boopadoop for Crosby; the cynicism of vocal machine-gun fire when Bogart, nervously assuming a prison-break frown, hurried toward the bar. For Dan Prader they were silent; this generation of caddies just didn't know him. Yet, fifteen years earlier, at the height of his career, he had belonged to this club just as he had to every other organization which, though he might never have had any use for it, seemed a distinction or, above all, cost money.

You made the money. You were supposed to spend it.

In those days, he reflected, the caddies hadn't ignored him. They had lined up at the hedge, jerking their thumbs sideways and yelling with a frantic twang:

"They went thataway . . ."

It was still early; the big room was almost empty. About half a dozen members stood at the bar while a platoon of colored waiters in white suits bustled to and fro in the grillroom adjacent, laying out a lunch of hot and cold dishes on the large buffet beyond. A captain of waiters glanced quickly at Dan and identified him at once as a nonmember. Approaching, the captain asked politely whom he wished to see.

"Mr. L. C. Bulow, if he's in the club," Dan said.

"I think he's in the cardroom, sir. Who shall I say is calling?"

Dan gave his name. In a few minutes the captain of waiters came back to say that Mr. Bulow would be out shortly: would Dan kindly take a seat?

(16)

A small, unseasonable fire was burning in the big stone fireplace; Dan seated himself in one of the leather armchairs in front of it. For a moment he let his mind coast off, remembering the old days when he'd lunched here with the gang. He jerked his thoughts back. Jill was always telling him not to dwell on bygone things and she was right. He sat straight in the upholstered chair—he rarely slumped, even when perfectly at ease—and clasped his fingers, thick as ropes, in front of his belt buckle. Bulow was certainly taking his time: he played a lot of bridge, probably he was in the middle of a rubber. . . .

Idling thus, Dan became conscious of three members in a group not far away, three men he knew: he dealt with the task of remembering who they were. Why, they had occupied these same chairs long ago when he'd been here; they didn't look so different now except that the fat one was fatter and the gray one had turned white. Three old cronies, all retired: Nesbitt, a boozy, quizzical, old-time director; Rex Garr, a tiny snip of a man who had made a fortune out of pictures which, like himself, had been shorts; Fats McArdle, the third, had been a top cameraman in his day . . . but there was something wrong with all of them, something Dan couldn't define at first but which was making itself felt.

"Hello, Dan."

Dan slowly swiveled his head around. He wasn't sure which of the three had spoken but since they had noticed him he nodded round the group.

"Rex! Fats! Nes! How you guys been?"

"Fine, Dan, fine," Nesbitt said in a bored way. He was eating a sandwich: he called the captain of waiters and ordered coffee. Dan looked away again, wondering about Bulow. Garr's voice, thin and raspy, reached him.

(17)

"Been working?"

Dan looked at him in surprise. This was a question which you only asked a man in picture business when you knew he had.

"Sure, some . . ."

"You're looking good," Nesbitt said in a sincere way which he still managed to make ironical.

"Thanks."

Dan was beginning to remember about these three. Each, in the old days, had had his own reason for the daily visit to the club: Nesbitt had come to drink, Garr to brag of his money, Fats to phone his bookmaker . . . but these were only outward reasons: the real truth was that these three men were ghosts. They came to the club to mock those who still kept up the illusion of life.

"You," they seemed to say to those about them, "you will soon realize that you're no different from us. These thrashings of your will are only the convulsions of an animal that has been knifed. Look at us. We won the game, and still we amount to nothing."

Dan tried to clarify this memory about the three old men. He studied them, unconsciously and rudely, and the three cronies, for their part, did not overlook any details of his appearance, the sweat soils on the Stetson he had laid beside his chair or the frayed place where his slash-pocket jacket had been mended. They took satisfaction in such evidences of hard luck in any person, let alone in big, tough Dan who had been such an arrogant louse when he had been Up There. From the hard, brown look about him, the toughness of the skin on his wide cheekbones, the clearness and quickness of his eye, it was evident that Dan still hoped. He kept his body fit, battled against idleness, refused to accept the inevitable. What difference did it make? Soon he would be the way they were, only worse, much worse, because, of course, he had no money. . . .

It was dangerous to kid a man like Dan, yet the temptation to do so was great. All three flirted with it, Garr finally accepting the gambit.

"Zanuck sent for you yet?"

"Huh?"

Dan stared at his tiny tormentor in uncertainty, not sure that he had heard correctly.

"I just heard you were in some deal." Garr appended casually. "Some big picture you had coming up."

Dan's red-brown eyes grew smaller; they seemed to pull closer together. The big nose which kept them apart jutted like a weapon, pointed straight for Garr.

"First I heard about it," he said guardedly.

Nesbitt quickly put in, "Wasn't it in the Trades, Zanuck talked to Danny? Wanted him to replace Marlon Brando in some epic?"

"Cut it out, guys," Fats McArdle said under his breath. He alone was not legged up to this mocking of a man down on his luck; to clear himself of complicity in the unpleasant sport he rose and waddled to a phone booth.

Among these pensioned derelicts themselves, such kidding was the worst of form. Each by the traditions of their comradeship allowed the others their small affectations. If one man, in a burst of egotism, ventured the remark that he would soon be working again, the others accepted this, knowing that the twitching nerve would soon subside. "Going back to work" was just a form of conversation.

Dan turned from Garr to Nesbitt. The muscles of his powerful shoulders tightened. His hands closed into fists, then unclosed. To hit Nesbitt would be homicide. But how he wanted to! How he longed to pick up the thin, mean man, with his sharp, flushed, drinker's face, and throw him through the plate glass window.

"Mr. Bulow! Telephone!"

Dan half rose from his seat but to his surprise Bulow (though he must have seen him) failed to acknowledge his presence; Bulow came out of the cardroom with a harassed look and went to take his call on the bar phone. He seemed to assume that by ignoring Dan he could make him invisible.

Fats came padding back.

"Warcry ran out."

Garr and Nesbitt nodded sympathetically.

"Who expected anything else?" they seemed to be asking.

"I've got a good one in the fourth, though," Fats insisted.

"You mean Golden Hind? They'll have to chase him off the track so they can start the next race."

"Pepsodent. You like Pepsodent?"

Fats looked secretive. "I'm not saying. Wait till the fourth, that's all." But somehow he let it be felt that Pepsodent was the right choice.

Garr smoked fast to hide a chuckle; Nesbitt coughed into his drink. That was the wonderful thing about old Fats; he still thought he could win. Every day, win a little, lose a little, the fortune he had made through twenty years of looking through a lens was draining into the pockets of the bookies.

For the past half-hour the club had been filling with a noisy, cheery noonday crowd made up in part of prosperous business and professional men, in part of their more freakish, anxious and animated co-members from the entertainment trade: writers, producers and actors. The area in front of the bar was crowded and as Bulow, finishing his call, started back to the cardroom, he tried to hide himself in this crowd, angling his course so that he would not have to face in Dan's direction. What the devil was wrong with him? He had been cordial enough a few weeks previous when Dan had come to him with a desperate plea for a loan.

The bastard was afraid of another touch!

Dan got out of his chair. He crossed the room in two or three light bounds, moving on the balls of his feet; he caught Bulow by the arm at the door of the cardroom and spun him around. His air was friendly, almost playful, but his hold was much too tight for friendliness. In this immense grip Bulow's little arm was nothing: he wriggled helplessly; his lower lip dropped down; his body sagged. He was a precise, nattily dressed man of medium size with a sallow face covered with a web of premature wrinkles as if his flesh had been pressed too long against a wire mesh. He was a former actor turned realtor, extremely niggardly but shrewd and quite successful at his new trade. When Dan had come to him in distress Bulow had lent him fifty dollars (Dan had asked a hundred) not out of generosity but so that he could brag of having befriended a man once as well known as Dan had been. By mentioning the loan he could obliquely call attention to his own success, in contrast to Dan's fallen state.

Now he regretted a thousand times over that he had ever made the loan. The muscles of his arm spasmed in Dan's grip. He lost his balance as Dan spun him around. With a deceptively gentle and friendly look Dan peered down at the startled man.

"I didn't come to ask for more but to pay what I owe," he said. "Here, now take this and get it cashed for me and I'll square up."

Letting go of the realtor, who staggered back, Dan pushed a

(21)

paper into his hands—the check he had brought from the studio. In his haste and rage, to which he had been partly whipped up by the goading of the cronies by the fire, he hadn't thought to separate the check itself from the invoice describing the services rendered. Seeing Bulow look at the typing above the perforated line, he regretted his carelessness. Out of vanity he would have preferred that the other think he had received the check for acting rather than the type of job for which it had been issued. Still, never mind. The main thing was to get the money and get out of here.

"Well, is it all right?" he demanded.

Bulow flinched.

"Why sure, Dan, sure. I guess we can take care of it. Heck, I'm glad to see you. Sorry you had to wait so long. Those vultures in there had me hooked and I guess I sort of forgot about you. How have you been, anyway?"

The realtor brought out this speech in jerks, flicking his eyes right and left to take note of anyone who might have seen Dan spring on him. His color was coming back but he was still discomposed; he fumbled eagerly for words which would restore a normal feeling to this confrontation. He was afraid of Dan. How could you know what to expect from an idiot who made his living falling off a horse? The way he'd jumped across the room: the way he'd grabbed him! He was like a frigging tiger! Maybe all those falls had made him saddle-happy.

"Can you get it cashed for me?" Dan insisted without friendliness.

"Why, maybe, maybe so," Bulow said. He took out a fine French handkerchief and rubbed his face as if to scour away the wrinkles and his fear of Dan at the same time. "We're supposed to be limited to fifty bucks a day, you remember

(22)

how it was," he went on confidentially. "But I'll talk to the manager. You know, Ad Sykes. He remembers you. We were talking about you just the other day, and he may do it. You stay right here. I'll go and see. Then maybe we can have some lunch . . ."

He edged away, instantly vanishing in the crowded room. More men had been coming in all the time; the air was full of smoke and talk and cocktail smells. Now and then the sweet odor of close-cropped, rolled and watered grass billowed in from the ninth green and fairway as members, reaching the turn, entered the club for lunch.

Dan remained standing by the cardroom door. He stood staring out over the heads of those about him, out of place in his outlandish, shabby clothes, intractable, walled up. He was considering Bulow's invitation to lunch. Bulow had started out by snubbing him, now he wanted to pretend everything had been all right. He was a coward, only bold to those who he believed were helpless or beneath him: if you hurt or frightened him he wriggled like a cur and tried to cozy up.

Dan looked longingly at the huge buffet, the roasts dripping gravy in their rich-looking silver platters, the cold tongues and turkeys and aspics, the colored boys standing deferentially behind the gleaming napery and tableware, raising the covers so members could inspect the hot dishes. He would have loved to taste this food. He would have liked above anything to hear some shop talk, eat with the other guys, the successes, as an equal. But to stay on charity, because Bulow had acted badly and now wanted to make up for it, this was no good; to eat that way would spoil the great feeling, his for today, of having money in his pocket, of being his own man.

"Well, partner, here you are."

Bulow was grinning. He stood there holding the money,

$422.05, wrapped in the invoice which (perhaps out of tact) he'd turned face down. Now he was even trying to talk western style in order to show what a buddy he was, apparently unconscious of the fact that Dan had worked for years with a fair amount of success to eliminate these westernisms from his own speech.

"Thanks," Dan said coldly. He counted out the fifty that was owing, rammed the balance into his pants pocket. "I can't eat with you," he said. "I've got a date."

Bulow was visibly relieved but still not quite at ease with their relationship. "Come over any time, Dan," he went on quite decently. "This is your old stamping ground, remember, pal; you ought to drop around more often."

"I may do that," Dan said. If he ever did it sure as hell would not be to see Bulow.

He shook hands sourly and briefly and left the grillroom; as he passed the caddie enclosure an unidentified urchin voice inquired where he'd left his horse but Dan did not stop to search out who had spoken. He climbed into his Buick and after half a dozen grinding tries with the starter got it going and drove carefully out the big gate, past the smooth sunny greenery dotted with the little figures of men playing: men who had nothing better to do than swat a ball around a cow pasture.

Dan drove with care. Having spent much of his life on horses he did not trust cars; he neglected engine repairs to spend money on lifeguard tubes. On the road he hugged the righthand lane, sitting way back and clutching the upper part of the wheel with both hands. His top speed when in motion was seldom over forty-five miles an hour; on the Freeway, where everyone went seventy, he slowed down to thirty, grinding his teeth and the gears at the same time, and glaring straight ahead with his Indian-looking eyes.

At one point in the trip, he fished out his roll of money and looked at it with appreciation. With a roll like that you could do things. You could go places. It was satisfying to be well supplied with money. He would never, he decided, be without it again.

One thing about his lovely wealth annoyed him—the invoice which he had stupidly let Bulow see and which was still there, wrapped around the wad of bills. Dan pulled it off, crumpled it, and threw it out; it blew along the Freeway in the backwash of the car, immediately absorbed in the highway scurf of empty cigarette packages, sandwich wrappers, beer bottles and what-not. Yet the invoice was not like these faceless and meaningless objects. It told a story. It presented in a sense the profile of a man—a portrait in arithmetic which, after deductions for tax withholding, social security, and a donation to the Motion Picture Relief Fund, was itemed:

Two days	$ 74.90
Extra time	47.15
Mount and rideout	50.00
Falls from horse (2)	250.00

3

The story of Dan's progress from ninety-dollar-a-month cowhand to motion picture star was often related in the days of his fame; it was given out ever freshly in personal interviews with the star himself, broadcast on the radio and distributed in mimeographed handouts by the Monahan Studios, his employers at that time. His descent from public favor had been less publicized: it followed a Hollywood pattern so familiar that no one had thought it worth examining. The truth was that, having squandered the large sums of money he had earned, he had recently been reduced to making a living by the same means he had used when he first broke into pictures: doing stunts. Josephine Dillingham Heston, later his wife, had been responsible for his rise, just as when hard times came she had assumed the task of maintaining his hope, ambition, and physical fitness so that a return to greatness still seemed possible.

Jill had been a script girl working eight-day westerns at Monahan. She was holding script on one called *Devil's Out-Post* on the day when Dan was first summoned from a Vine Street boarding house to perform a routine fall and rideout; she had been impressed with him and on the last day of the picture, when he was scheduled to double the star in a fight scene, she had taken him aside.

"Listen, when they yell cut don't move. Stand in your marks and talk, brush off the other guy's clothes or something; then look over to me and smile and say 'Hi, kid.' Say anything, just so they hear your voice."

"Who's going to hear it after they cut?"

"Just do what I'm asking you," Jill said. "What have you got to lose?"

It was an unofficial test, made with the friendly compliance of a camera operator and soundman who neglected to stop rolling when they were told to. Dan was given a studio contract and he and Jill were married a few months later in the Church of the Good Shepherd with the personnel of Dan's stuntman's boarding house in attendance. Shotgun Emmet arrived in a stagecoach with the four Dollarhyde brothers and Steece Livermore brought his trick pony and made him lie down on the pavement when the bride and groom came out. But the best gag of all was pulled by Jennings Cole, a special effects man from United Artists who wired Dan's car with a bomb which went off when he stepped on the starter, letting out a terrifying blast and a thick cloud of blue smoke. Jill began sobbing right then and kept it up halfway to Tia Juana.

"Knock it off, honey," Dan said at length. "The boys were only kidding. They didn't mean any harm."

"That's not what I'm crying about," Jill said between sobs.

"Well, then what is it, for God's sakes?" Dan demanded.

"It's only that—I guess no girl in the world ever had such a wonderful wedding."

Such anecdotes as this made pleasant telling; they had been included, with minor expurgations, in Dan's publicity. Dan himself, enjoying their flavor when he saw them in print, often repeated them; he told his son, Harold, stories about Bannerman's boarding house and the people who lived there. But always and eminently he paid tribute to Jill. "That little gal," he stated in an interview for the *Saturday Evening Post*, "is the reason I got some place." Nor had the change in his fortunes caused his loyalty to tarnish; even on the slight spree, for instance, which he allowed himself after cashing his check, he had not forgotten her. By no means. His first act, for instance, on leaving the Lakeview Club had been to visit a Hollywood importer where he bought Jill a present: a sort of pendant made of Mexican silver, centering an Indian's face cut out of real turquoise or some stone just as good. Only when this was safely his, wrapped in tissue paper and buttoned in his shirt pocket, did he pick up some things he needed for himself . . . principally a new Triple X Stetson, valued at forty dollars marked down to twenty-five for him by J. C. Gebbard of the Sunset Saddlery; it was a new color, Colorado Fawn. With the hat he had picked up a few shirts—even Jill had admitted that he needed these—and a pair of boots that were halfway respectable. At fifty dollars the boots had been practically a gift but, as Gebby pointed out, Dan had brought him plenty of business; often in the old days he had outfitted an entire company at the Saddlery. Gebby had never forgotten. He still kept a photograph of Dan over the cash register.

Old Geb always gave his friends a break on prices; his loyalty in this respect had induced Dan to buy one item which, perhaps, might not have been strictly necessary, but was a stand-out and might lead to jobs: a tight slash-pocket jacket made of mackinaw cloth, faced with a double row of concha buttons. Jill would be sure to say it wasn't worth the seventy-eight fifty it had cost but she'd be wrong as usual: a jacket like that was a once-in-a-lifetime opportunity and Gebby had thrown in the conchas—worth at least six dollars—free.

(28)

Dan got a pair of frontier pants to round off the outfit. He had been tempted to donate to charity the old, trashy clothes he'd worn coming in, so distasteful were they to him now, but at Gebby's suggestion he had allowed them to be mailed home. Well, Jill could give him credit for that much economy anyhow, and the old stuff would do to work out in.

Togged in his new trappings, Dan cut a splendid figure in The Cinch. As he looked around the modest bar, quiet now, but rapidly filling up with its regular customers (mostly crew people, bit-part actors, and extras from the nearby studios) a spirit of confidence and generosity moved him. He felt more than ever that the woman whose face and sloping, giving-in-type shoulders appeared so attractive, was worthy of some attention.

"Wingy," he said in a firm, jarring voice, "take the little lady in the corner a drink with my compliments. And the broad with her, too."

"Yes, sir. Coming up, sir," Wingy said cheerfully.

He could afford a few treats; he felt that there was no use worrying about money. He had failed, it is true, to do well in the betting room where he had stopped briefly after leaving Gebby's. Fats McArdle had mentioned the horse, Pepsodent, and Fats was no fool. Also, Pepsodent was a toothpaste and his radio sponsor, when he played the Ringo Kid, had been a toothpaste manufacturer. It had seemed like an omen and if he'd had sense enough to bet the horse across instead of on the nose he would have been all right: the damn camera, in fact, was all that beat the Pepsodent horse—a photofinish. Jill would certainly forgive the dent in his bankroll when she saw the pendant, proof that he'd been thinking of her. . . . But would she? She could be tough at times, she could be god-damn tough! Needing some confirmation of his own belief in

(29)

the pendant's efficacy he took the gift out of his pocket and unwrapped the tissue paper that protected it.

"Wingy, take a look at this."

The one-armed bartender moved away from another customer, with whom he had been chatting.

"By God, Mr. Prader, that's a beautiful thing."

"Little giftie I picked up for the wife," Dan explained. "I figure she'll like it. Women kind of go for those things, wouldn't you say?"

"The woman who wouldn't go for that wouldn't appreciate good things, Mr. Prader," Wingy said. "I wish I could afford to take one home myself."

Dan was both pleased and reassured. He rewrapped the pendant and put it out of sight.

"Quit kidding. You could afford to take home diamonds."

This was true. The Dollarhyde brothers had all done well —beside Wingy there was Collin, a stuntman, Wick, an insurance salesman and the fourth, Art, smartest of all, who owned the stable where he had once boarded Thunder.

A picture of the famous horse was displayed in a row of other stills, some of them almost as old, above the bar mirror.

"To the Dollarhydes—from Thunder."

It was a beautiful picture: the black stallion stood at a fence rail, his ears forward and his neck turned toward the camera. Through years of practice Thunder had learned how to pose: Dan had bragged of him that he could upstage most actors and any leading lady. In the picture he let you miss none of his points—the powerful slope of his shoulders or the bulge of his quarters or the compactness of his strong, short back which a stock saddle would completely cover. He was a quarterhorse bred of a Morgan-Arab strain, for weight and

(30)

power combined with a capacity for bursts of speed and sudden stops: the Morgan showed in the great curving neck, the Arab in the beautiful, small, tapering head under the wide brows. His eyes were gentle and intelligent, his glistening body charged with male sexuality for the benefit of the horse world and with courage and strength and intelligence for the benefit of humans.

Thunder had been six years old when the picture was taken, just coming into his prime: at that time he had been as well known as Dan himself, one of the half-dozen most celebrated horses in the world. He had been the best horse Dan had ever owned, the best horse, he often thought, that any man had ever owned; every time he saw the photograph he missed the stallion with a deep pang of loyalty and longing.

"We'll be together again some day," he thought.

Sometimes to comfort himself for his loss he pictured Thunder where he was now, twenty-two or twenty-three years old, on the Nevada ranch of a friend who had taken him when things got tough and put him out to stud. Hell, yes: Thunder was a hundred, a thousand times better off and happier on the free range up there than in some lousy boarding stable or even working in pictures. Dan could imagine him running on the springy earth covered with rich grass, through wild, sweet air that smelled of mares and waterfalls. Thunder romped on the hills at dawn and stood in shady canyons when the sun was hot; in the afternoon he browsed beside fast streams which broadened into yellow shallows, easy to drink from, and at night the mares bunched round him as he stood hipshot under a cottonwood or lay on the moist earth and slept.

"That horse has it made now," he told Wingy.

From Thunder's lovely image his eye strayed to the portrait

next to it—Ernst Lubitsch, signed slantingly across the cigar:

"To Wingy,
> *Gesundheit!*
>> *Ernst."*

"You sure used to get a bunch of directors in here," he told Wingy reminiscently. "I got myself more'n a dozen jobs in the old days, standing right here at this bar."

"That's before you was the Ringo Kid, Mr. Prader. After that you didn't have no trouble getting jobs, sir," Wingy said respectfully.

With Wingy it was never "Dan" or "Danny-boy" the way it was with some of these punks who wanted to show how familiar they could be. With him it was "Sir" or "Mr. Prader."

"They still come in," the bartender added, "only not to see their pals the way they used to—they come in when they want to hide out." Lowering his voice slightly he added, "Lucky Mansfield's in the back room now with Miranda Dobbs."

"He is?"

"Roy Sowells is with them," Wingy said. "I guess you know him too, don't you?"

"I know all of them. Known 'em for years, Wingy," Dan said, his eyes blinking as they always did when his mind was working at top speed.

"That's what I thought, sir," Wingy said. He did not say it as if he were definitely planting an idea. Yet, looking back on it, Dan wondered if he had been.

Wingy knew the score. From the trade gossip passed across his bar he knew which people were working and which weren't; how much those who were working had been paid, and how badly those who weren't needed a job.

(32)

It was no time to be stand-offish. Lucky had risen to become one of Duart's most important directors; here was an acquaintanceship which should certainly be renewed, explored for future developments. True, Dan remembered vaguely some disagreement he had had with Lucky on the set of *Border Badmen,* the last picture he'd been in that Lucky had directed —but an old beef was not necessarily important: Lucky by now might have forgotten all about it. Miranda also was a friend: she and Dan had worked together when she was a flip, sexy kid, just starting to go places in pictures while he had been on the way out. He had taught her how to handle an upstaging male juvenile and she had been grateful. Well, this would be her chance to show her gratitude, put in a word for him with Lucky.

But he himself must make the first move! He must and he would. He'd go and shake hands with old Lucky. Two cronies from the great days. Shouldn't such men stick together?

He must act now, while the idea was fresh. He had never been good at selling himself: he couldn't bear to crawl to those On Top. But never mind. This was a chance, perhaps a heaven-sent one, to improve his condition.

4

With a few strides Dan crossed the barroom. He pushed aside the old-fashioned red curtains screening the dining alcoves in the rear. While he stood in the doorway peering round, a party of three people at a nearby table, a handsome brunette woman and two men, took note of his presence.

"Why, Dan Prader! You old horse's end!"

Miranda Dobbs was smiling up at him, her smooth mouth spreading into a lovely sensuous O.

"Dobbsy! How are you, honeypie?" Dan said with a fine affectation of surprise.

He remembered reading something in a column about Miranda having a romance with Mansfield. Possibly it was because of this that they were dining in a hideaway joint like The Cinch—also why they had brought along Roy Sowells. Miranda, whose divorce from some society jerk was not yet final, was particular about avoiding gossip.

But now was no time to worry about matters of this kind.

"You look great, but simply great," Miranda was saying. "You know these gentlemen, don't you? Roy Sowells—Lucky Mansfield."

"We know each other," Dan said heartily. "And how! Hi, Lucky. Hello, Roy."

Big Roy Sowells half rose from his seat. "Greetings!" he said. He was a baldish fellow who had once played football for S.C., later serving with greater effort and fewer plaudits as first assistant on the early Ringo Kid pictures in which Dan had starred.

Lucky Mansfield, bone-thin, reserved and wary, remained seated; he nodded in a manner which was not exactly rude but was not friendly either—just superior and exasperating.

"Sit down, Danny-boy," Miranda said with a reproachful look at Lucky. "Give us the scoop. Where have you been hiding?"

"Oh, I got me a cave up in the hills," he kidded back,

pulling out a chair. "I hole up there when the going gets rough."

Miranda laughed as if this was very funny. Her pleasure in Dan's company seemed to increase in direct proportion to Lucky's mounting taciturnity.

"You haven't changed," she said to Dan. "Except you're more beautiful than ever. Where'd you get the pile of threads?" She touched the sleeve of his bright new jacket. "My! And concha buttons yet. What kind of cave is this you're living in? Have you got a weaver up there with you?"

"I've been working," Dan said, grinning. He was afraid Lucky might have got the wrong impression from his phrase about the going being rough: if they thought you couldn't get a job they never wanted you. He added definitely, "Just finished at Columbia. Got one coming up at U-I in a couple of weeks."

"That's swell, Danny," Miranda said. "I'm awfully glad. And Harold's doing well too, isn't he? I see him on the lot sometimes."

Dan's face took on the wooden look he always got when anybody talked about his son, Harold.

"Hey, Wingy!" he called, wishing to change the subject. "Some drinks for this table!"

"Coming up, sir," Wingy called from the bar.

"Skip me," Roy Sowells said. He patted Miranda's arm and sauntered off to the john.

"We've got to go pretty soon," Lucky said.

Dan turned rather worriedly to Miranda.

"You'll stay for this round, won't you?"

"Of course," Miranda said. "We all will. It's wonderful to see you, you old horse-pistol."

She began to chat about the last time they had worked together, possibly to stir up Lucky. Dan looked at her hungrily and she sparked back at him prettily, pretending to mistake the desire in his glance for polite social interest. One star who'd never had makeup poisoning, Miranda was allergic to nothing except lack of attention. The red knit dress she was wearing gave her dark skin a bloom like camellias and showed off her big breasts and tiny waist; only the faintest suggestion of a double chin betrayed her age slightly—not enough to bother anyone except a first cameraman. In a few years, perhaps only a few months, she would begin to have a middle-aged look, but now she was perfect, vulnerable, and ready.

If Lucky had really been romancing her Dan envied him. He suddenly disliked the director intensely—his little mustache, his superior, knowing manner, his pale skin and polished nails, even his salt-and-pepper suit and the red scarf he wore with it. It struck him forcibly that Lucky was not being cordial: his own manner altered correspondingly.

"Lucky," he burst out, "are you teed off that I sat down with you?"

"Of course he's not," Miranda put in quickly.

"I'd like him to answer, Dobbsy," Dan said. "I want to get this straight, because if I am not wanted I can go. I don't aim to intrude."

Wingy brought the drinks that Dan had ordered, putting them down beside the empty dessert plates and half-filled coffee cups of Lucky's party.

"We're glad to have you, Dan," Lucky said with the most civility he had shown so far. "But as I say, we were about to leave."

The answer seemed to satisfy Dan temporarily. He nodded

(36)

several times. The excitement of the day had dimmed his wits as if he had been drinking. He took a nip of his soda pop.

"Mud in your eye, Danny-boy," Miranda said.

"Thanks, honey, thanks a lot," Dan said, eyeing Mansfield. "Tell me one thing more, Lucky. Have you got anything against me? Anything we ought to settle?"

Mansfield did not draw back from the implied threat the way most people drew away from Dan when he showed irritation—the way Bulow, for instance, had done. He sat looking at the bigger man with cold antipathy.

"Not that I know of," he said truculently. "Something with you?"

"Hell, no, man," Dan said heartily. He felt relieved. Lucky was loosening up somewhat; now, if ever, was the time to make his move.

"Lucky," he cried, gripping the director's forearm, "you know what I can do. Is that right?"

"You've been up there with the best of them, if that's what you mean," Lucky said. He signaled for his check.

With an effort of will, Dan suppressed his annoyance.

"That's the truth, man," he cried, "and you're the one that knows. I can ride and I can act. The old body's still the same. See this? No lard there, my good friend. . . ." He hit himself a blow on his flat belly with his fist and glared at Lucky. "See what I mean?"

The director, adding up the bill, did not reply, but Roy Sowells, who had returned from his trip to the men's room in time to hear the last part of this speech, put in tactfully, "You sure look as if you lived right, Dan."

Dan put back his head and roared with laughter.

"You can say that again," he declared stoutly. Once more he addressed Lucky. "What I mean is," he went on, "I'm available. No use dishing out a lot of crap. I've been working, but I could work more. You just said yourself that I'd been Up There. Well, I can be again. One good part is all it takes. I'll knock their brains out and you'll get the credit."

He felt that he was saying too much, not exactly phrasing what he had in mind. His approach, so far, might have seemed too much like bragging. This would have to be corrected.

"Lucky," he said. "Man to man, now. We've had arguments maybe; who cares? We've made pictures. We've done things these bellhops they call directors now could never do . . ."

At least the approach was honest. It was on the right track. Miranda's big eyes glanced from Dan to Lucky; she laughed in a throaty, flattering way. Dan could feel she was on his side. He leaned forward. His face was now only a few inches from the director's.

"Here's the situation, Lucky. The salary is right. The talent is right. And I'll tell you something most people don't know. I'm through with stunts. Give me a role, I don't care what it is. Give me the lines to say, and see what happens. Sure, I can throw some nag ass over tip, but who wants that? Lines, man! That's when the people shove that folding stuff into the box office. They remember. And how they remember! The name of Prader stands for entertainment. Spot me in, Lucky," he concluded, letting his voice roll out. "Just one break— and we'll show them something great the way we did the last time."

"You mean," Mansfield inquired coldly, "something as great as that rescue scene in *Border Badmen*?"

The friendly light faded out of Dan's eyes. He now remembered with amazing clarity the arguments he had had with Lucky on this picture: the scenes they'd fought about, and Lucky's stubbornness and stupidity.

"No, Lucky, no. I didn't mean that rescue. But—have it your own way," he continued, forcing warmth back into his voice in a manner which he felt sure Jill would have admired —she was always telling him he was so tactless with the people who could do him good—"Hang it on the rescue scene and leave it go at that. That is, if you don't want to remember the poker game out in the backroom . . ."

"Poker game?" Lucky said vaguely. "And what in your opinion," he said in his offhand, superior manner, so infuriating to a person who had tried to be friendly, "just what was wrong with that poker game?"

Dan pressed his lips together. He had made an effort; now he gave way inwardly. Lucky had gone too far. He had tempted him once too often.

"Direction!" Dan said firmly. "Direction, Lucky! That's what was wrong with that scene. And nothing else. Just a little matter of direction!"

Lucky stared at him. He looked from Roy to Miranda.

"You would have done it different, I suppose?"

"I would!"

"Boys, boys," Miranda said delightedly.

"Weren't you guys leaving?" Roy inquired of Miranda and Lucky—but the director did not take the hint.

"This I would like to hear!" he said, studying Dan. A tightening was noticeable now in the director's waxy face.

"All right, partner," Dan said. "Look: instead of all that chatter about who cheated who when they woke up next morning, why not something like this? They wake up, see, and he reaches over . . ."

"Great," said Mansfield, winking at Roy, "let's reshoot the whole picture. Hell, it was only made in nineteen twenty-seven . . ."

Miranda touched Dan with her silky leg to prod him on.

". . . He reaches over," Dan said. "I mean the character that I played—Butch. He reaches over and the other guy is still sleeping. So Butch just takes an ace out of the other guy's sleeve. That tells you the whole story without a line of dialogue. Get it?"

"He's right," Miranda said, who had never seen the picture. "I remember the scene, and he's absolutely right." Her love affair with Mansfield, cooling recently, had reached the point at which she liked to see him lose his temper—and was ready to assist toward this end.

Mansfield ignored her.

"I don't write scripts, I shoot them."

"That's right," Dan said. "I guess that's what you do. Directors nowadays are nothing but bellhops, as I just said," he went on, forgetting that he had specifically excepted Mansfield from this category. "The real directors wrote, the ones I worked with. They were creative people . . ."

"You mean the washed-up bums that made your big horse operas, *Coyote's Hole* and *Eagle's Dong* and that stuff?" Mansfield said. He was now openly angry. Miranda laughed again. The altercation was developing beyond her expectations.

"I mean guys like Willie Wyler. You think he doesn't write?" Dan demanded. "Don't fool yourself. He writes! That's why he makes masterpieces, not crap. He works with pantomime. And Howard Hawks! He's a bum, I suppose? I've seen old Howard sit down on a set and rewrite a whole goddamn script while he was shooting it . . ."

(40)

"How did you get to see him, were you on a studio tour?"

Dan did not see fit to answer this. "Believe me," he said, "when they named you Lucky they named you right. The luckiest day you ever had was when some regular director was too busy and they let you take a second unit out. There's a lot of second unit men shooting first unit today, that's what's the matter with our business . . ."

"Now, Mansy, control yourself. He's too big for you," Miranda cautioned as Mansfield rose from his chair.

Eyeing Dan, who had not moved, Lucky decided to take her advice.

"I've had about enough," he said. "Come on, Miranda."

Miranda brushed Dan's body as she got up. By way of fare-well she put the tips of her fingers on his cheek, fingers which carried with them the faint, indefinable scent of an expensive woman.

"Now you've done it, you character," she said. "Aren't you sorry?" She made a pouting mouth at him, then calling, "Lucky! Lover! Wait for me!" she turned from the table and ran after the director, her heels tapping on the tile floor. Lucky was almost through the red curtain when she caught up with him and took his arm: with a reproachful, flirtatious look at Dan she sashayed, her full flanks swaying deliciously, out of the room.

5

Dan sat bent forward at the table, plunged in gloom. Well, his intentions had been good; he'd tried to say the right thing even if he had not gone about it in a skillful way. He'd tried; he'd tried for Jill's sake, more than anything, knowing how much a job in one of Lucky's pictures could have helped their fortunes. Was it his fault that he'd failed? It was hard to stomach arrogance, insults, and mockery, especially from one of Lucky's caliber—a nobody, really. Never, never had he been able to crawl on his belly, to accept humiliation. He remembered how he'd once faced them all, the lawyers and the yes-men and the studio top brass, one day long ago when they had called a conference to discuss renewal of his contract. He had faced them with the same anger lashing in his guts that he'd experienced just now when Lucky spoke to him so coldly, so disdainfully.

"Gentlemen," he'd said, speaking with a dignity that hid his rage, "it boils down to this: either I get my salary plus ten per cent of all the Ringo Kid productions or you find yourself another boy."

His agent, Nol McClure, had looked at him in terror; this last speech had not been part of the act they had rehearsed so carefully. Nor had it been in line with Nol's final plea, as they were entering the studio gate. "Danny, this time for God's sake let me do the talking!"

Old Quib Monahan, the studio boss, moved a chaw of tobacco from one cheek to the other. In those days they had called Quib "King of the Quickies": he had pioneered in low-budget westerns and the small studio which he controlled made nothing else.

"I'm sorry, Dan, we've tried to explain why we can't do that, not for you or any star. If you stick to this demand, we're parting company."

"I do stick to it, Quib," Dan said. "I'll stick to it to the end," and Quib had slowly nodded his bald dome. He'd flipped a switch on his desk and said to his secretary, "Call Stage Two right away and have Shortie Williams come over here!"

And then, right there in front of Dan, Quib had told Shortie he was the new Ringo Kid!

All the trouble he'd had since had really grown out of that conference, the hazards set up then, by that one afternoon's negotiations—perhaps by that single wrong speech of his—snowballing through the years. Shortie, of course, had gone on and up. But where was Quib Monahan today? Retired—running a turkey ranch somewhere near San Diego, and the lawyers and the agents who had witnessed his, Dan's, downfall, they too were scattered or in other jobs, many of them no longer in film business. Such a fate, he felt sure, waited for a man like Lucky Mansfield. Big men could take suggestions, jerks resented them—jerks who would most likely wind up in the garbage can. While Roy Sowells ordered another drink, he went into a waking reverie in which Lucky, broke, and wearing ragged and soiled clothes, approached him as he entered a fashionable restaurant and asked for a handout. At first Dan pretended not to hear the derelict's plea, then he turned back and gave him three dollars, peeling the money from a roll he had won on a horse. The people on the sidewalk looked at him in admiration and he heard somebody say, "It's Dan Prader, God bless him: the Academy Award Winner . . ."

"The stupid jerk!" he said aloud.

Roy swung slowly around to face him.

"Who?"

"Lucky Mansfield. Who else?" Dan said with great feeling.

Roy settled back into the pads of flesh which had replaced the canvas and leather upholstery of his football-playing youth. He showed no disturbance at being left behind by the director's hasty exit with Miranda: it occurred to Dan that, if Roy had been carried as a chaperon, it had been arranged in advance for the other two to split off after dinner.

"Maybe . . . maybe. But first of all, you shouldn't have given such a play to Dobbsy. She acted like she kind of likes you, and that made him madder still. Second of all, why did you tell him you were through with stunts? There's a stunt job coming up at Duart you could handle fine: two or three weeks' work, and you might even ramrod."

"If it's with Mansfield, I wouldn't want it."

"It's in a Von Kramm picture. Maybe you could get Harold to speak to Von Kramm about you."

"I'm not interested in the job. And above all I'm not interested in Harold."

Roy persisted. "He could speak to Von Kramm. That's about all it would take. Harold rates just as high as Lucky— maybe higher. They say he'll be directing Deluxes soon; Lucky is still doing Specials."

Dan's son, Harold, a director at Duart, did not use the name of Prader, being known professionally as Harold Heston.

(44)

"I'm not talking to that phony, so let's forget it."

Roy shrugged; he made one more attempt.

"You need the job . . . why not quit crapping around?"

"I'll never call him."

Roy looked at him in puzzlement. He had not anticipated this resistance to what he regarded as a sensible idea. With Dan's interests at heart, he went on in blundering but kindly fashion. "You raised him, didn't you? Who are you going to for help, if you can't go to your own kith and kin?"

He had intended saying more but broke off suddenly, appalled at the fury in Dan's face.

"Who asked you to sit with me, anyway?"

"You were the one who sat with us, remember?"

"Well, never mind who sat with who. You stink, and this conversation stinks."

"I'm beginning to believe you're right."

"Then why don't you take a powder?"

"If that's the way you want it."

"You're damn right that's the way I want it."

"Okay, then. So long, Dan."

"So long."

"There," Dan said in a loud tone, addressing the room at large as Roy paid for his final drink and left the bar. "There is a football-playing bum. One of those guys that never grew up. I'm glad he's gone."

Wingy Dollarhyde cautioned, "We're all friends here."

"Are we?" Dan demanded belligerently. "How you gonna prove that?"

"Doesn't need proof, Dan," Wingy insisted. "Either you're a friend or you're not. To me you're a friend. Am I wrong?"

Dan stared at him uncertainly, then roared with laughter.

"You're not wrong, Wingy," he said. "Not a goddamn bit

wrong. We're friends and you know it. Have been for years. Am I right or am I right?"

"You're right, sir," Wingy said, relieved.

Dan laughed again, more moderately this time, and with this laugh he felt his anger at Roy leaving him—and even his disgust with Lucky Mansfield: at the moment it was hard to remember why he had been angry with either of them.

He pulled out all the money he had and laid it on the table in front of him.

"Wingy," he roared in his tremendous voice, "I'm buying drinks for all."

6

It was then, in the intoxication of friendliness, in the liking and comradeship of those about him, that he had remembered the young woman at the corner table. Her name, it turned out, was Josie, and she and her companion, a relative named Miss De Lap, were dental technicians from Atlanta, Georgia, visiting in Hollywood.

It was pleasant to discover that Josie, in spite of her apparent youth, was not too young to have seen some of his pictures.

"You were my favorite, Mr. Prader," she said with a subdued trace of southern accent.

Dan ordered Wingy, in kingly tones, to put money in the

jukebox. He excused himself from Miss De Lap and danced, at first reservedly, then with abandon, with the brownhaired beauty, Josie. He discussed taking her to Mocambo.

Bored with her friend's flirtation, the older woman left: she had a date to see *The Robe* with a friend from Mobile. Dan and Josie ordered steaks, then had a final round of drinks— Orange Crush and Scotch old-fashioned. Mocambo was now definitely on the near horizon. Josie went to the ladies' room, weaving slightly, delicately tipsy; when she came back to the table she cuddled against Dan and he kissed her, their lips clinging for a protracted time. Now out of funds, he started a new account, charged the final drinks and the dinner, then made Wingy cash a check (which both of them knew would bounce) to finance the Mocambo expedition.

The entire clientele of The Cinch, which he had treated twice, toasted him as he led Josie out, his arm around her waist, her acquiescent body closely pressed to his. In this posture they stood on the corner looking for a taxi, for in his role as a current star (which he maintained for Josie's benefit) the old Buick would never do.

No taxi stopped but, with a squeal of brakes, another car did—an old sedan with two women in it. Dan, looking over his shoulder, saw the woman sitting next to the driver of this car leap out and bear down on him, bent forward like some predatory animal. Dan was shaken. His quickness of mind, which he had frequently retained even in situations of great physical hazard, left him: the familiarity of the crouching, speeding figure and yet its unfamiliarity, its devilishness as a transformation of a person he knew well, plus its unexpectedness in this place, at this hour, all conjoined to freeze his nerves; he gaped, then made a clumsy lunge forward.

"Jill . . ."

"Leave go of me."

Jill's voice was not particularly angry. It was matter-of-fact, the voice of one with business to attend to. She spun out of his grip as an agile open-field runner eludes a charging tackle. Josie, suddenly released by Dan, staggered away a few steps. Slightly stupefied by alcohol and amorous feelings, she was in no way alert to her danger.

"Honeyman," she said, "who's this?"

"I'll show you who it is," Jill said. "It's his wife, that's who." She seized Josie by the throat, her clawing hand slipping to the front of the lady's dress. Jill spun her victim round, this act accompanied by the sound of tearing cloth.

"Ouch! Help. I want . . ."

"Now, Mama, wait. Jesus . . ."

". . . Police! . . ."

Dan's hand fell on his wife's shoulder—a hand large and powerful enough to have broken her in half but which did not have even the effect of slowing her up. Jerking her head sideways, Jill sunk her teeth in the fleshy palm till she felt bone.

"I'll honeyman you. Whore!"

"Oh, God . . . won't someone . . ."

"You didn't need help when you stole my husband."

Nursing his hurt hand, which was bleeding profusely, Dan could not help admiring the proficiency with which Jill backed her larger opponent against a lamp post. The dental technician's soft possessible flesh showed pinkly through her torn dress; her hair had fallen about her face which, as Jill pummeled and scratched, she tried to cover with her arms. Finding this did no good she embraced Jill, then tripped her; both women fell to the sidewalk, rolling over and over; Dan stood

(48)

helplessly by. People from nearby bars ran out to see what was doing, and Mrs. Arden, who had parked her car, came over to watch, but she too was an outsider now, relieved that she did not have to exhibit any connection with or concern for her recent passenger.

"Is it for real?" an elderly man in an electrician's cap inquired.

"You know it," said a youth in an apron—the busboy from The Cinch. He added reflectively, "Ladies like that should be on TV."

Jill was now pounding the head of the dental technician against the pavement. "You homebreaker. Take that."

"Hey, Yellow . . ."

Dan had caught sight of a cruising cab which, fortunately, swerved in. With the help of the busboy, he pried Jill from the now half-conscious Josie, then half-carried, half-dragged the latter to the cab and placed her inside.

"Where to?" the driver demanded, looking up and down the street. This looked like the kind of call where the cops might grab your fare away from you.

"The lady will tell you," Dan said. He shoved a bill into the man's hand. "Get going . . ."

Now that the girl was out of sight, incentive to further brawling seemed lacking. The onlookers strolled off, leaving Dan and Jill to face each other. Both were out of breath—but this did not seem too important since, at the moment, there was little to say.

Jill was the first to recover.

"A tramp. A dirty—ugh!"

"Now, honey."

". . . At least I knew where to find you!"

With a last burst of strength she tried to kick him in the groin, an intention which he perceived in time to forestall. Then a terrible thought came to her.

"The check. Did you cash it? . . . Where's the money? . . ."

"Gone."

"All of it?"

Dan took a last look in his pocket; he hoped Jill wouldn't find the dough from the rubber check Wingy had cashed.

"I guess so, Mama. Every goddamn last cent of it."

Jill screamed and struck at him. When he held her off she leaned against him, crying weakly and with utter despair. "I might have known . . ."

Clumsily and guiltily but with infinite love he stroked her head, dodged her sporadic kicks and blows, led her to where the car was parked.

"Come on now . . . I'm sorry, but hell, what difference does it make? I'll get some more, plenty of it, so don't take on."

"Don't take on, he says. What about the stinking rent? What about Bond's Market? What about . . ."

"I got another job coming up, Ma," Dan said crisply, "so come on. Quit all this nonsense and let's go home. It's getting late."

7

Dan fell asleep as soon as they got into bed but Jill was wakeful. She'd had nothing in her stomach for many hours but the cookies she'd snatched before leaving home; lying beside her husband, listening to his contented breathing, she remembered the Olympia oysters she'd hoped to surprise him with, their celebration dinner that had not come to pass. She grew angry all over again and her empty stomach writhed; she went out and got the oysters and ate every one of them, then sat in her kimono in the kitchen for a while.

A draft blew under the door; the fog sniffed at the cracks of the little house; the shapes of the gods who hunt at night for the weak places in the hearts of men and women crawled and shifted in the shadows around her.

She had not given in to Dan; her love of him rather than his superior strength had beaten her temporarily. She had been hungry for him; now she had him back, unconscious but her own. In the morning she would make him face the music, she would give it to him properly.

Just let him explain about the money! Just let him tell her about that floozie.

Already she had answers ready to combat the lies he would invent. He'd try to make love to her, of course; not that she'd give in. Or not at least until he was well humbled and his

(51)

need of her sharpened—her need, also, to prove her superiority to the tramp she'd caught him with.

She could hardly wait for him to wake up . . . yet, what a mess. The sweetness of conquering him, shaming him, punishing him . . . and then, oh, then rousing him, drawing him into her in an agony of forgiving and possessing: all this, the savage but beloved and unpredictable way of their lives had been quite wonderful as long as she'd been able to believe in him, to trust; as long as he'd sworn and she'd accepted his oath that it never, never could happen again.

But she couldn't believe now. She could love, yes; she would never stop loving. But she couldn't go on having faith, saving and slaving, dragging the little cart with the food in it he would not get home to eat.

She had set so much store on his promise to bring the stunt check home. So much had depended on it. That was a real betrayal: even if he'd had the woman he should have brought home the money. Then their partnership would not have seemed so unfair. There was so much good in him; such handsomeness, such strength and laughter. But what would happen when the zest of fighting left her altogether? Could they go on together then?

Jill was afraid. She squeezed her arms over her breasts, shivering in the thin kimono. "Get out of here," she said to the demons in the shadows, but they wouldn't leave: she felt their moldy breath on her; she heard the scratching of their claws.

It was not one thing but so many things in combination: age coming on them and all, and Dan's crazy actions making a new start impossible. Every time they got going a little and it seemed as if they might make it back up, his pride and recklessness would boil and he would go on the loose and spend the money that had been death in the not having and the risk of death in the making.

She felt so tired. She felt old, old. . . . She drew her hands down her face, exploring to see if there might be any youth left in her. Yes, she would battle if it could be fun again, but it was no fun: it was coldness, it was hopelessness. Harold gone. Harold in a sense not their son any more. If the dear Lord in His mercy had spared her this one punishment the whole devilish journey might have been worthwhile. Harold! Her whole heart yearned for him. She rocked back and forth. She could feel his chunky body in her arms the way he'd been when she'd sat in this very room and suckled him. Then she could see him a few years later, playing out in the street with the red wagon. And what a man he was now! How he'd risen! There was not a mother in the nation who might not envy her her having such a son.

But . . . but she had lost him!

A fierce determination came to her. She got up and made herself a cup of tea, then sat and drank it, plotting. The squirming went out of her stomach. She felt strong again. When Dan woke up she would do something, she thought—something she had never dared to do before; she would do it partly out of pity for him, the big stupid lug. She would make him realize the part he'd played in driving Harold away! Either that or . . . tell him she was leaving. He had to come down to earth sometime. He could still get work in pictures—what form of insanity made him think he had to be a star or featured player?

An actor!

Hell, he'd never been an actor the best day he ever saw!

Light was filtering under the blind. Down the street she heard the whunk, whunk of a starter, such a starter as only old heaps like theirs had and the other cars of Lefferts Drive except for the red jobs of the call girls and the flashy Pontiacs and Mercs of the racetrack guys.

Whunk, wait. Whunk whunk wait. Finally a start and go, boy, go.

So! Another day had started, another big slick day on Lefferts Drive. That whunk whunk and off would be the Qualens, Mr. and Mrs., a handsome elderly couple, very happy people, much in demand for ballroom scenes and such. Every morning about dawn they went out in the old car dressed in the same formal elegance as the bona fide society people Dan had run with for a while (like the Countess Sari de Sahn, that fraud!), the people who were at that hour probably returning home to the chateaux in Beverly Hills . . . but not the Countess Sari de Sahn because the Countess, though a Hungarian, was buried in the Cemetery of Campo Verano in Rome, her millions willed to some little Lesbian milliner.

"Here, Winky. Here, Winky, Winky, Winky . . ."

It was day for sure when Miss Tremaine, the librarian, went out to call her quail. The dumb bird had broken its leg and Miss Tremaine had repaired the injury with a splint, taping on a piece of wood or metal so that the quail had one thick leg and one thin. Helping it live, Miss Tremaine had come to love it and had given it a name. She had clipped its wings so that the quail could never leave her. Easy for them, who could keep loved things close by helping first, then crippling them. True love for lesser creatures meant not this but help that turned them loose, strong and free, to fly away forever. Jill envied Miss Tremaine but pitied her more, pitied also the wild bird that lived under the old maid's house like a chicken, coming out for its meals when called.

Well, it took all kinds to make a world. Jill got up. She

could have sworn she heard her knees creak. Dan stirred in his sleep; soon he would be out in the kitchen looking for something to eat, as was his way. Then, oh, then . . .

Jill grinned. She pulled off her kimono and then her night-gown and stood rubbing her sides and the back of her neck, the soft gray dawnlight glimmering on her body.

She felt better. She went into the bathroom and took a shower, came back dripping wet, carrying the bathmat which she laid in front of the stove. She turned on the stove and was standing in front of the warm open oven, drying herself, when Dan walked in rubbing his eyes and yawning. He had a bloody handkerchief around his bitten hand.

"Got anything here to eat, honey?" he inquired in a matter-of-fact tone and Jill said in the same tone, "Not for you, you bastard," and threw the half-warm kettle at him.

Then they were off.

8

The walls of the studio were high and thick, the gates made of iron, watched by cops. People came and went, beautiful girls in summer dresses, laboring men, craftsmen of various kinds, agents, contractors, caterers and all kinds of money-men, their careful, wolfish faces lined with greed, dressed like vacationists in wide-shouldered suits and hand-painted neck-ties, all with gold wrist watches and tie clips and gold Dunhill lighters, all with some project bubbling in them, some smart trap for cadging the money that frothed inside the walls, the gates, the sound stages like suds in a washing machine.

All these people had the knowhow. They had identity cards or special passes which admitted them to the contest within. Without such a talisman they were turned away. No matter how important they might be in their own eyes they were sent scampering and told to come back when they had the right papers.

Once, Dan remembered, he had worked in a studio when strikers charged the gates. Then machine guns had been mounted on the walls. Chains had been strung across the gates and deputies with sawed-off guns stationed in front of them. The strikers had upset the cars of people trying to drive in, and the cops who usually lolled around peacefully, joking with equals and gesturing ceremoniously to superiors, had then been militant men with the clenched faces of fighters; they had thrown tear gas bombs, they had clubbed men's heads to prove that, whether you liked it or not, the studio had an existence apart from the rest of the world.

Dan stood in the sunlight in his splendid clothes, suddenly hesitant. Physical hazards which would have appalled ordinary men were the daily grist of life to him: not so these walls, these gates, these faces of preoccupied strangers.

In the old days he had never noticed that a studio was cut off. In those days the gates had always been open for him, the gatemen and receptionists respectful, even hero-worshiping. Now, he was reluctant to give his name to the girl at the reception desk. She would be sure to recognize the name and realize he was the sort of person she had dealt with many times, one who had come down in the world. He would do it, of course, but he wanted to put off the moment: he stopped and bought a *Hollywood Reporter* from the rack on the sidewalk, then stood with his back to the big wall and the sun warm on him to read the chatter of the trade.

He had decided to renew neglected contacts, try for work at RKO and Paramount—two places which, because of fear of refusal, he had not applied to recently. Since his night of adventure he had known he would have to do something constructive to restore his standing with Jill.

The quarrel which had started in the kitchen and continued in the bedroom afterward had followed a familiar pattern, yet there had been something new in it—a kind of tiredness. Dan had expected her to attack him. He could deal with this. He'd had a secret weapon—the beautiful Indianhead pendant he had brought her. He produced the pendant at exactly the right moment—just when Jill was saying that he squandered money on clothes and whores, but never spent a cent on her—but to his amazement she threw it on the floor, smashing the Indian's nose and bending the silver setting. She behaved as if she had gone insane.

Later, more in her established fashion, she had capered in front of him naked, angrily taking inventory of herself as compared to the woman she had caught him with. Was there something wrong with this or with that? Any reason why he didn't still want to make love to her?

And Dan, seeing her weave a dance of desire before him, had known the renewal of the fierce need of her which—emotionally and spiritually as well as physically—was the dominating pull of his life.

He could not imagine how he would live without Jill. Other affairs to him were merely a celebration of the excess energy and health he drew from her, his wife for such a long, wonderful stretch of years.

Yet this time she had threatened to leave him, not wildly and in a passion as she had sometimes done before, but wearily, almost helplessly. This in itself was different and frightening. But there was worse to come. For even after their relationship had been established again and everything had seemed all right, she had gone on talking and accusing him; she had refused to accept his promises that he'd be different.

This time she had said one thing that hurt him in a mortal place. She had been reciting the crises in which, against her better judgment, she had stood by him.

". . . even when you drove the boy away, turned him against you . . ."

Dan had waged battle over this remark—but there was truth in it. The most deeply rooted and incomprehensible sorrow of all the years, and the only one against which he had built no defense, was that Harold had renounced his father-hood, even taking that cursed name "Heston," his mother's maiden name. It had been a terrible rejection, making the division between father and son almost complete. They no longer visited each other's homes or communicated in any way. Dan had suffered more than rejection—he had proof, he felt, that Harold hated him, this the strangest of all, since the love for his son and the pride he felt in him had never slackened.

The thought of Harold weakened him. He could not face the girl inside there, at the desk, until the weakness passed. He folded the paper and put it in his pocket, watching a limousine pass through the gates where a group of crewmen were coming to work with their lunch pails.

He had always wanted a child—above all a boy. Both he and Jill had felt sure that Harold's birth would mend what-ever had been lacking in their marriage and for a time it had even though Dan's career went forward at an ever accelerated pace. When he had been too busy to play with the boy for a while he would sometimes call a break in the middle of an afternoon in order to go home to see Harold. He didn't want any son of his growing up neglected. He wanted more kids—though none had ever come. It had been his pride to provide well for his family. Somehow in the progress of a career which he conducted with a reckless arrogance and an insatiable appetite for gratifying his senses, he had acquired the prosaic ideals and sentimental moral values of a small-town businessman and he saw nothing inconsistent in the relationship between such standards and the fact that he spent his time leaping from precipices, being shot at with blank cartridges, and causing horses to turn somersaults while galloping.

Sundays and holidays, as his publicity agent announced to the world during this period, were devoted to his family, particularly his son. The statement was accurate. Locking the electric gates of the big place in the Valley where his photograph was frequently taken, prettily posed with Harold, Jill, and big, black Thunder, he would play determinedly with the kid who, thin, big-eyed, and rather timid, would be waiting without either anticipation or distaste for this weekly appointment with his famous father. Endlessly and obediently Harold would then swing a baseball bat or ride or box, sometimes target practicing with one of Dan's big six-shooters, held in both hands; it was so heavy, though, of course, so beautiful and the best gun that money could buy. He would try to win Dan's approval, blankly and awkwardly cooperating, hoping with an empty and usually fruitless yearning that Dan would tell him he was doing better. As for Dan, he also rather strangely sought for a reward from these stubborn self-appointed sessions of parenthood, some proof that Harold loved him or at least admired him, as all the rest of the world seemed to do, but all that came his way most times was the tiniest of smiles some days, a flickering pinwheel beam of warmth sparking up for a moment from somewhere inside Harold as Dan, after patting him on the head, ordered the gates unlocked and rushed off to his next appointment.

"So long, Dad."

Why had they always been saying so long, good-by, see you when I get back? Why hadn't somebody told him that the appointments that sliced up his time in such a glittering fashion had meant nothing when stacked up against a son?

Standing against the studio wall with his eyes closed, looking half-asleep or drunk to those who hurried past him, Dan recalled the kind of boy Harold had been. There had been a kind of song inside his spindly body, gay, lonesome, fearless, and sad; his days had marched or danced to a rhythm different from anyone else's. That was the way it was with a kid. Harold had even hummed the tune, always humming or whistling, running up and down the stairs, prowling along the fence, getting the bat or the ball, waiting for something no one had supplied or for some person who never came.

What had that song been about? If he could remember, Dan thought, he might find out the truth about Harold, but the song was gone now, lost in the roar of the years. It had been brave. He knew that. He had not understood it then. One of his criticisms of Harold had been that the kid lacked guts. That had been wrong. Who could fathom the incalculable bravery of kids? . . . Dan remembered when he had first become aware of this. It had happened one day when having some time off between pictures, he had gone one day to fetch Harold from school in the huge car with the steer's horns on it: he had parked outside the gate and peered in. School had just let out and the kids were playing a kind of tag game shoving one kid, the littlest, who ran after them, sometimes pushed to his knees or sent cruelly sprawling on his face, but never giving up, chasing the others as the rules of the game called for him to do. Dan observed with horror that the little kid was Harold. He started to get out of the car. He wanted to walk out in the schoolyard and defend his son. But something made him keep away. He had to see how Harold would make out. After a long time the other children tired of the game and Harold, catching sight of his father, got his lunchbox and jacket and came trotting over.

"What was going on there, partner?" Dan inquired as they drove home.

"Oh, nothing," Harold said. "They do that. That's the way they play."

"I don't think it's too good," Dan said. "You're the smallest. No reason why those bigger kids should shove you around."

"Oh, I don't mind," Harold said with the air of one possessing an inestimable treasure. "They only do it to me because I'm your boy and you're the Ringo Kid. That's why they do it. I don't pay attention to them."

9

Harold had been bright in school. He avoided the sports for which Dan had laboriously trained him but made the swimming team and the high school debating team. His senior year he had a friend who owned a red Ford hop-up on the turtleback of which was painted:

PASS WITH CARE YOUR DAUGHTER
MAY BE IN THIS CAR

Painfully conscious of his own lack of education, Dan had planned for Harold to go to college; he was more annoyed than gratified when a family friend who was a cutter at Columbia gave Harold an apprenticeship. Dan tried to talk the kid out of it but Jill backed Harold up solidly and Dan, losing his temper at the blocking of his own dream for his son—and what he thought of as frustration of Harold's career—said some things he didn't mean.

"A celluloid slicer! It's a disgrace . . ."

"What's disgraceful about it?" Jill demanded calmly. "It's a job. Without cutters who could paste up the routines you call acting?"

This stab goaded Dan still further.

"I won't have a son of mine latched in a cell all his life with his eye glued to a Moviola."

(62)

"He won't be there all his life," Jill said. "He'll get ahead. Lots of cutters get to be directors or writers, some producers even."

"Maybe if they've got a personality, yes," Dan conceded. "Not if they act superior to other people because they read books all the time."

"How do you expect him to get educated if he doesn't read?" Jill said. "He'd read in college, where you want him to go."

"He'd read a better class of stuff," Dan said.

"You might be better off if you'd read some of that stuff," Jill said, "and spent less time putting a shine on a stock saddle with the seat of your pants."

"That's all," Dan yelled. "That's all I want to hear. If he takes this cutting job I wash my hands of him. I'm through."

Following this talk he had done a bad thing. He had gone to Norman Wynn, the cutter who had offered Harold the apprenticeship, and asked him to withdraw his offer. He had made threats as to what would happen if this wasn't done.

"I'll run you out of the industry," he yelled.

"All right, Dan," Norman said quietly. "You just better go ahead and do that. I'm plumb tired of working anyway."

Norman had taken off his glasses as if he expected Dan to hit him. He sat blinking in the gloom of the small, damp cutting room—the cell in which he had been confined for twenty-five years by a peculiar kind of life sentence which permitted him to go home most nights and a good many Sundays but not to have thoughts or interests beyond the clips of film hanging in front of him. The cutter was as broad and tall as Dan but his body was now no body at all, just a shell bent almost double by arthritis and by so many years of stooping over. "Listen," Norman said, "if you want to stay friends with Harold you'd better not try to stop him. That kid is going places."

Later Dan admitted to himself that he'd been wrong, but where Jill was concerned (and perhaps with Harold too, since he seemed to share much of his mother's temperament) once you had made a mistake it was made forever. Old Norman had been right about Harold's abilities. The kid had zoomed up, propelled in part by a combat-film job during the war in which he worked as editor for a famous director, who later said a good word for him to top studio brass. Harold's first picture, *Rim of Sky,* rumored to be a flop before release, turned out a smash hit. Since the day when Dan objected to his going to Columbia, Harold had broken off relations with his father.

All of this had been unfortunate, not irreparable; Dan had explained to friends that Harold had changed his name because he didn't want to cash in on the old man's reputation. He had bragged to everyone about Harold's success, always believing that the misunderstanding which had divided them would iron itself out. Surely love when it existed between a man and his son could never be completely blocked off—the love and pride he himself felt so deeply, and the feeling in Harold he had been so sure was love, or hoped it was.

Dan's hopes had been blasted by a happening which revealed an unsuspected savagery in Harold. Dan got a few days' work in *Blade of Castile,* an historical picture which Harold was directing. He was doubling the hero in a sword fight when Harold took exception to the way he was performing. Harold had stopped the cameras in the middle of a take and ordered Dan to leave the set. "All right, everybody," Harold said through the loudspeaker, "you saw what happened to this man. Don't let it happen to you. Let's go for another take and see if we can get it decent. And remember, you other guys, if I see anybody dogging it, he can go and turn in his time the same as Prader. You're supposed to be swordsmen, let's see you do some swording. Everybody ready? Okay, roll 'em . . ."

The arcs lit up, the cast moved into action positions, and the slateman stepped out with the slate again. The assistant nodded to Dan who got out of the company and walked stiffly toward the back of the stage, unbuttoning his ruffled coat.

Dan knew there had been nothing wrong with his work. Harold had made an example of him out of spite.

He had never told Jill what had happened that day; when she finally heard about it and questioned him he passed the whole thing off as a minor quarrel, taking the blame on himself for quitting the picture—an explanation which Jill, knowing his temperament, was quite ready to accept. Dan had been rather fearful that Harold himself would tell her about it, for the two still visited sometimes (though with the new, fashionable life he was leading Harold didn't seem to find as much time as formerly for these chats with his mother), but to his relief she had not referred to it again.

No, he could not bear to tell Jill. For in spite of her nagging, her temper (and what redhead didn't have a temper!) at the faults he had, she still had sided with him in this estrangement from the boy—and Dan for his part had never wanted to do anything, say anything that would damage the relationship between mother and son. That was why it had hurt so much when Jill had accused him of "driving the boy away": the remark had just popped up unrelatedly in their quarrel over Josie, the dental technician. (He still laughed, though, every time he thought of that catfight out in the street: no woman had a chance with Jill in a catfight!)

(65)

But did she really think he'd driven Harold out? She might have been nursing such a grievance for a long time, unsuspected, and if she had, he was in danger. Then she might really leave him; that is, unless by some great stroke he restored her trust. He could not be rude to the idiots who ran the studios these days, he could not and must not hold out for an acting job but must take any kind of work, even another stunt, if it would bring in money.

If he couldn't . . . but no use thinking about that. Still, if he couldn't, then it was all up with him. Then he knew he'd come to the end of the line.

Resolutely he walked into the RKO reception entrance and inquired for his old friend, Hugo Blessing.

"Mr. Blessing is no longer with the studio," the girl reported. "Did you wish to see anyone else?"

Dan thought it over. There was Rush Connors in publicity . . . Wilbur Friend, the unit manager, and others he knew well: but maybe these too were no longer on the payroll or had moved to other jobs, it was so long since he had contacted them. However, he took a wild chance, asked to see Johnny Hocumb, former location man.

The girl hesitated, then dialed a department number.

"Is Johnny there?" she inquired.

Dan looked at her in surprise. That was an odd way to inquire for an important man. He wondered whether Johnny had been dating her.

"Mr. Prader to see you," the girl said into the phone. She listened a moment, passed the instrument to Dan. "Johnny wants to talk to you."

At first Dan could hardly hear what was being said due to a series of thuds and crashes, as if from the fall of heavy objects, a disorder which seemed to be taking place where Johnny was working.

"Dan! Say, what's the good word? Long time no see."

"Just passing by, John. I figured if you weren't busy . . ." Hocumb sounded vaguely embarrassed.

"Why, Dan, I'd like to see you, I sure would. But I kind of changed jobs around here and they keep me pounding . . ." (A heavy boom substantiated this, almost too literally.)

"Well, if you're tied up . . ." Dan said.

"No, just the old grind. You know how it is. But say, will you be around in a couple of hours, maybe around twelve? I go to lunch then and I'd sure like to see you . . . Have to rush some, though: we're only supposed to take half an hour . . ."

"Sounds like I got you at a bad time," Dan said, a whack, then a crunch at Johnny's end making his words an obvious understatement.

"A little bit, Dan," John admitted, "but I'd sure like to see you any time. Try me in a couple of days, huh? Sorry, I got to go now, Dan; we're not supposed to use this phone for personal calls . . ."

"What is John doing now?" Dan asked the girl as he hung up.

"He's working in the mail room, Mr. Prader," the girl explained.

The mail room! What a job for a man who had been a three-hundred-a-week executive!

"I didn't know . . ."

The absurdity that he, Dan, had been about to seek employment from a mailroom clerk did not enter his mind. He was aware only of his sympathy for Johnny. He knew how the guy must feel.

"We had a sort of purge around here," the reception girl said. "Some of the guys took anything they could and just held on."

Dan thanked her and turned away. He had thought of going over to Paramount, but as he walked down Gower Street he gave up this notion. In the back of his mind the past three days had been the memory of Roy Sowells telling him about the job at Duart. There were several reasons why he hadn't wanted to show interest in this job. First, it was a stunt spot, not acting; second, Duart was where Harold worked—but why in hell was that important if, as Roy had mentioned, this was a Von Kramm picture?

He could at least phone Harold and find out what the score was.

To do that would be asking help. It would be looping back into the past just as if *Blade of Castile* had never been. Would Harold turn him down? Hell, he might not even take the call. He had a secretary, Dan supposed, an office, and all that crap; he was a big wheel out at Duart.

All of a sudden Dan felt a fierce yearning to talk to Harold anyway. Never mind if he refused the call. Never mind anything. He walked into a phone booth and got the studio operator.

"Mr. Harold Heston, please."

A girl with a pleasant voice asked who was calling. Dan longed to say, "his father!" but instead barked:

"Mr. Daniel Prader."

"Just a moment, I'll see if Mr. Heston is free to talk."

Dan gripped the receiver hard, the harsh grooves in his cheeks deepening. But Harold sounded neither hostile nor friendly—just casual, as if a call from his father were the most ordinary thing in the world.

"How are you, Dan?"

For years now, at the times when they had been on speaking terms, he had not called him "Dad" or much less "Father" —either of these terms, it would seem, indicating too close a relationship.

"I'd like to come out and see you."

"Well, sure, fine! Only—I'm kind of busy right now, Dan."

So that was it—rejection!

"It won't take long, goddamn it," Dan said fiercely, angry and supplicating at the same time.

"Well—okay. Only, you want to tell me what it's about?"

"Can't I come out and see my own bastard relatives without giving out a song and dance what it's about?"

These words were on Dan's tongue but, with extraordinary control, he withheld them.

"I'm going back to work, kid," Dan said in a manner which, because of his defensiveness, sounded more superior than he'd meant it to. "I heard there was a stunt job coming up out your way."

"Why, not that I know of, Dan."

"What about the Von Kramm unit?" Dan inquired, remembering what Roy Sowells had told him. "Isn't he shooting some horse opera with a lot of outdoor stuff in it?"

"Well, hold on now," Harold said crisply, "I hadn't heard of it—but wait now. You know old Von, don't you? Why don't you give him a ring yourself?"

"I might just do that," Dan said icily, his heart sinking again. Every actor or rider out of work called big directors like Von Kramm. Most likely Von's secretary had orders to refuse such calls.

"Wait, now, Dan . . ."

He heard Harold asking someone in his office if Von Kramm needed stuntmen. Evidently Harold then picked up another telephone since Dan could hear him repeating his question differently phrased, in some new direction. Then his voice returned to Dan's line.

"Come on out, Dan. They'll talk to you."

"Where? When, Harold?"

Dan was almost yelling.

"Right away. There'll be a pass on the gate for you. You can go right up to Von's office. No sense taking the trouble to come way up here, is there?"

No sense!

"Who wants to go up there?" Dan rasped, letting out his pent-up feelings now that the favor had been done.

"Well, okay, Dan. He'll see you," Harold said, definitely cool now. "I'm afraid that's all I can do."

"Thanks, anyhow," Dan said, "and give my best to your wife."

But Harold had already left the telephone.

10

Before starting for Duart, Dan rang his exchange; Bobbi gave him word that Mr. Sowells had called.

"Call him back at the studio right away," Bobbi said. She added, "Gee, I hope it's something good, Dan."

A large cheerful woman with two sons in the Navy, Bobbi was the type of exchange-operator who mothered her clients, especially the stuntmen for whom she had a special sympathy.

"I'm keeping my fingers crossed for you, dear," she said.

The call from Roy, according to Bobbi's timing, had come in early in the morning, almost two hours before his own call to Harold. Was this coincidence, or was something cooking for him at Duart? No sense returning the call now, as long as he was going right out there.

He left the Buick in a large parking lot in front of the Administration Building and walked confidently forward. At least this time he would not have to stand in front of some receptionist, fumbling to remember whom he knew inside.

At Duart, studio cops instead of girls serviced the reception windows. The cop at Dan's window left his booth and came round to shake hands.

"Mr. Prader! It's good to see you, sir!"

"Good to see you too, pal," Dan said heartily. He was grateful for the greeting though he didn't remember the cop: just some old-timer who had probably known him long ago.

"They're waiting for you upstairs, Mr. Prader. Mr. Von Kramm's office just phoned down. And here's this, sir," he added, handing him with a slight gratifying flourish his yellow pass on which the word *Interview* was stamped. "Not that you need it at Duart, Mr. Prader."

Dan thanked him and stepped inside. The cop's friendliness increased his optimism as he took the elevator up to the third, the director's floor. They did things the right way at Duart. If there were any worries about TV or bad boxoffice the executives of Duart kept them out of sight. This was motion picture business, the greatest business in the world—subject to changes, to ups and downs perhaps, but gloriously stable in

(71)

its basic structure, proof against anything short of an H-bomb. Even the beautiful little elevator, with a good-looking uniformed girl to run it, gave you that feeling: the girl's sweet smile when she opened the door for you—then the great hall beyond with doors stretching off to right and left, every door with a famous name lettered on it under a glass plate. The only unseemly note was the presence of a workman who had just finished removing one name—that of some unfortunate celebrity who had died or made a bad picture. No doubt, however, at a place like Duart, the name which would be substituted for that of the casualty would be as impressive as that which it replaced.

Dan walked along swiftly in the direction the girl told him to take, reading the names. The carpet under his feet was deep and soft and the air he breathed had a faint but exhilarating perfume in it, the smell of paper and ink and cigarettes, of food brought up on trays from the executive dining room, of secretaries who could afford the same perfumes as stars—the smell of bustle and decision and, in short, of the Upper World: a smell which Dan had almost forgotten. It was good to sniff it again, to be a part of all it brought to mind.

REGUS VON KRAMM

Dan opened the door boldly and strode in. A secretary with gray hair, who looked kind, efficient and, above all, expensive, was pouring a cup of coffee from an electric percolator.

"Mr. Prader?" she said in a pleasant manner, obviously recognizing him, just as the cop downstairs had. "Would you care for a cup of coffee while you wait?"

Dan accepted the coffee. He was slightly dashed not to be admitted right away—the cop's statement as he handed out the pass had seemed to indicate he would be—but he had been out on many interviews and it was always the same: you hurried like hell and then you waited. He expressed this view to the secretary and she smilingly agreed with him. They were chatting about western pictures and Dan, putting down his cup, was telling her about a stunt he'd done in *The Man from Brimstone* when the door of Von Kramm's office opened and Roy Sowells came out. Roy had on a white T-shirt, a pair of old gray pants, and blue sneakers; he looked as if about to start drilling a football squad in calisthenics except that he carried a worn, bulging leather briefcase.

"Hi, kid, how goes it?" he said, sticking out his hand.

Dan got up and shook hands cordially. He was pleased Roy had apparently forgotten the slight difference which had developed at their last meeting.

"Swell, Roy, swell. And with you?"

"Same old grind," Roy said.

Dan wondered what Roy had been doing with Von Kramm. He looked inquiringly at the secretary to see if he could go into the director's office now, but to his surprise Roy took him by the arm, motioning to an office on the other side of the secretary's room.

Dan hung back slightly. "I was supposed to see Von," he told Roy.

"He's busy right now," Roy said amiably. "Anyhow, he thought that you and I could have a talk. Then we'll go in and see him, just as soon as he's free."

He led the way into the other office and closed the door. The office was a small one; it contained a worn leather couch, two chairs, and a desk. Roy sat down in the swivel chair. He put his hand up under his T-shirt and scratched himself vigorously.

"Did you call your exchange today?"

"Yeah," Dan said. "I got your message just before I started up here. I'd just talked to Harold and . . ."

Roy grinned.

"It's a kick, you getting Harold to call Von. Remember, you got mad when I suggested that. Huh, kid?"

Dan said, "I need a job, that's all."

He took the stiff chair facing Roy. He sat down in it bolt upright, his big hat in his lap and his feet planted firmly out to each side. He looked serious and slightly hostile. He was not pleased at doing business with Roy instead of Von Kramm, if business was to be done.

"Well, sweetheart," Roy said, "you got one."

He took a folded mimeographed sheet out of his pants pocket and tossed it across the desk. It was headed.

Desc. Stunt Work Prod. 2411 (Now casting.)
Dir. Von Kramm.
Assist. R. Sowells.

"This is what I told you about," Roy said. "Only I didn't know then I was going on the picture. I've been talking about you all week."

Dan felt a warmth toward Roy, coupled with excitement. Good old Roy. Roy had been plugging for him, working in his behalf without his knowledge—and after a quarrel too, good friend that he was. He had never needed to call Harold —Roy could have fixed this for him. And a spot like this, on a Von Kramm picture, would be big!

He ran his eye briefly over the enumerated stunts, twenty-four in all, each calling for from one to six men. No ramrod was listed.

Roy said, "You want to ramrod and do a couple of stunts?"
(74)

"Are you kidding?"

Roy's eyes, the color and size of nailheads in their screening folds of flesh, looked into Dan's with a glint of complicity and utter frankness.

"They're in a spot," he said.

Dan nodded slowly. They would not have come to him first for a job of this size; they would have talked to other ramrods first, a lot of them maybe.

"Who have they been talking to?"

"Howard Strayer. Ace McClure. Others."

"What's wrong with it?"

Roy leaned over the desk. He stabbed a fleshy forefinger on the last item on the page:

24.   (Sc. 267—268—269—270)

Mounted man to jump from cliff.

"That's the one," he said.

He reached into his briefcase and got out a bunch of color stills, spreading them out beside the inventory of stunts. All the stills showed the same thing—a section of tan cliff and blue sky, with ocean below. From the scale of feet noted on a strip of tape at the left side of the still Dan could see that the height of the proposed jump was more than seventy feet.

"It's high," he said.

Roy said, "You did more than that in 'thirty-six, in that soap opera about the Daltons."

"That was in the old days," Dan said.

He tried to conceal his excitement. He would take the job, of course: both he and Roy knew this. The only things he had to find out was how bad the stunt was and how much money he could get for it. There was still some element about the proposition that he did not understand—the baldness of Roy's approach, maybe. Roy was certainly pushing this at him. "If it's so great," he said, "why did Strayer turn it down? He's a good hand."

"He's chicken when it comes to jumps," Roy said.

"Ace ain't chicken," Dan said. "And he likes to make a buck."

"These guys are spoiled, I'm telling you," Roy said almost plaintively. "They won't jump out of a window ten feet high unless you've got a fireman's net under it, and even then you've got to insure with Lloyds of London. They're chicken and they're superstitious. A couple of jerks died on the lot last month and you know the old crap line that death in picture business goes in threes. Who's next? So that makes it all the tougher."

Dan said, "I'm not superstitious and I'm not chicken, I just like to know what I'm doing."

He looked at the photograph again. The cliff lipped out a little at the bottom but still not enough to matter if the takeoff was right.

"Where is this location?"

"Place called Todos Santos, Mexico. Fishing town with a resort hotel in it, about a hundred, hundred and fifty miles north of Acapulco. We got everything we want down there. I haven't been there, but that's what they say."

"I'd like to go down there and take a look," Dan said. "I don't want to sign on blind. It's a tough stunt."

Roy took thought.

"Dan," he said, "do you want this spot or don't you?"

"You know I want it."

"Then grab it."

Dan felt the skin on his scalp tighten; he clasped his fists, then slowly unclasped them.

"Grab it, huh?" he said. "Just like that?"

"That's what I'd do," Roy said.

"I don't work that way."

Roy shrugged. "It's a sweet spot, Danny-boy."

Dan said, "I worked blind a few times in the old days. That was the nearest I ever came to getting killed. No more. I need the job, I need it bad. But you can get yourself another boy."

Roy probed for some real or imaginary irritant in his left ear, his eyes fixed upon outer space.

"Will you take my word this stunt can be done, that it's not impossible?"

"That might be true," Dan allowed. "I'd just like to know some more, that's all."

Roy said, "Look. Suppose you went there personally. Suppose you saw it. Man, I know you like a book. You'd come back and say we had to pick another location. Or you'd crab about the dough. Something. That's how you are, sweetheart; you're tough, real tough."

"Is that bad?"

"It's bad when you're not working," Roy said. "It's goddamn bad. You're that way with everybody, that's the hell of it. The guys in town who could do you some good you insult and the ones you don't insult you make a pass at their girl or something. Sure, there's a few places you can still work—where they pay off in lock washers and seashells. You were thrown off a picture on this lot right in the middle of a take; don't let's forget that, honeychild."

There it was: *Blade of Castile* again, the black memory of the worst day, the worst happening in his life, thrown up to plague him.

Harold.

"That wasn't—that was a personal—"

"I know—I know," Roy said. "But all they remember here

is, you got thrown off the lot. Where work is concerned in this town you can't get yourself arrested—you, the best stuntman that ever put leg over a horse. And a star, once, in your own right."

"I'll be a star again, boy, and don't you forget it," Dan said.

"Don't quit eating till you make it, you'll get thin," Roy said brutally. "What bothers you? You'll have a chute for the takeoff, two by twelve planks, greased on the bottom so the horse can't balk. What more do you want?"

"A platform," Dan said.

This was a slip. It indicated, as a slight twitch of Roy's pudgy, alert face did not fail to record, that Dan had already decided to accept. And they had not even talked dough yet!

"What do you mean, a platform?"

"One like I had in the Dalton picture. A platform with a runway in the back so I can get the horse up on it and a trap in front so I can trip a lever and dump him on the chute when I'm ready to go."

"What's the matter with riding him on?"

"No good. He can slip and—lots of things. With a platform he has to hit the chute in the right position for the dive."

Roy rubbed his face.

"I don't guarantee the platform," he said. "But I'll do my best. What else?"

"Who do I double?"

"Florian Pipps. He plays the heavy."

"I get SAG scale for that. Two-fifty a week for ramrodding."

"That's okay," Roy said. "What else?"

Dan stared at him. The job was fine. It was a top spot, one that would do everything for him that he'd been hoping to get done. Yet taking it this way was bad, with Roy high-pressuring him under the guise of friendship. And the worst of it was that the things Roy had said to him were true.

"How much for the stunt?"

"One grand."

"Fifteen hundred," Dan said.

"I've got no authority to go beyond a thousand," Roy said, "but I'll tell you what I'll do. I'll suggest twelve-fifty and I think they'll take it. I can almost swear they will. Okay?"

Dan took a deep breath, let it out slowly.

"Okay," he said. He lifted his new Colorado-fawn Stetson with both hands and set it on his head. He felt less like a man who had put over a successful deal than one who had surrendered something. There was no dignity in this and no way to recapture dignity. He had to sign on, not as a skilled craftsman who could rig his own hazards and decide how to handle them but as a hireling, doing what he was told.

As he got to his feet, facing Roy for the sealing handshake, he remembered his apprentice days and how, as he had just said to Roy, he had occasionally worked in this way and he knew again the fear that he always experienced, not in the work itself but in the moment of agreeing to do the work. He looked down at the colored stills and tried to picture the cliff with the sky above it and the sea lapping softly at the bottom of it. He saw a horse with a man on it, himself, suddenly appearing, arching out over the edge, out into nothing. Seventy feet! The story of an ordinary building was nine feet so seventy feet was the height of a good-sized hotel or close to it—the St. Francis in San Francisco or the Hollywood Knickerbocker. Water, hit from such a height was like concrete; it could break a man's back, smash his body like a paper bag unless he hit it at just the right angle.

(79)

He dropped Roy's hand, feeling the safe, solid floor under his feet and pushing back at the fear of the horse, its legs stretched out in the chute, flying toward the edge of the world. Once in Tia Juana he had gone to the bullfights with a friend of his who was a bullfighter, but was present that day as a spectator, and this bullfighter, who had killed a thousand bulls, had said that when he sat in the stands and saw the bull come out to another fighter, down in the arena, he always felt that he himself, down there, could never face a bull. Dan felt that way about the leap from the cliff, watching himself do it in imagination. And Roy, now—Roy pushing the job at him; was Roy really so damn friendly after all? Wasn't he maybe scoring to make up for the quarrel in The Cinch?

Slowly the fear passed—never, he hoped, to come back again; he grinned at Roy with a dry mouth. Roy slapped him on the shoulder.

"Von will be glad to hear about this," Roy said. "Let's go on inside and say hello to him."

Von Kramm's office supplied Dan with a script of Production 2411, Screenplay by Frederick Rogiot, from a story by Lucius Dewitt. Dan read it carefully, analyzing it from a box-office point of view as well as for the stunt work involved. Like most people in picture business he held himself to be a shrewd judge of story values.

He told Jill, "I don't see where it will make money. It's too mean. Too much killing and not enough romance."

"That's all they make nowadays, seems like," Jill said. "Meanness! I wouldn't want to go much to movies any more, even if we had the money. They've forgotten what *heart* means in a picture."

Dan agreed. The pictures in which he had starred, espe-

(80)

cially the few he had made independently, had always had plenty of heart. Now, sitting with Jill in the kitchen (their most used room) with the script of Production 2411 on the table between them, neither reminded the other that some of Dan's pictures had not made money either. Possibly there could be such a thing as too much heart in a picture.

During the days following Dan's talk with Roy Sowells, he and Jill were together more than usual. He stayed away from The Cinch and Bellyful of Blues and, except for occasional trips to Dollarhyde Brothers' stable in the Valley, spent most of his time at home; he visited the studio only once—to ask again about the platfrom for the chute—but was given no definite assurance as to this. Roy said he was still working on it. Several evenings he and Jill went over to the Ardens' to watch television and one night when the weather was hot they picnicked on Zuma Beach, building a fire out of driftwood and roasting wienies and potatoes. Many fires were winking along the beach like the lights of tiny, temporary homes and there were, of course, a lot of high-school and college kids in swimming and later sitting around the fires; the kids brought battery radios and ukuleles and even phonographs with them so that walking along the beach you would hear thinned-out shreds of music mingling with the silky rip of the surf. Dan and Jill had planned to swim but felt too hungry at first and after their meal too sleepy; they rolled up in a blanket and lay on the sand in an embrace which might have seemed ridiculous at their age if there had been anyone around to see it, but which both enjoyed; they listened to the waves awhile and then dozed off. Both were depressed about their coming separation; they had seldom been apart—but it would not be possible for Dan to take her with him on location, except at his own expense, which was not to be thought of. He was careful not to mention his uncertainties about the job ahead but Jill sensed that he was bothered about it and tried once or twice to make him tell her what was wrong. The night before he left he was as edgy as an overtrained fighter; it was an effort both for him and Jill to keep from quarreling but they made it somehow and their farewell was affectionate.

The Duart company was scheduled to be in Mexico about two weeks.

11

Like many young Hollywood couples who felt the need to escape from the tensions of family life and to provide themselves with new topics of conversation, Harold Heston and his wife, Nancy, spent much of their time going to parties. They seemed to enjoy parties about equally, though of course Nancy had more time for them since Harold seldom had much time off between pictures and when working, had to be on the set at an ungodly hour in the morning. Often he would go home from a party early, leaving Nancy to be brought along later. Freddy Rogiot, the writer, would bring her, or whatever man she had had dinner with. Nancy did not exactly flirt but the appearance of flirtation had to be there, at least, when somebody was decent enough to take you home. She would plant a kiss on the escort's cheek and jump out quickly, before he got too interested, holding her latchkey in front of her like a dagger.

Being at a party was different from being in a café or on a set. There were the kind of parties covered by *Look* or *Life*: three-ring-circus type parties given by professional party givers or rich people trying to crash Hollywood where shashlik, fortune tellers and champagne were available and the guests, since they were present as a condescension and, in a sense, anonymously, behaved badly but talked for days afterward about the sensational time they'd had; in contrast to these but equally inclusive were the doings given once or twice a year by some important figure in the industry (not below executive-producer level) where everyone, being on exhibition, spent his time posing or currying favor and went home exhausted, swearing never to do it again. From these reservoirs of party-goers (lists of whom could be obtained at a price from a party-guest agent in Beverly Hills who made his living supplying addresses and private phone numbers) smaller, more compatible groupings were constantly forming, dissolving, and re-forming: the Smart Young People's group, the Ranch-Householders' group, the Horse, Boat, and New York-Theater group, and the myriad interweavings of these various groups, with an overlap into Los Angeles society, radio and TV. There was also a pitiful, hard-driven group of famous singers, men and women, who had made the destructive mistake of entertaining free of charge and, since they were now asked everywhere with this objective in mind, knew what lay ahead when they spied one of their own sort at any gathering and passed between each other a harried look which asked the question "When do we go on?"

Best of all party groups were those brought together for one occasion, by a single host or hostess well placed in the industry though not quite at the top: parties where a Name was not enough but where, in order to obtain an invitation, you

(83)

had to have good manners, talent or intelligence, or all three —failing which you had to be at least a bona fide friend. Nancy had a theory that the distinguishing feature of these really "good" parties was that incidents took place at them, little dramatic happenings which one laughed at or remembered: it was impossible to say whether the incidents made the parties or the parties made the incidents, they happened, that was all. For example take the hilarious thing tonight, at the Fines'. Greg Fine, a producer at MGM, was giving the party as a farewell to his wife, Dorothy, who was going to Europe; dinner had been delicious and after dinner Springfield Folger, the columnist, had risen and rapped on his glass. Everyone stopped talking, of course, and Spring who by this time was definitely stoned, made a speech worded in the lush pseudo-intimate baby talk he used in his column and his radio m.c. job, saying how the party was in honor of Dorothy's trip and how they all loved her so much.

"And now," he wound up, raising his glass handsomely to the hostess who sat in a daze at the head of the center table, overcome with finding herself, for the first time in her life, an object of public attention, ". . . and now, Dorothy, we take our leave of you. Dear person: We will miss you, Dorothy and—shall I confess it? Yes, we envy you, I know I do. Ah, the Campagna! Ah, Piccadilly, Montparnasse, the Bois! You'll soon be seeing those magical places in all their enchantment while we poor slaves go drudging on right here, down in the smog. Have a good time, dear, and hurry back. I think that's all I have to say except one phrase that says it all. Good-bye, dear Dorothy, good luck and . . ."

Spring collected all eyes, waited for a beat of one, a beat of two—and then with startling effect the hoarse gangster voice of Brod Barton, who, when he had a can on, always played his hoodlum roles offstage, punched: "Bun voyage . . ."

Everyone howled. The feud between Brod and Spring had started years ago, God only knew what about, but it was famous and Brod had certainly picked the right moment to score. Spring broke up. Spring was really more than a shade homo, though he always denied it: he broke up and stamped his foot.

"Thanks very much, Brod," he said, "thanks for filling in. I'm sure we all appreciate it . . ."

"Bun voyage . . ." Brod repeated wittily, and the guests howled some more. The phrase was, of course, just what Spring in his cute, effete way, had been about to say before Brod beat him to the punch.

"Perhaps you'd like to rise and lead this toast, Brod," Spring said. "I'm sure I'm completely finished."

Dorothy Fine blushed, burst into tears, and left the table. This solemn moment, sentimentally dedicated to her leave-taking, had turned into a comedy scene in which the guests eating and drinking at her expense guffawed, stamped, and thumped each other's backs in their joy at the byplay between Spring and Brod. Dorothy rushed for the bedroom where her female friends followed to reassure her. Nancy thought that Dorothy was certainly making the most of her wrongs but, not wishing to seem without sympathy since Greg, obviously, might be helpful to Harold some day, went up to her and told her Brod should be machine-gunned. Freddy Rogiot was waiting at the foot of the stairs when she came down—a short, somehow pearshaped fellow with a wavering, bemused face and large, damp hands; a former RAF hero, he had written an intellectual novel about the Battle of Britain which Christian had liked. It was funny, she reflected, as she raised her arms to dance with him, how many of her friends, the people she liked best, although she only saw them out at parties, dated from her life with Christian Mist, her first husband; she also realized, making the physical adjustment required when dancing with Freddy (he danced smoothly but with an odd rhythm, due to a combat hip injury) that Christian would have liked Freddy as much as his book. Like Christian, Freddy was all in one piece, spinning on his own axis—a man of talent, not the driving sort that Harold was or mature and fulfilled like Christian, but charming and intelligent, boyish and (outmoded word!) gallant.

Gallantry! . . . She wondered, moving to the music, whether she would have appreciated this quality or many of the things she now prized most in life if they had not come to her as legacies from Christian's world—that massive and irrecapturable world which now seemed so remote. She had never, she felt, quite deserved it; she had been a starlet just promoted to her first dramatic role when she and Christian met. He had been the greatest actor of his generation, perhaps one of the greatest of all time—or at least, that was what everyone had said. She had fallen in love with him the first day they worked together on the set of *The Impostor* when he put his arm around her and told her the way to read the line "Possibly you're right, old boy." He was at that time fifty-eight, yet filled with a youthfulness of feeling, needing, wanting. His face was so empty and ravaged that it had the appearance of not being a face, of having been shot off, perhaps, so that nothing was alive in it but his eyes, the only eyes of a complete, whole man, she thought, that she had ever seen. He was a drinker; his body was puny; his hair came out in handfuls; he was a miser, a part-time Communist, and in many ways a fraud, cynical and ferocious, but she loved him for the greatness in him, for his suffering and his understanding of human beings and the truth that came through everything he did, even the bad things, and every scene he played, even the most ill-written and unimportant scene of some picture which was itself of no moment.

She loved him but she never deluded herself that her love was returned. He had married her because he had to have someone with him; there was something ahead of him he could not face alone. This was his need. It had been enough for her.

In their brief marriage, as she looked back on it now (and lately, for some reason, she had looked back on it more than was good for her), she and Christian had not communicated much with each other, certainly not through the medium of words or interests held in common. She had sent her mother back to New York and moved into Christian's house on Rexford Drive, a Spanish house with high ceilings and big bathrooms; here she and her husband invented a way of talking to each other, speaking sentences which were themselves like empty rooms set with a few small pieces of ill-chosen furniture.

Christian Mist had died of cancer in the middle of their second winter together and Nancy, numb with desolation (she had fainted at the funeral, to the enrichment of late afternoon editions), found that she was a celebrity: The Young Widow. She had gone back to work, but with only fair success; with a sense of obligation, since the studio had kept her on the payroll (out of deference to Christian, she suspected; it would not do for some columnist to find that The Young Widow had been cast off) she did anything the Front Office required: she posed for cheesecake stills, she christened ships, she was voted the girl whom the delegates to the National Electric Appliance Sales Convention would most like to be on a desert island

(87)

with. This last honor, she sometimes insisted, had been her outstanding consolation until, visiting in the lunchroom at Duart, she met Harold and life began to be different.

12

"How is she?"

Nancy, sunk in reverie, looked up at Freddy blankly.

"Who?"

"Dorothy, of course."

"Oh," she said, pulling herself back into the present and feeling somewhat spiteful in consequence, "loving it to pieces, I would say."

"I thought it was a bit rough for her," Freddy said in a surprised tone. He was always springing to defend assaulted or insulted womanhood.

"But I saw you laughing," Nancy said to prod him on.

"I was, I was," he said sheepishly. "But I felt badly about it. Doesn't matter, though, of course."

"It does if you feel that way," Nancy said gently, herself feeling like a mother, almost, to Freddy.

"Oh, come off it, Nancy."

"No, I mean it," she insisted. "It's a sweet point of view. Just the sort of thing I love you for. See?"

She leaned back softly, peering up into his face, and Freddy, immensely pleased, beamed down at her with his wobbly eyes.

"Oh, do come off it," he said again.

Rab O'Grady danced by with Miranda Dobbs: "A new twosome," as the *Rambling Reporter* put it next day. There had been rumors that Miranda's Thing with Lucky Mansfield had gone blah.

"I have some news for you," Rab said and Nancy—as another couple chose this moment to edge between them— pantomimed "See you later." She made Freddy dance her over to the buffet where in addition to bottled drinks served by Carlos, a barman from Romanoff's, there was a silver punch bowl with a huge slab of pink sherbet tilted into it.

"By the way," Freddy said suddenly, "did I tell you I'm shoving off to England?"

His large hands juggled the tiny punch cup; his face seemed to be dissolving into it. This was his way of making announcements—he lurched into them just as he did into dance steps.

"Whatever for?"

"Have to. Studio dropped me. Oh, they were jolly nice about it and all that, but I won't stay without papers and they know it."

"Papers," she knew from the past, was Freddy's phrase for "contract."

"Freddy—this is impossible. I just don't understand."

"Happened, though. Truth of God."

There was a crimson divan across one end of the room on which another couple was already sitting, the girl on the man's lap, but there was room enough on the mountain of upholstery for six more couples; Nancy, with her arm through Freddy's, led him there.

"It *couldn't* have happened," she said with great earnestness. "They were so pleased, I thought you told me, with the screenplay."

Freddy's face hardened. When he looked like that Nancy could understand how he must have looked flying the Spitfires eleven, no, thirteen years ago.

"Only the last one. Can you fancy it? Zeld sent me a note, said it took an Oxford man to write a decent western. He had Zeidman give me a lot of rot about it being studio policy to drop all options at the moment, and all that."

"Perhaps it *is* policy."

"Can't help it. I'm off in a fortnight."

Nancy felt an unreasonable alarm. She had counted on Freddy, she did not know in exactly what way: one more of the precious links between her and the lost life with Christian.

"What are you going to do?" she said quietly.

"Write some fiction."

"The one about Dunkirk?"

"Hardly."

"But I'm mad for that one."

Freddy said vaguely, "Dunkirk's had a bit written about it. This one will be about Hollywood."

"You never told me about that one."

"It's been a dark secret. I have packets of notes."

He smirked, then said shyly, "You're in it, you know."

Nancy put down her glass.

"I say, do you mind?" he demanded with sudden anxiety.

"Of course not."

"You don't exactly look pleased."

"I'm pleased. Also flattered. But I'd be more flattered if you'd told me all this about leaving before you—before it was decided."

He took her hand—his own clammy as a fish, as usual. She wondered why men with clammy hands always wanted to be clutching someone. Yet for some reason she was moved, al-most teary.

"I'd given it a thought. I even thought of asking whether you'd care to go with me."

"Why, Freddy. Is this a proposition?"

"Proposal. I believe that's the correct term."

"Thank you. And when did this occur to you?"

"Been occurring for months," Freddy said. "Why not, now? Can you think of any reason?"

"Let me see—" She appeared to take concentrated thought. "Well, for one thing—I have a husband."

Freddy said, "I'm rather fond of him."

"And I love him."

In spite of the tone of banter which she, at least, had been using (you couldn't tell about Freddy) she had felt obligated to make this statement and it was not in the same tone: it did not fit.

"Naturally. Still, that's not a reason."

"No? But it *could* be one. I mean, from a conventional point of view . . ."

"It could be," Freddy said looking at her with eyes which now wobbled not at all. "But not necessarily."

Nancy took a deep breath. She had a longing to enjoy just for a second or two the senseless pleasure which passed through her. It had been a long time since any man, above all one like Freddy who was reticent almost to the point of tor-ment (which made it, of course, far more flattering), had indi-cated that he was in love with her.

He was amazingly youthful in most ways. She withdrew her hand.

"Freddy," she said, looking at him with exactly the proper

archness, "this is the nicest indecent proposal I have had to-night."

"Will you meet me somewhere?"

"No."

"Will you, at least, let me tell you why I'm going? The real reason?"

"You just told me," she said firmly.

"But not the real reason. I'm leaving because of you. Because I can't remain and—"

"Now Freddy, darling—"

"Please, Nancy. I must see you somewhere, just for a few—"

He looked so desperate that she put her hand against his cheek.

"I've already told you once tonight that I love you and that's enough. At this moment I have a violent urge for another brandy punch. And there's somebody over there that I must talk to . . ."

13

Rab O'Grady was standing at the buffet, giving a performance. Apparently there had been an aftermath to the Brod Barton-Springfield Folger encounter: Rab and some other pranksters had obtained a bunch of vegetable tops from the kitchen, they had made a bouquet of them and sent them by a

(92)

servant to Spring, who was sulking in a corner, with a card which said "Bun Voyage from Brod." In a burst of rage, Spring had gone up to Brod and tossed the bouquet in his face. Brod had swung on him and the pranksters had had to close in quickly to prevent manslaughter. Rab O'Grady acted out the complete episode—Spring's bravery and Brod's dumbfounded, then furious reaction; he made it all very funny without ever becoming part of it or losing his own controlled, rather sinister elegance. Nancy, laughing with the rest, wondered as she had many times before why no producer ever put Rab in a comedy, he would have been so good in one, just as he was in everything else.

Rab could play dramatic roles or Hopalong-type westerns with equal facility. His real name was Paul Rabner Gradich and he was not Irish but Slav: he had arrived in the United States as the lover of a famous, aging European star who had refused to work in Hollywood unless the studio that wanted her also signed her youthful protégé. The star had gone home, disgruntled, in six months; Rab had stayed. At first, as Paul Rabner, he lived in a white tie and tails, playing dukes, card sharpers and gigolos; as the vogue for such characters lessened Rab fell into unemployment but revived professionally when it was discovered that his spare, athletic frame looked well in dungarees. He was an excellent horseman and what was left of his hardly perceptible Belgrade accent could pass for a brogue as easily as it had once been slanted for Spanish or Parisian. Born of an aristocratic family which he had charmingly depreciated (". . . anyone with three pigs was a Baron in my country . . .") he had good-humoredly accepted the Irish name which the Duart publicity department conferred on him.

The results had been gratifying. The Rab O'Grady Fan

Club, an international organization, had members in Pakistan, Dubuque, Iowa, and—what was more important—County Athlone. Nancy had first met him in Christian's house; Rab had been one of Christian's few old friends who had stuck with him after he had begun dabbling, as it had been thought so smart to do in the days of the Grand Alliance, with the Vine Street outposts of communism. He and Christian had argued by the hour on this and other issues while Nancy, sitting with a crossword puzzle or a game of solitaire, had wished she'd had enough education to talk with her husband the way Rab could. She had been jealous of him and disliked him as a phony: his conceit, the lifts on his shoes, his false name, everything about him had irritated her and she had wondered why Christian bothered with him—yet it had been Rab who fended off the photographers who closed in to record her collapse at the funeral; it was he who had brought her home later and helped her, with phone calls and visits, through the first anguished weeks of widowhood. Later they had seen each other less, hardly at all since her marriage to Harold; their contact was resumed by chance when they ran into each other one afternoon at Kahn, Inc.—Harold's agents. They greeted each other like the old friends they were and Rab took her into Scandia for a drink: she spent an hour telling him how happy her marriage was; she described the MG, the Bellaire house, the boxer—telling him everything, in fact, except that she had been thinking of getting a job.

Rab had now apparently either guessed this or found it out from Ollie (the Aga) Kahn in the time that had intervened since their meeting. Having finished his story about the vegetable tops he took her arm and guided her straight back to the crimson couch which was apparently to be her conference center for the evening. He said, "They're interested in you at Duart."

Nancy was taken aback. She had discussed with nobody outside the agency the business that had taken her to Kahn, Inc. However, she concealed her surprise.

"Do you mean it?"

Rab assumed an air of mystery.

"Few people know that O'Grady is the No. 1 agent in this town. For my friends only. Without charge."

"But when did you do this agenting?"

"When you had a second daiquiri with me last week I said to myself, the marriage is happy, the new home is delightful. But she is just a little bored."

"And being bored, she rushes for the gaiety of a camera. What a logical guess, Rab. It's standard procedure, isn't it? Not that I'm admitting anything, you beast . . ."

"You want to know who mentioned you at Duart?"

"Naturally."

"Then listen—"

He narrated in his moody, dramatic fashion, how he had been in the office of a "certain producer" (a traditional character in Rab's anecdotes) when her name had come up for a role in an O'Grady picture . . . and how he, Rab, had endorsed her.

All of this might well be true. The Aga had said he would acquaint Duart with her interest in working. The mention Rab had heard might be a result of the Aga's presentation.

"—But what sort of a part?" she demanded. "This is so exciting, Rab—"

"A part perfect for you, baby. You are a young housewife . . . I do not know how to say this . . ."

"Please, Rab!"

". . . You are losing your husband. Or he is losing you. I am not sure . . ."

"Then it's *not* perfect, either way. But do go on."

"You are southern. From Louisiana. Good?"

"Yes," she said, frowning with the effort of imagining the part—even the dialogue—and herself reading it with just the faintest, chic suggestion of a drawl. "Yes, I think I could do that. And this is in your next picture, Rab? It would be just too perfect to do something with you . . ."

Rab said the role was for the picture he was scheduled to make after *Leatherlegs*. It was to be a costume picture, he was playing a pirate, Lafitte, who had saved New Orleans; her part, if she got it, was to be the second lead. She listened with intensity, giving off little cries of approbation and interest. From the crimson divan she could see Freddy Rogiot dancing rather glumly with Miranda Dobbs, who did not understand about his hip (damn her, Nancy thought, she's making it difficult on purpose; no one could be so stupid with a man by accident).

Through the open door of the library on her left, a quite different scene was revealed: here the men, Harold among them, had gathered for canasta, gin, and what she called talent talk, a Hollywood practice of which she thoroughly disapproved. The Fines might as well not have wasted money on a dance band; hardly any male partners were available. (Freddy had once said this sort of thing could not happen in Europe; women were too well thought of there.)

"How long ago did Christian die?"

"Whatever made you think of that?"

"But I think of it often, as you do," Rab said with seriousness.

"Yes," Nancy said quickly. She added, "Three years and nine months—"

"And how many days?"

"What is this—widows' statistics week or something?"

Rab shrugged in a manner that was an apology. Rab had as many shrugs as some actors had suits of clothes. She put her hand on his arm to make him understand, in spite of her words, that it was all right.

"Eleven days," she said. "I think—yes, eleven."

"But it is better now? Much better, eh, sweetheart?" Rab said.

"I hardly think about it at all now," she said.

"I think you are happy, maybe. Happiness is always boring, just a little. Especially at first."

"Of course," Nancy agreed.

"With a man like that Christian you got spoiled," Rab said. "Even I got spoiled a little just to be his friend."

"He lived a lot," Nancy said. For days at a time, now, she had been able to keep from thinking about Christian in the sense of concentrating on him. Yet it was a relief to be able to remember, to talk about him with a person who had known him as well as Rab had.

Rab made a gesture as if shaping a theater marquee in the air. *"Positively his last appearance,"* he said, quoting the funeral announcement which, ordered in Christian's will, had appeared in the Los Angeles papers. "He lived, sure. But whoever *died* like that? Give yourself a little time."

Both, looking at the library door, saw Harold come out with the Aga. Rab immediately stood up.

"I must have one dance before that devil husband grabs you. He's a swell boy, sweetheart."

"That's what I've been telling you," Nancy said loyally.

"Give the other time and it will pass. Meantime, if you want to work, Ole Uncle Rab is in your corner. No commission necessary."

"You're sweet, angel," Nancy said. They danced; over his shoulder she blew a kiss to Freddy Rogiot: Freddy was still lurching along, comfortlessly enveloped in Miranda's lovely flesh.

The music stopped. Greg Fine, it seemed, wanted to make an announcement. He stood by the piano, on which he had rapped with his seal ring.

"Don't go anywhere, please, anybody," he said firmly to the room at large. "Frankie's going to sing in half an hour."

There were delighted exclamations. Miranda applauded. "How divine—I just adore Frankie," she said.

Greg, beaming, motioned to the orchestra to resume playing; he strode off to make the same announcement in the next room.

14

Harold did not dance with her right away, as Nancy had rather hoped he would; catching her eye, he waved his cigarette by way of greeting, then continued talking to the Aga. What, she wondered, could they be discussing? Even the industry tradition of bringing business affairs into social gatherings did not make it necessary to spend two hours after dinner mulling around with your agent. She was about to work herself into a mood of annoyance when her instinct checked her; possibly they were really discussing something important. Otherwise why would the Aga devote so much time to him? There was another indication, too, that something was in the wind: tonight, just as they had finished dressing to go out, Miss Frobisch, E. T. Zeld's secretary, had given Harold a standby call, Zeld being one of those insane bosses who liked to work at night. She had ordered Harold to check with her every hour on the hour no matter where he was. Directing pictures for E. T. or in fact working for him in any capacity meant that you could never be far from a telephone. Still, the standby call could be another indication of some front-office move in regard to him.

It was exciting, certainly, being a part of a career on the make instead of one that had been previously crowned with laurel. Nancy watched Harold as she danced, admiring his quick, dark handsomeness (as indeed, she admired everything about him) but feeling, as usual, left out. She had not told him her wish to work again: the few hints she had dropped regarding this had been ignored and she sensed that he would oppose her. Why, she wondered? It could not be out of jealousy, because he objected to her having an interest other than himself? Such a conclusion did not seem fair to Harold; it was an ordinary conclusion and the outstanding fact about Harold was that he was not ordinary. There was talent in him—that special thing which now alone excited her. It was not the great universal talent of Christian, in which values were positive and all men found brotherhood, but a limited, intense ability for which he had found exactly the right channel. Then again, they had been able to talk—they had been, that is, until he began working so hard. Almost nostalgically she remembered how, when they first met, they had discussed all the subjects which, in Christian's massive world, there had been no sense discussing: her ideas about life, about books and music and people. They had ridden bicycles together on Sundays, they had gone to little theaters made out of remodeled stores and garages where plays were acted by bright and beautiful and undiscouraged young people—kids, Nancy regarded them as now. They had gone swimming—the one outdoor sport he seemed to care for; they had danced a lot in unfashionable places where there were big, not too crowded dance floors. Nancy had liked Harold a lot right off because he had a boxer pup, Bobo, and took such good care of him: she also became fond of Bobo and took comfort in him when her own dog, Jasmine, died. Something glittering, wonderful and rewarding stirred in the warm climate of their growing love—just out of reach: it seemed closest sometimes when they were quarreling and then it was gone again.

Nancy could not tell why marriage had not brought this undiscoverable yet necessary element into their lives; it hadn't, though, and daily now its outlines became vaguer, its intoxicating promise further from realization. Instead of the indefinable closeness which had once seemed a possibility they had bonds, agreements, understandings. They had projects. The house was a project—the smallest house in expensive, fashionable Bel-Air: too expensive for them but a chance they had a right to take, Harold's career was going ahead so splendidly. The car was a project—Harold had wanted a Jag but they'd settled for an MG. Why, why was her career the one project which had been taken off the agenda? She hadn't cared at first: if Harold wanted her to stay home she would stay: it was only in the last six months that she had become uneasy about this, finally (and secretly) rebellious. A vacuum had

(100)

settled round her like the Nothing that had happened when she'd lived in Westwood and gone out to lessons. She didn't mind not having made herself a Name in her own right or sacrificing the precarious celebrity of being a great man's widow but she couldn't pretend: there was no use going to hen parties and baby showers, playing tennis with women who played better than she did and gossiping on the telephone as a method of convincing herself that she was of use. She had been of use once, she knew what it was like: Christian Mist's tragic waiting had not excluded her, she had shared it; now she waited alone while Harold rushed by. He needed her for lovemaking: for the rest he seemed quite satisfied if she admired him; she did, but this was not a complete program for a full life. Nor were parties, flirtations, the pleasure of belonging to the inner circles of an industry which the whole world regarded as worth while and fascinating quite enough to give her the feeling she'd had when she'd been a girl growing up in New York City or studying to be a secretary or, later, modeling for John Powers: the feeling of being a real person.

15

A man who was playing *The Thing from Outer Space* at U-I and had grown an apostolic beard to fit the part, cut in on her; Nancy leaned away from him to keep from getting scratched, wondering with a sudden spasm of fear whether Rab or the Aga would mention her job-hunting to her husband. She had cautioned him to secrecy, but then you never knew . . . it would do her no good if Harold heard about it from another person, an outsider, before she herself had found the proper way to broach it to him.

Would tonight be the time? She put the vexing question out of her mind; she wanted to enjoy dancing, even if she had to do it with a Space Monster; she so seldom danced. The floor was gradually becoming crowded as those males not engaged in high-stake card games emerged from the library; Nancy danced with the College Element: a producer's assistant who had gone to Harvard and a producer whose tailor made him look as if he had. A dignified man who had won the Academy Award in the role of a bishop told her a dirty story and an agent who looked like an ant-eater spilled punch on her Dior dress. Finally a soldierly financier whom she and Harold had met in a café cut in, dancing as if he were leading a military band and happened, entirely by accident, to be pushing a woman on his stomach. He was about to finance a picture in Africa, he said, and thought her husband might be "borrowed" to direct it . . . Now at last Harold, answering her distress signals, came over; the Englishman, letting the phantom band stop in the middle of "Rule Britannia," surrendered her with a bow.

"You must come to Kenya, old man," he said, patting Harold on the shoulder. "I've just been telling your wife about it."

"What's about Kenya?" Harold asked as they danced off.

"He wants you to direct a picture for him. He's quite sweet."

"Kenya might be all right."

(102)

"And I might as well have been there all evening. I haven't set eyes on you."

"But I've been watching you, my pet, and you've been doing fine, just fine."

"Thank you. Whatever were you doing with the Aga so long?"

"I'll tell you later."

They were in front of the crimson divan. Because she could see something was bothering him she stopped dancing and, seating herself, pulled him down beside her.

"Harold? . . ."

"Not the right place to talk about it, though," he said.

Harold, she knew, would talk about anything, anywhere, except his employment at Duart.

"You mean they didn't renew? That's what the Aga was telling you?"

He nodded. So this was the "new deal": to have no deal at all.

"Is he sure?"

"Quite sure. He's known since yesterday."

"But he must have said something more than just *that*."

"He didn't exactly say anything. But he's not worried."

"Darling, I'm very glad. We're in the breadline and the Aga isn't worried. I'm so relieved for him."

"It's not as bad as that. Just that theater business is way off and the studio has a pile of dough in this new wide-screen process, Cinemirror. They're not renewing anyone except stars."

"As a matter of fact," she said, remembering, "Freddy's option was dropped too. He says he's going back to England."

"Probably where he belongs," Harold said. Lately he had shown signs of petulance about Freddy.

(103)

"But they'll keep you on a week-to-week basis, won't they?" she persisted. "Or does the Aga think you ought to make a change?"

Harold looked around to make sure nobody was eavesdropping. During her five years in Hollywood Nancy had become accustomed to this wide-sweeping look, in restaurants, at parties, in studio anterooms—the look which cleared the air of invisible eyes and ears.

"That's just what we were talking about, if you want to know," he said, dropping his voice. "I can go to Paramount any time for more money. But the Aga thinks Zeld wants me for a special job. He wouldn't say just what it is."

"Oh, Harold—what do you suppose?"

"I haven't got the slightest idea," he said, "but we'll know soon. Maybe even tonight."

The orchestra had begun to play a rumba and he rose: he liked to rumba.

"Do you suppose that's what the call from Zeld was about?"

He did not answer, concentrating on the subdued, intricate steps, and Nancy, too, fell silent, enjoying the dance though she resented, in an inarticulate fashion which many of his words and actions now inspired in her, both the manner in which he had assumed that, since it was now his whim, she must dance with him, and his refusal to answer her question. Much of their former capacity to share experiences had been diminished or extinguished by this absent-minded superiority on his part, a manner which excluded ordinary courtesies as if they were not worth observing or as if she, for some shortcoming she could not pin down, did not merit their observation. Still, still—couldn't they revive those moments, the communication that had made their courtship pleasant, their marriage basically possible? From the skylines of cities, the spirit of lonely places, from music, plays, automobile drives at night, sometimes even from people—they still drew and took pleasure in sharing an identical excitement: yet he no longer sought or seemed to attach importance to this sharing. She had often heard him complain of his father's arrogance and intransigeance and the hurt these traits had caused him in his boyhood: she wondered now, even as she smoothly and sensuously matched her movements to his, whether he weren't inflicting the same failings upon her.

The music stopped; he brought her a highball. She knew that in a moment he would look at his watch, say that they must go. It was eleven o'clock: they had dined, he'd had his business talk; they'd had one dance together. This, in his eyes, constituted the full gamut of an evening out—not so in hers.

"Did you call Miss Frobisch?"

"Yes, she said to check with her again about twelve."

"But darling, let's be sane. He certainly won't want to see you after *midnight*."

"You never can tell about E. T."

"He's a maniac."

"Maybe, but he pays the bills. And regardless of tonight, I've got to be on the set early tomorrow—"

With a hand on his wrist she forestalled the inevitable raising of the watch. Tonight, her instinct told her, he would object if she suggested coming on later with Rogiot nor did she, for once, want to suggest this.

Dorothy Fine, fully recovered from her bout of tears, expressed regret that they were going. She stood beside her husband in the hall, both declaiming almost in unison "But Frankie's going to sing in just a *minute* . . ."

And it was true. As the parking boy brought up the MG

Nancy, already half regretting her docility, heard through the French windows behind her the firm preliminary chords of a piano, then the famous voice beginning "The Young in Heart."

16

Did Harold appreciate her sacrifice in leaving without protest? She hoped so: possibly because the sacrifice itself engendered a warm feeling in her she felt unusually fond of him: some degree of insensitiveness was to be expected from a person who had himself experienced little gentleness. To Christian, fundamentally a gentle man, success had been taken for granted: to Harold it was a major objective, almost an obsession. Was that so unnatural? He had come of age in a world where success or the lack of it was the difference between splendor and humiliation: his boyhood had been conditioned by this pressure, his family eventually divided by it.

Harold had Hollywood in his blood; option or no option, he himself was a success, would be an even greater one. Nothing could stop him. He was a success and he was the most attractive man she knew, far more so than Freddy, far, far more so than Christian had been, Christian, whom she had loved so much better. And in the small car, wishing to make the most of the attraction she was feeling, she moved close to her husband or as close, at least, as she was able in view of the division caused by the bucket-seats: she reached over and put her hand between her husband's shirt front and his skin. Not only bucket-seats but other troubles could be thus defeated, troubles which were by no means all of Harold's making. Her flirtation with Freddy Rogiot, for instance, (though till now she had not consciously applied "flirtation" to her relations with Freddy, what other word was there?) had gone on long enough. And Rab . . . well, Rab . . . he was sympathetic and well-meaning but he too probably thought lightly of her marriage. Here again she had been to blame: neither Rab nor the Aga had been the person to consult about resuming her career. The Aga's encouragement had removed her project from the status of a reverie but it would not be real or in any way truly feasible until she had Harold's approval. Perhaps tonight . . . she leaned over suddenly and kissed him.

"Now, baby," he said warningly, but took a hand off the wheel to pull her closer.

"Now, baby," she mimicked, "what's the matter—are you afraid we'll get pinched for necking?"

"I'm afraid we'll get pinched, period," he said.

He had been driving slowly on Sunset Boulevard where a few traffic cops might still be working even at this hour; now, entering into Bel-Air through large stone gates resembling those of a mortuary he unwound the MG on the curving, banked strips of macadam named like perfumes or ballets: Bellagio, Copa de Oro, Tortuoso.

Yes, she thought, perhaps tonight . . .

Harold cut the engine, the car coasting noiselessly, with the slight bumping motion of a bobsled, down their own driveway and into the garage; she knew that when he cut the light he would turn and take her in his arms; she became excited almost at once and deliberately exaggerated her excitement in order to please him. They sat kissing for several minutes; then she gave him a pat and quickly got out. She liked to precede him to the bedroom where, while he delayed downstairs making a drink or letting out Bobo, the boxer, she used the interval to prepare for love, then "made an entrance" from her dressing room, wearing gold slippers, perfume and a serious, inventive air which Harold called her "bed expression." In their increasingly strained life together his desire for her had, paradoxically, heightened, while for her sex had become important chiefly because in its development (provided, like a Chinese drama, with stock characters and an unchanging dénouement) she, though barred from more professional enterprises could be at the same time a performer and a member of the audience; the bedroom with its subdued rosy light and kingsize bed became a sort of sound stage where she played her most interesting and, as she sometimes thought, her most successful scenes.

Was this perhaps the real flaw in their relationship, she wondered, that love was a performance, from her point of view? The pleasure, of course, was real, the pangs which sometimes rippled through her almost unendurable, but always satisfaction had to be channeled through acting and indeed became acting so that even in the middle of the most violent delights she wondered whether they were still in love. She would have been jealous at the thought of Harold turning to another woman—indeed, it was hard for her to think of such a possibility—but at the same time she had encouraged other men to flirt with her in a way that was amusing but not entirely good for her marriage. For make-believe to dominate her here, at the source of intimacy, where all unreality should have dissolved, was frightening, implying as it did that her own inner life was either at a standstill or itself a distortion, a fantasy.

Yes, no longer paid to act, she had invented a way of acting which had the power to corrupt as well as to divert—had cast herself moreover in a role which had existed in life but which was no longer either true reality or inspired creation: the role of Harold's wife.

She snapped on the lights in the living room, coming suddenly to a decision: tonight she would not go upstairs! Instead, while she was still in the mood which preceded closer intimacy she would try to reach some conclusion about their lives. She tossed her mink stole on a chair and went into the combined kitchen-and-pantry of this new house they had been so proud of and in which she was no longer sure she wanted to live; she found whiskey, ice, and glasses and put them on a tray, then made two sandwiches, it was so much easier to face vital problems when you had something to eat and drink.

She carried the tray into the living room, and sat down to wait for Harold; she leaned back decoratively in one of the big white chairs and on her face was an expression of inner searching which people now identified with her and remembered about her just as they had once remembered her voice and long thin legs and the way she had thrown her head back when she laughed: the inheld violence that was "her look."

17

"Easy now, pal, what's the big rush? That's it—Hey, man!
. . . Can't you knock me down?"

The boxer, a beautifully compact projectile of bone and
muscle, threw himself again and again at Harold, loving the
game, rebounding from the damp lawn with each knockdown
to try again, shamefully smearing his master's dinner coat
with his wet paws. And Harold ducked and blocked, stepped
in and out as if he were battling a human opponent.

"Once more, kid . . . that's the way . . . what's stopping you?" With an abrupt change of mood, he tired of the
game, slapped the dog sharply when Bobo, overexcited, refused to understand that it was over. Both stood breathing
hard, Harold with his hand on the dog's collar, looking down
at the scatter of lights on the landscaped levels below him—
the hotel to his left and the soft invisible expanse of the golf
course. Just under him, on his own property, was the small
hedged sun patio where Nancy lay for hours each day, slowly
turning a beautiful golden brown. Surely she must be ready
by now: to prolong anticipation he waited a moment longer,
then went inside.

Something was wrong; there was no light upstairs; to his
surprise, Nancy called to him from the living room. He

turned toward her, his eyes not yet adjusted to the light, his clothing disarranged.

"I thought we might have a nightcap in here. Do you mind?"

She handed him a highball, offered the plate of sandwiches. It seemed to her that a vital hurdle had been passed when he took one. He sat down, looking at her uncertainly.

"Darling," she began, "I was just thinking: if we have to economize there's something I could do to help."

"Why do we have to economize?"

"I mean, with the new situation at the studio and all. Oh, you're all wet."

"I was playing with Bobo."

"That dog. Why do you do things like that when you have on good clothes?"

"You don't have to throw a tizzy just because my option wasn't taken up. I'm not leaving Duart, you know; there's no talk about that."

"But things aren't *certain*. Perhaps I'm a dope but I like to know where my next dollar is coming from."

"The next one will come where the others have come from the last four years," he said, controlling his irritability, "and where seventeen hundred and fifty come from every week— the motion picture business. I guess we can get by on that."

"You really ought to take that coat off, it's soaking. I hope those smears come out. All I mean is that I'd like to help you if you need it. I'd like to be some use."

She's restless, he thought; this isn't anything she cooked up tonight, it's been coming on for a long time.

"You are of use. This is where I need you—right here."

"But sweetie—"

(111)

"When we got married you said you were disgusted with acting—fini."

"I was. I don't mean that I'd take it *seriously,* the way I did then."

"If you don't take it seriously, what's the use? What chance have you got with the gals that do take it seriously? You'll be crocheting samplers while they're playing kick-you-in-the-nuts."

"Sweetie, that's perfectly true. Only don't you see, I wouldn't care. I'd be on the team, helping *us.* I wouldn't be going to baby showers or getting a wax pack, waiting until you had time or weren't too tired to take me out."

"My God," he burst out, "honestly, Nancy, this is the oldest complaint of wives. They feel neglected. They—"

"Well, most of them—"

"—never go out. What—"

"Are and don't!"

"—crap. You aren't and you do. We went to Ciro's last week. We went to the Fines' tonight. And suppose you didn't go out, would our life be lousy on that account? When have you ever taken the attitude that we had to be gadabouts? I can't stay up every night till four o'clock, you know, and be on the set at eight."

"You know that's not what I mean," she said. "You have to make everything so *typical.* This isn't typical, neglected wife vs. overworked husband. It's us and we're not typical."

"You're sure talking as if *you* were."

She had wanted so much to avoid a quarrel and now without warning they were halfway into one. To gain time she picked up the paw-splotched coat he had tossed on the new divan and made a show of rubbing at the spots with his handkerchief.

(112)

"I guess there's no use talking about it, then."

"Why not? Let's talk. Only let's not kid we're going to go hungry. A contract's not always the best deal at a studio, just as long as you stay on salary. There are directors in the business who won't take a contract and they haven't missed a day's work in years. So point one: we don't have to economize. What's the next point?"

"Us."

"What about us?"

"I feel left out, that's all. I hate it."

He bit into a sandwich but his mouth was dry, he couldn't chew. He put the sandwich down, thoughtfully nipped on his highball.

"Left out in what way?"

"By your success."

"A minute ago you had to put your shoulder to the wheel because I was a failure."

"I never said that. I know we'll be all right. Even saying 'your success' is too glib and all that but I'm all alone most of the time, even when you're here. That's the part I can't stand."

"How would your going to work fix it? It would only be a new way of walling us up from each other, only you'd have your wall too."

She put the coat down, turned quickly toward him.

"Walls are the whole trouble. What can we do about them? Go to a psychiatrist? That costs fifty dollars an hour. I'd rather go somewhere and work for fifty dollars a day."

She spoke harshly now, in contrast to his own rather sudden quietness. Why was he so afraid that if she went back to acting he would lose her? Obviously that was his fear or he would have been reasonable, have seen her point of view—he often did, if it did not really matter, did not threaten the cage he

(113)

had built around himself to keep love out. He needed love—
nobody more than he, but she could not break down the cage
and she was getting tired of trying.

"I'd honestly rather you didn't, Nancy, though, of course,
I . . ."

"—I don't think you—"

"—realize. We could talk to the Aga, of course."

"I *have* talked to him," she said, avoiding his eyes. This
seemed the most damaging admission she had made so far.

He nodded. Her exposure of this intimate problem to a
stranger did not seem either to surprise or anger him.

"And—?"

"Oh, nothing definite. But there's a part coming up at Duart . . ." She felt it would be best not to mention Rab's
services as an agent-without-commission.

"The Aga thinks it would be good for me," she said.

"Great! In a bead bra, I suppose, doing a samba in a
musical."

"It's the part of a young southern housewife."

"You're southern, I suppose?"

"You could suppose I was an actress. Then I wouldn't have
to be southern. I could *act* southern . . ."

"Pardon me."

She ignored his sarcasm.

"He wanted to talk to Zeld about it, but I said I'd have to
ask you first."

"Well, you've asked and I—"

"Darling—"

She slipped to her knees beside his chair. "Can't you see
how much this means to me, not to be left out, just to have
something to do? If I'm restless, it's a worry to you too: you
think you're not enough of a success. Then you drive harder
(114)

and harder. You shut yourself up more and more. Pretty soon we might get like those wives and husbands who are hardly on speaking terms. Wouldn't it be better if I had something to keep me busy?"

"Jesus, Nancy—"

"No, let me finish . . . If you're against it I'll give it up, you know I will, but then I'll be unhappy and that will hurt you. I never was unhappy, really—except after Christian died. But not lonely. Even then I had records, I had books . . ."

"Books!"

He smiled in an infuriating manner. In spite of her protests to the contrary he had always conceived of her widowhood as a period of public sorrow and private debauch just as he thought of her modeling days as a series of brief photographic sittings, alternating with feverish sprees. Possibly, she had sometimes thought, he had ornamented her past with imaginary sins so that, accusing her, he could console himself for his jealousy of Christian.

"Yes, books! . . . Oh, you won't understand, you won't seem to although you do. You could imagine it. If this scene were in a picture you could direct it perfectly and make everybody cry. But in yourself you can't understand it. You were born in the life I was always trying to get into. No one ever kept you from getting a job when you wanted one."

"You're wrong. Somebody did."

"But you got the job anyway, didn't you?"

"Yup. But it cost me."

"This is costing me," she said in a low voice. "It's costing me . . ." She was about to say, "our love," but held this back, it sounded so deliberately dramatized and cheaply so. But might it not be true? Again fear at the prospect of losing what she had gripped her and she turned from him and, still on the floor, sat at right angles, leaning her head against his knees.

He stroked her hair lightly, looking down at her body so daringly exposed in the provocative dress, thinking how desirable she was, especially when stirred. But the excitement which brought them together in this way stemmed from the same pressures which were inexorably forcing them apart.

"What the hell. If you want to go to work, go to work."

"Harold . . ."

"I mean it."

He carefully removed her head from his knees and her hand from his ankle. He put down his drink, looked in the box on the occasional table for a cigarette, failed to find one and crossed to the mantel where he found one and lit it. All this time his wife sat on the floor looking at her husband as a district attorney might look at a prospective juror whom he was about to dismiss for cause.

"Are you sure?"

"What do you mean?"

"If I'll tell you you'll get angry."

"No, I won't," he said with anger.

"You see?"

"All right," he said, modifying his tone. "Tell me."

He forced a look of amiable, husbandly expectancy into his eyes.

"I think you're agreeing to let me work because at this moment you want to go to bed with me."

"That's what I thought you'd say," he said. "All my motivations are based, according to you, on my yearning to get you in the feathers."

(116)

"—But how can we be *honest* if you promise everything *then,* and later take it back?"

"I haven't promised anything. Not right now I haven't. I just said you could work if you wanted to. Is that a promise?"

"Well," she said with sudden resignation, "it's your decision. So make up your mind."

"And whatever I say, you'll go along with it?"

"I'll try."

He looked at her uncertainly where she stood in front of the white couch which had cost them twelve hundred dollars at Sloane's, her arms at her sides, her eyes streaked with mascara and her beautiful half-bare body turned square toward him. She would try, too: she had a lot of loyalty in her. And he knew that if he took her in his arms then she would go to bed with him and the quarrel would be forgotten for a while in their closeness, only to reappear at some future time. It seemed better, if possible, to get it settled once and for all.

"Don't do it, then."

"Oh—"

"I'm sorry, Nan . . ."

She buried her face in her hands, then raised it and looked at him.

"That's final, sweetie?"

"I guess so," he said miserably. "You know I want to say yes. But you're right, I'll take it back. And I'd have to take it back. Two jobs in one family may work, if they're ordinary jobs—but not the kind I've got or the kind you'd get. Hell, in a week we'd be clawing at each other like cats in a barrel. Why should we kid ourselves?"

With her face turned away, he heard her say in a low voice, "Yes, I wonder why we do . . ."

Silence fell on them—fell on them and lasted longer than

a silence should if the subject which it interrupted is to be further discussed. It was broken, finally, by no word or action of either, but by the telephone.

Nancy was the first to rouse herself. With a grimace she handed him the mouthpiece.

Miss Frobisch's voice, warmly executive, said pleasantly, "Now, dear, you were supposed to check with me. I called you at the Fines'."

"What time is it?" Harold barked, immediately tense.

"Twelve-fifteen, dear," Miss Frobisch said. "He's in with Von Kramm and Louie Zeidman but they're tapering off. I think he'll be ready for you in half an hour . . ."

18

She'd been right, of course, he thought, holding his watch under the dashlights of the MG so as to see the time: eight minutes, employed in getting out of his dinner jacket and into a sports coat, plaid shirt, and slacks, left him twenty in which to get to the studio: just enough. She should be privileged to work if she wanted to. She had not really been doing badly when she "gave up her career" for him—or not as badly as she'd thought at the time: her conclusions in regard to this had been much influenced by things he'd said, while appearing not to say them. Things such as "Before long you'll get a better part . . . ," when the part she'd had was a marvel of good luck, or ". . . I liked you in the scene, you were just swell except right at the end—you know? The spot when you . . ." Thus he had swung her his way, finding methods of increasing the discouragement which affected all young actresses so easily. The wrong kind of praise could do it to them, even the wrong kind of look. Then after their marriage he himself had artfully suggested that perhaps she'd like to keep on as if she herself had had the contrary idea, and she, after some weeks of hesitation had said with conviction, "No, dear, I've decided . . . I'm through with all that. I just wasn't made to be an actress, I guess . . ."

He charged down the winding roads, banking around turns he had negotiated in the opposite direction less than two hours earlier. He wondered why he hadn't mentioned to her till tonight how his father had once tried to block him in his own career: a point he had gone into at some length with Abe Limbagh. Abe, now in private practice, was a therapist he'd known in the Army; he'd gone up to see him a few times after work and they'd smoked and chatted companionably with their feet up on the desk in Abe's small office.

"I'd put it this way," Abe said. "Your feelings about your father are less oedipal than occupational: you didn't know it then, but you two were professional rivals before you were five years old . . ."

Did everything within fifty miles of a sound stage take on an occupational slant—even the relationship between father and son, man and wife? Abe was, no doubt, a very wise, well-integrated fellow; he'd tried to be helpful, but at the same time the problem hadn't been settled. Was this situation with Nancy also a problem of competition? Was it true she felt "excluded" or did she want to go back to work so that she could stop being a retainer, as it were, and be a rival? Driving

(119)

rapidly past the darkened, expensive houses of Beverly Glen he tried to analyze his own feelings about this. No guy naturally liked to have his wife covered with body makeup kissing Gable on some safari set, but that was silly too: Nancy wasn't the cheating kind, nor was his objection to her plan based on any such glib superficial fears. It was far more than that: somehow deep in his being was the conviction that the industry in which he had succeeded so well was also the enemy of his chance for eventual or stable happiness. Sometimes he dreamed of leaving it all, saving enough money so that he and Nancy could go away some place where he could get into another business, direct for the theater or write plays or books.

The theater was not a world apart, at least from what he knew of it. The people were real, they stood in front of other flesh and blood people and spoke their lines, and in their personal lives they were also a part of the main stream of humanity, they lived and worked in cities in which entertainment was an employment similar to other employments. It was different for motion picture actors. They were a caste; the idolatry accorded them, while it gave them a feudal status like royalty in foreign countries, cut them off from other people with the result that they were restricted to consort only with their own kind. They even had a city or at least certain portions of a city set apart for their use and their big salaries were paid in a currency which, what with taxes and high living costs, could not be fairly circulated away from this (as it were) Ghetto area: the Tiffany Ghetto where talent instead of race was the fatal strain which locked you off behind the Pale!

To be sure, The Ghettoites could make love, like those prisoners in Mexican federal penitentiaries who take their families to live with them on barren islands, but they must make love only to each other, with the result that inbreeding sapped the vitality of their already limited caste; they could laugh, but not with the innocent or healing laughter of the great world: their laughter was prison humor, its hilarity incomprehensible to an outsider—like Brod Barton's "Bun Voyage" tonight. Also there was a rule about such laughter, a rule which the stooges and the court jesters knew how to capitalize; it was no good unless someone was hurt by it.

Harold throttled the MG down to a throaty hum, remembering the first time he had heard that laughter. He had been taken by a chauffeur in his father's immense cream-colored car to visit Dan at the studio: when they arrived his father had been busy, as usual, so he'd been taken in tow by a publicity man who conducted him onto some other sets and presented him to the players working there, never introducing him by his own name—which all people love to hear, and no one more than a child—but with the standard formula:

"This is Dan Prader's son . . ."

In those days he had always felt that his father's friends were disappointed in him and he did not blame them. It did not seem right that a big-eyed skinny kid such as he, self-conscious in a store-bought cowboy suit (how much better he would have felt if he could just have worn ordinary clothes!) should be the offspring of a great bull of a man like Dan.

Finally the red lights over the door to his father's sound stage had gone dark, meaning that the take was finished; the publicity man had led him down into the great barnlike interior until they reached a spot of intense concentrated light —the place where the company was working. Here the p.a. made a mock ceremony of presenting him to Dan while a photographer shot candids of the scene.

"Hello, son," Dan said in his booming voice, and Harold had piped, "Hello, Dad. I just met Shortie Williams."

A guffaw went up from the hangers-on, the half-dozen parasites who in all situations accompanied Dan in those days.

Dan's face had stiffened under his makeup and he had dropped his son's hand. The boy, Harold, realized sickeningly that he had pulled a boner. Shortie was his father's arch-rival in western roles, already being groomed (although the blow did not fall till months later) to take his place. Because of this situation, Dan had felt that some prankster had coached Harold to mention Shortie. Later on his mother, when he confided his misery, had explained all this to him—but he did not understand at the time what wrong he had done: he only knew of the sickness that choked him, then the hate for his father, as Big Dan, with the laughter of his stooges ringing in his ears, stalked off, immense, handsome and unforgiving, without a word.

It was something, of course, to be the son of Dan Prader, the Ringo Kid. At school fellows and girls were always asking him questions: was Dan really part Indian? . . . Did he have a cave where he hid out in Arizona? . . . Did his famous horse, Thunder, live at home? . . . How many men had Dan killed? . . . Did he do all those stunts himself? . . .

To the last question Harold could proudly answer yes. That was a wonderful thing that made Dan different from other actors. As the more sophisticated among his playmates knew, other actors had "doubles" but Dan let no one take his place in performing dangerous deeds before the camera. The newspapers were always writing about this and showing pictures of the things Dan did.

Sometimes mothers and big sisters wanted to know about Dan or wanted Harold to get signed pictures of his father for them or even fix it so they could meet him. This he occasionally did and, if the sisters or mothers were pretty, Dan was always very nice to them. He was nice to Harold, too! Lots of times he was swell! . . . Oh, it had been something to be the Ringo Kid's son, all right . . . like at commencement when Dan rode Thunder onto the school grounds and did roping tricks, then put Harold up behind him, allowing him to cling in terror and glory to his belt while Thunder reared and pawed, then turned and galloped off with him while all the kids cheered! Later, to be sure, they teased him in the recess yard, to make up for it . . .

Harold had liked it best when they had had the house on Beverly Drive—the family's first move when they had left the place on Lefferts. Then he could run over to other kids' houses and play. After they moved to the Valley there had been a high chainlink fence all round "the estate," as Dan called it, a fence with barbed wire on top and an electric gate and there hadn't been anyone to play with much. Sometimes his father sought to cure his loneliness; he would make an appointment to see him and come home from the studio (if he didn't phone at the last minute to say he couldn't) bringing the stooges, his leading lady, and anyone else who happened to be around. With this claque to supply applause Dan would demonstrate the various accomplishments which any boy, let alone the son of a famous star, ought to have been glad to learn, but which he, Harold, had detested and at which he was a continual disappointment both to himself and his father. Not that Dan was mean about it. He would pat him on the head and tell him to practice harder. And if he did well he was allowed to go on sets or locations, if not too far away, himself becoming part of the claque while his father, this time for real, again ran through the induplicable feats, the trick riding, the tumbling, the target shooting with his beautiful pearl-handled Colts, and

(123)

all the other tricks which no other man could do as well and no puny boy would be able to do, not even if he practiced the rest of his life.

"We're pals," his father would say to the guys from the studio. "We ride and play like pals. And some day Harold is going to take my place . . ."

The boy, Harold, hadn't known how to tell him that he didn't want to take his place, ever; he just wanted to be let alone.

19

To hell with Abe Limbagh. He'd been a different type of guy in the Army. Abe had been getting sour, getting yellow, sitting with his expensive cordovans up on a mahogany desk and telling him what he, Harold, already knew: that he had to get his old man out of his head. "Surgical removal of the relationship . . . just don't ever see him. Forget you've got a father, at least for now . . ."

He'd admired the ruthlessness of this, yet resented Abe telling it to him. He hadn't made Abe feel the truth, that he had a father no one could forget, no one could surgically remove: a guy like a rock or a cliff, with roots that went down to the middle of the earth, a guy you couldn't kill, who couldn't get old, who destroyed people just by walking past them while they rushed to knock themselves to pieces on his iron frame. He hadn't wanted Abe to tell him how to stop feeling the way he did about Dan but only to tell him it was okay to go on feeling that way. After that "surgical removal" routine he'd walked out of Abe's office never to return.

Oh, long ago he would have talked. He would have talked especially to Dan. He would have told him, would have made a clean breast of it if there had been time but there never had been time even if Dan had liked to talk which he hadn't. So as a consequence of this odd state of affairs the revelation of his own rebellion had come in an unfortunate manner, at a première of Dan's picture, *Motherlode*. Bleachers had been put up for the occasion outside Grauman's Chinese Theater and when Jill and Dan and Harold drove up in the cream-colored limousine, the crowd had cheered just as they cheered Dan at the Santa Claus parade or when, at football games, he rode around the infield between the halves, standing up in the car and waving his hat. Dan had ordered a white dress western coat just like his own made for Harold and Jill also wore western attire and when the crowd cheered Dan waved his hat as usual and Jill smiled graciously. Harold alone had failed to live up to expectations: he had done nothing.

"Wave to them," Dan commanded, but Harold shook his head.

"I don't want to," he said.

"That was a hell of a way to act," his father told him afterward. "Don't you know how to act at a première?"

"I know. I didn't want to, that's all."

"What's the matter, aren't we pals?"

"No," Harold said.

Dan looked tired. He wagged his huge head. "All right, son, all right," he said wearily. "I'm sorry . . ."

Harold had known then that his father was hurt. He had known also with a feeling of intoxicating strength that he himself, thin, undersized and timid, and in fact no match in any way for this handsome, ruthless, yet tenderhearted man, could hurt him, perhaps destroy him . . . and how he longed to hurt, maim, destroy him! For the first time then the savage urge to blot his father off the earth had taken hold of him, the urge which returned when—after having gone to considerable trouble to obtain for Dan a well-paid stunt job in *Blade of Castile*—he had humiliated and harangued him and ordered him off the set. This rage, this secret and vile lust had become even in his boyhood a fountainhead of strength. From that moment he had felt that he, too, would be a person, that he would be successful in some way: when in high school English he had encountered a novelist's statement, "Every man longs to kill his father," he had become so terrified at this exposure of his secret thoughts that when the statement was discussed in class he had declared it was absurd, that no normal person could believe or accept it—and the teacher, to his secret glee, had agreed with him. He sometimes wondered how it would be if, during one of his father's acts of dare-deviltry, he could arrange to have the cable break on which Dan swung above a canyon or fire a bullet into Thunder so that the huge horse fell and crushed Dan. Plans for his father's destruction had haunted him, even when he was in the Army, yet he never questioned in himself his passionate love for Dan, his admiration for him, borne out by his tendency to brag about him at every opportunity in the brick foxhole at Astoria, where he had sat out the duration, making training films.

"Remember the Ringo Kid, the original one? That was my dad."

(126)

After the clash on the *Blade of Castile* set he'd had a waking fantasy; while he finished the day's work with a new double in Dan's part he had dreamt that his father had been ill and that he, Harold, had led him into a western equipment store and bought him an immense silver saddle. "I've got a horse for you too," he had told his father in the dream. "You can ride him easily. He's Thunder's son . . ."

Dan's fall from greatness had been so gradual that at first Harold had hardly noticed it. The family had sold the Valley house, moved into one only slightly less pretentious further out (the third time the Bekins trucks had backed up to their door: there were to be two more times, the last back to the house on Lefferts) where Dan could still keep horses and have a place to practice his stunts. This first reduction had been caused by Dan's argument with the studio which produced the Ringo Kid series: the demand for a share of the profits which had caused Quib Monahan to replace him in the role of Ringo—yet he had merely been amused by the notion that Shortie would perform his duties adequately.

". . . They'll never teach him what it takes . . ."

Harold had realized with incredulity that Dan, in his most secret being, felt that no one but he had what it took.

His own name was Heston now. His wife was Nancy Heston. The era of exaggerated spending, lavish places and fancy cars in which his father had flourished was gone: a family was not only the right thing but the smart thing for a picture personality to have.

Nancy, he knew, had once, at least, gone by herself to visit Jill and Dan; the old folks had her picture in their bungalow. He had discussed the whole situation with her quite frankly—frankly, that is, except for one or two things which for some reason he could not tell her: such as his satisfaction

(127)

in the fact that his father had trouble getting jobs and was often in need of money, that he was no longer powerful or formidable but in a way, in spite of his health and strength and his miraculously continuing good looks and virility, somehow pitiable and beaten.

Harold recalled the first time he himself had realized that Dan was no longer a menace to his own aspirations. Before he had gone into the Army and long before the family argument about his accepting the cutting job at Columbia, he had been driving a borrowed car into Hollywood to take a girl to a Christmas dance; he had followed a side street in order to get across the boulevard ahead of the nightly parade but had miscalculated; the bands and floats had trapped him at the corner and he had been forced by an arrogant porkfed cop to sit there and watch the whole preposterous carnival, the starlets shivering in ballet skirts and blowing kisses, the Walt Disney cutouts on wheels, the Santas with their motorized reindeer. Suddenly a great roar went up from the crowds packing the sidewalks: Shortie Williams, the Ringo Kid, was passing. Shortie sat there like a king, a cocky little broken-nosed cowhand, bowing politely to left and right, accepting the ovation as proof of the success he had made of the Ringo Kid role: people had stopped remembering, no doubt, that any other actor had ever played it. Shortie was a big man now, a very lucky waddy who had known better than to ask for anything he couldn't get. Then a chill twisted Harold's guts; Dan was riding in the float behind Shortie's. Dan's float, a sort of grotto, looked sorry and cheap: probably refurbished from last year to save expense. There was a throne on the float and on this throne Dan, who had failed to get a hand from the spectators, was working to get laughs. He fired his six-guns. He waved his hat. He put his thumbs in his ears and flapped them, challenging the crowd's indifference with his own mockery. Then, to Harold's horror, he took off the big Stetson and stood on his head; he jigged, upside down. He did a spread. He kicked his booted heels in the air. The people stared, uncomfortable and uncomprehending—a generation of movie-goers who had already forgotten him. There were some snickers and a few half-hearted claps; then some kid razzberried and another fellow nearby yelled "A-aaah, tie a can on it." The crowd now laughed more boldly, more voices took up the yell, A-a-a-a-ah-h-h-h-h! Tears streamed down Harold's face, yet he had never hated his father as he did at that moment. He stood up in his car and cupped his hands. "Ya-a-a-ah-h-h-h-aa!" he yelled over the heads of the sightseers and the tourists, the grownups with kid brains and the fond parents from the sticks lifting their children up to see the movie celebrities go by.

"Ya-a-a-a-a-ah-h-h-h-a-a-ahhhhhh!"

How could you explain the wish for a man's destruction when the object of it was not a sadistic drunkard, let's say, but an easygoing, charming man who, though impractical perhaps, vainglorious, spendthrift, foolish, had been for years, by the force of his personality, the idol of every boy in America, the living embodiment of what a father should be? Then, obviously, such a wish was highly improper, to say the least; Abe, looking at his shoeshine with one eye closed, had called it a dramatization of puerile feelings of inadequacy. Screw inadequacy. If it had not been for his father and his father's maniac actor's vanity, he, Harold, could have lived normally, he could have grown up the way other kids grew up, and his mother, whom he pitied for so much but most of all for her loyalty to that jackass, Dan, could

(129)

have had the things in her life, the few basic, humble, simple things which she and every woman wanted and needed for her happiness.

He turned into the great gate of the studio, raising a finger to the cop who stepped out of his sentry box to identify him. Dramatization! That was a word people were always applying to situations in Hollywood where nothing was supposed to be quite real and where it could be safely assumed that since the citizens of Hollywood were employed in manufacturing a product which was make-believe the stresses produced in their own lives by the processes of this manufacture were also imaginary. If this were such a logical assumption, why didn't the lawcourts make it, why didn't the tax auditors make it when they racked up the score that took the prize out of the game, why didn't the doctors and nurses make it at the high fee clinics where they doled out the nembutal and the shock treatments and the bulletins advising the public that their idols had reported in for a routine checkup but would soon be as well as ever?

He had made up his mind long before he ever talked to Abe Limbagh that he would keep on turning off the radio whenever it played "Stardust," the damn tune his father had always been whistling. The way to keep his anger at Dan within bounds was to rise so far in the industry that no competition with his father could ever affect him. He would have to be so brilliant and ruthless and praised and respected that Dan's huge body and sensational courage and above all his kindliness and his capacity for being hurt would shrink to a pinpoint, no longer a threat, so that even Dan's destruction, if it could be arranged, would be unnecessary, an anticlimax like one more Academy Award after you had already won a couple of them.

(130)

Unfortunately, he reflected, parking the MG on the strip of concrete lettered with his name, he still had to win his first. He knew he could do it, given the right opportunity, and he hoped profoundly that the Aga had been right and something good was on the way for him. This summons to a conference at midnight—and it was, already more than that, almost one o'clock—might be it, or it might quite definitely not be. No way of telling. E. T. Zeld was unpredictable; that possibly was what made working for him such a challenge. E. T. never personally praised an employee when face to face with that employee but the Aga had reported that E. T. had liked *Dust Riders,* had called it a swell directorial job.

"You can go right in," Miss Frobisch said. "They're waiting for you . . ."

20

At one end of the huge room, adorned like the hunting lodge in *Mayerling* with animal skins and horned heads, E. T. Zeld strode up and down, squeezing a small rubber ball which he occasionally tossed into the air or flipped to one of the persons present; anyone thus singled out was expected to catch the ball and toss it back. E. T.'s hobby of the moment was big-game hunting and he felt that practice with the ball developed his quickness of eye.

E. T. was a man devoted to hobbies: besides shooting he

had taken up successively aqualung diving, mountain climb-
ing and steeplechasing, becoming highly proficient at each
before dropping it for a new pastime which, in order to appeal to him, must contain the element of danger. In a com-
munity where indolence bred physical softness he had kept
himself tough, outnerving his competitors when he failed
to outthink them, running the huge Duart plant with its
three thousand employees and its hundred and fifty million
dollars of invested capital like a small lonesome Army post
in which, with all communications cut and he himself in sole
command, the garrison had volunteered to fight to the last
man. Financiers, offended at his authoritarian habits and
occasional expensive mistakes, sometimes attacked viciously,
bombed him with proxies, rolled up liens like mechanized
divisions: always they retired in confusion with Zeld jeering
at them from the ramparts. He had little ability to anticipate
public taste but a vast resourcefulness in shaping it: he had
put sex into westerns, made the first West Point picture, the
first gangster pictures, invented the modern, fast-paced musical. On the personal side, he was a generous encourager of
young talent, a loyal friend to anybody who had ever done
a decent job for him, a patient and sometimes inspired creator
when he could easily have settled for being a mere organizer.
Women admired but did not like him; he found them ex-
pendable; he had never "created" a woman star; he made
pictures for men. Harold knew that he himself had not yet
advanced far enough to have Zeld's confidence but it was
something, at least, to have drawn attention: E. T.'s remark
to Kahn about *Dust Riders* was, in the scale of values at Duart,
a battlefield citation.

As he entered the conference room Zeld, without verbal
greeting, took him by the arm and led him up to a young
    (132)

woman seated in a stiff chair at one side of the vast carved desk. "Isabel," he said in his penetrating voice, "I want you to meet one of our most promising young directors—Mr. Harold Heston, Miss Isabel Carnavon."

Harold bowed in what he hoped was a promising manner and the young woman chirped "How do you do." She was small, freckled, bony, and untidy—a sort of female Huckleberry Finn. She peeked up at Harold with a pixie, disarming look in her small eyes which were set so close together that they seemed to have taken cover in the same hole.

Zeld said, "Miss Carnavon is doing a closeup of *Leatherlegs* for *Scope* magazine. She will cover every phase of the production of this motion picture."

"Wonderful," Harold said. Miss Carnavon twinkled again. She opened and closed her hands in her lap as if catching an infield fly. Harold had never heard of her but realized she must be someone of importance; never before in his experience had a press correspondent been allowed to attend a Zeld night conference. E. T., however, immediately turned away; paying no further attention to Miss Carnavon, he marched in silence the length of the room and back again, squeezing his rubber ball and passing it from his right hand to his left.

Several men, among them large, bull-necked Von Kramm, pipe in mouth, and little Lou Zeidman, occupied upholstered chairs along Zeld's line of march. Zeidman, a young producer recently drafted from the Theatre Guild, looked worried. Though he had never ventured ten miles from a paved street or, until he stepped off the Super Chief, five miles west of the Hudson River, Zeidman had successfully produced a number of Duart's western pictures. He greeted Harold by name—a courtesy which the latter took as possibly indicative that they were to work together. Nobody else spoke to him.

Some issue to which the rest were privy had evidently been decided here.

Harold could not see any place to sit, so squatted on the floor next to Von Kramm's chair.

Zeld flipped the ball against the wall and caught it. He did not look at Harold but the others did, thus making it apparent that it was he whom Zeld was addressing.

"Here's the situation. Spiegel wants to borrow Ella Torme for an English picture. We haven't got anything for her and he has a hell of a fine script, so I'm letting her go. That means this Kraut has to go along to protect her. It can't be helped, Von," he said, turning to Von Kramm—evidently resuming a discussion which had been in progress before Harold's arrival. "I know you've been putting plenty into *Leatherlegs*. I just got the final script; Rogiot never did that good without help. You ought by rights to stay on the picture, but there's no one else to protect Ella. If you're handling her I won't be losing a star for the sake of a loanout. Will you help me out?"

Von Kramm took his pipe out of his mouth, shrugged, and put the pipe back again. When E. T. Zeld asked you to help him out it was an order.

"How many days' shooting you got left on *Lonesome Road*, Harold?" Zeld asked. He tossed the ball to Zeidman, who fumbled, then scrambled under the divan looking for it.

"Your coordination's lousy, Lou," Zeld said. "You should get more exercise."

"How can anyone get exercise working for you?" Zeidman said in a low voice. Zeld did not hear him but Harold was sure Miss Carnavon did and that she stored the remark up for future copy.

"We should wind up tomorrow night, sir," Harold said. His

throat felt tight. Zeidman came up with the ball but did not throw it.

"Then, as of day after tomorrow, you're taking over *Leatherlegs*. Lou will get a script for you. Talk to me after you've read it if you have any suggestions. For my dough it's ready to go."

This meant there would be no talk and no suggestions. E. T. sat down at his desk. He looked commandingly at Zeidman, who tossed him the ball. Zeld put it in his pocket. He turned to Harold. "This is a great chance for you," he said with grave, measured emphasis. "I told that halfwit agent of yours we won't take up your option, but we'll do a damn sight better, we'll put you to work. This can be a great picture—" his voice rose pregnantly, "a great, GREAT picture. It's LOADED: big, new, and has a gimmick at the end that will give you an orgasm on the wide screen." He turned to Miss Carnavon.

"*Leatherlegs*—in Cinemirror," he said, "starring Rab O'Grady and Miranda Dobbs, directed by Harold Heston."

He waited for some comment from her but Miss Carnavon either could not think of any or was unwilling to commit herself. At length she twinkled softly and remarked, "It sounds all right."

A look of ironic glee passed from Von Kramm to Zeidman. This was not the way you talked to E. T. Zeld. E. T.'s face underwent a slight contortion but he allowed himself no other sign of discomfiture.

He said, "I predict a gross of six or seven million dollars for this picture. We will première at the Astor in New York."

He bent over his desk and made a note, possibly writing down the name of the theater where he intended to première. He turned to Harold.

"Do you like the assignment?" he demanded.

"I think it's terrific," Harold said. He added, uncertainly,
—"Sir!" He wondered if the promotion just conferred entitled him to abandon this form of address; old-timers on
the lot called Zeld "E. T." or even "Elon."

This was his chance!

"I'm grateful and I'm delighted—sir," he said, trying to
steady his voice. "I know I can bring in a fine picture."

But Zeld had already lost interest. He was talking on the
intercom, giving his secretary directions about setting up
some film in his projection room. "A GREAT picture," he
said over his shoulder. "Good luck! Lou, get a script for
Harold; let him read it right away."

"Yes, sir," Zeidman said. With amazing boldness he approached the desk and, bending close to Zeld, spoke in his
ear. Harold watched Miss Carnavon. She did not move or
appear to be listening but again he had the feeling that with
some uncanny auditory power she could hear what Zeidman
whispered—hear and take note of it indelibly within her like
some kind of human tape recorder.

Zeld straightened up. "No, no," he said impatiently. "Not
in the least. What I said goes. I'll see you later . . ."

Zeidman turned away. Motioning Harold to accompany
him, he led the way out of the office.

"Know what I said to him?" he demanded when they were
in the hall. He spoke with great intensity. His face was gray
with strain.

"No. What?" Harold asked politely.

"I told him I don't want this genitation from *Scope* stooling
on my picture. I don't trust these genitations from New York
magazines. Paid spies. They come here to laugh at pictures.
He won't listen."

(136)

Zeidman swung round on his heel, tottering toward the parking lot; he seemed abruptly to be so infirm that Harold felt perhaps he ought to take his arm.

"He lets her sit in on conferences, to be nice. Why be nice? They come here from New York and go into your home. They write it down, every time you go to the john, to boob you. Everybody in the Stork Club gets a big laugh. 'Look at the things they do in Hollywood.' I'll be goddamned if she gets in my home."

"It's a risk, all right," Harold said.

"Publicity," Zeidman said. "That's not publicity, it's rape. But he can't see it. He trusts her."

Harold felt that the real matter that was troubling Lou was less a possible betrayal of confidence on Miss Carnavon's part than his own annoyance at the loss of the experienced Von Kramm as *Leatherlegs'* director. Well, it was too late for Lou to kick about that now.

He, Harold, had his chance. He was on his way.

The Duart lot was quiet, a deserted city: in rows along wide streets which dead-ended in neat little parks the huge, windowless stages stood like paddocked elephants, nursing their secrets: the only sound was a faint hum from the mills, the only lights the shaded glow of E. T.'s windows and an orange bloom in the sky over the backlot where some company was shooting night scenes. He and Zeidman said good night beside the parking lot and the producer, still sunk in depression, drove off in a Cadillac which seemed too big for him to handle.

Harold got into the MG. He flipped on the dashlight to look at the title page of the script. He had a furious impatience to read it at once, to search and memorize every word of these pages which, when transferred to celluloid, could mean success or failure for him. He detached the crew sheet clipped to the back cover of the script, listing what from a point of view of failure or success was as important as the scenes or dialogue: the men he was to work with. Roy, of course, was first assistant—that couldn't be better; Jake Abrams, a second he didn't know, was listed, but if Roy had him for second he might be all right. Shelby Deane was first cameraman, an older guy, but all good cameramen were older guys; you couldn't go into the ASC until death caused a vacancy. Seth Huntsman, one of the studio's best, was art director—all top guys so far. He ran through the rest of the list rapidly: *sound,* Jerry Martin; *special effects,* Sam La Brasca; *script,* Dolores Lansing; *greensmen,* Will Goff, George Hansen; *publicity,* Lincoln Hyman; *second camera,* Merv Perkins; *first aid,* Dr. I. C. Phillips; *wardrobe,* Cole Younger. Then, almost at the end of the sheet, he saw the name he had been wondering about, half hoping it would not be there:

Ramrod, Dan Prader.

21

A human being did not need much to live by, Nancy thought; she herself did not need much. It was amazing, with the infinite variety that life offered, how little you actually had to have. The only fate that was intolerable was to have nothing; the shame of this was such that you became confused, you could not make your situation clear; the words were not invented that could make the situation clear and if they had been you would not have known how to use them. She had tried, that night at the Fines' party, she had tried at least up to a point, but she had failed. She did not blame Harold for not understanding, she had made acting the whole issue when it was not; she was not an actress, she had known that even when she had been married to Christian, but the acting could have been a solution; when he refused to understand this he had stopped further communication.

She had given in. This, too, was part of the shame; she blamed herself for it, she told herself that she was pitifully lacking in courage. She knew she should have slugged it out, bashed her way through to him somehow; she should have made him see that when she wanted to go back to work she had not been trying to hurt their marriage but to save it.

Possibly, of course, he saw and pretended not to. This he might have done out of selfishness or the feeling that if she was an actress she would be competing with him in a business way—competing as his father had. The idiot! And why, when he was doing so well (and he had never had such proof of his success as this *Leatherlegs* commitment) did he remain so touchy on this score? Well, that part of him, of course, was something that she could not cope with—the part connected with his boyhood and his queer, strained family relationships. It was all in the past—or should be, by this time. Only, there was more boy in him than in most men, she thought, and this too influenced her, made her compassionate when she should have been firm: she had not had the heart to intrude on his jubilation with her own demands.

So there they were again, he with a new professional assignment and she, forbidden to act, acting at home, reading the lines of an admiring, companionable wife, pretending with him that there had never been a quarrel. She got up that morning and made breakfast for him and until he left to take the company on location she began to live once more the days of her life, polished and glittering as the spaces between the stars: the well of empty days through which she fell, faster and faster, while the rush of space burned the flesh off her bones.

"You know," she said one day quite casually, as if she had given it no thought at all, "I have another idea for me; while you're on location I might go to New York. Would you mind?"

"Why, no, I don't suppose I would," he said a little too carefully. "Why should I mind?"

"I don't know, you seem so fussy about anything I want to do by myself these days."

It was a Sunday afternoon and they were having cocktails on the terrace; Harold seemed very intent on the matter of mixing some more as he replied, "I must say, I don't see what you'd do there. It's June, you know. The shows will all be closing for the summer or re-cast with understudies and that's never any good."

"But I wouldn't be going to see shows," she said, taking the cocktail with a small, mechanical smile of thanks. Neither was looking at the other.

"Then what would you be going for?"

"Well," she said, "I could see mother. She must be a little lonesome, knocking around alone in that apartment. And I haven't seen her for over a year."

Harold nodded in a grave, appraising manner which, Nancy
(140)

thought, he must know infuriates me, it would infuriate anyone, it is so disbelieving.

"Yes," he said, "you could see your mother. You've got a point there, all right."

"*And,*" she went on, still with the thanks-for-the-cocktail smile on her lips, but slightly nervous now and annoyed at herself for being so, "I could do some shopping. You know how much I hate shopping in Beverly Hills."

"I didn't know," he said.

"Well, I do."

Harold emptied his glass, set it down and carefully refilled it.

"Saks Fifth Avenue out here in Beverly is different, I suppose, from Saks Fifth Avenue on Fifth Avenue?"

"Oh, it certainly is," she said, losing the smile. "Everyone who knows anything knows that."

"I guess I don't know anything, then."

"Does that mean that I can't go? I can't go to work at Duart and I can't go to New York either?"

"No. It doesn't mean that."

"I'm awfully glad."

Both looked out over the green gorge below with its expensive chimneypots.

"So you've definitely decided on it?"

"Not definitely. But I think it might be rather nice."

"How long would you stay?"

"I don't know, a week, two weeks. However long you're away, then when you're through working I'll come back. Is that all right?"

"I guess so."

Harold's tone disowned responsibility. He made a camera finder out of his thumbs and forefingers and, through the

(141)

aperture thus created, studied the gorge some more.

"You know, I wasn't dead set against your acting. I may have sounded that way, but I wasn't."

"Now, Harold . . ."

"No, honestly. I just thought, if you weren't going into it wholeheartedly, it might turn out to be a . . ."

"You were dead set against it. So don't change now."

"I'm not changing, I'm just clarifying. If you want to take a crack at . . ."

"Darling," she said sharply, with a dead tone in her sharpness, seeing his strategy and moving to forestall him—not with pleasure at her own cleverness, as in past combats, but with weariness, regretting that such moves were necessary. "You told me that I couldn't act. I accepted that. Don't try to trade now, your permission to act for my trip to New York."

"I wasn't trading."

"Well, don't. Because you told me I could go to New York. Didn't you?"

"I told you that I . . ."

"Did you tell me I could go or not?"

"I told you."

"Then it's definite," she said. "I'm going. And I've got news for you. I would have gone whether you gave me permission or not. I'm not a slave, you know, that you picked up at auction from Christian's estate."

She got up suddenly, upsetting her glass—surprised by the unexpected and angry and rather shoddy words of rebellion that came to her—"a lousy script," she thought, "but I can't help it." She went up to the bedroom, rather expecting him to follow, but she heard him puttering around in the hall closet, looking for his tennis racket: he evidently found it because in a minute he called up, saying he was going to the club and would have dinner there. Knowing he seldom liked to exercise so late in the day she reasoned that he'd gone to work his anger off; he must be more upset than he appeared.

Next day he did not refer to her outburst, he went to work early and again dined elsewhere. She fixed a date for leaving for New York but caught a summer cold and changed her reservations. She got out of bed to help him pack for Mexico but they were short with each other and even friendliness, the last day, was an effort. Harold had been on location over a week when she fixed a new day for her departure. She was lonelier than she had ever been in her life and grateful to Freddy Rogiot for delaying his own eastbound trip so as to be on her plane.

22

It was not an assignation nor would Freddy, in his wildest dreams, imagine that it would turn into one. She had not even promised to go out with him when they were in New York. "We'll see," was all she would say when he suggested dinner at "21." But it would be fun, there was no doubt about that—especially since no disloyalty to Harold was involved. Freddy had been a comfort; he had called up every day after Harold left to see how she was feeling. Finally, when her cold was gone, they lunched together: she felt she owed him that much at least. She hated traveling, really. It would be wonderful to have Freddy with her, to see to the bags and everything on the plane.

She packed the night before. The definiteness of traveling schedules frightened her: she always got ready long in advance, then dawdled nervously through hours of waiting. The house had been cleaned; the milk and paper stopped; the Kahn office notified of her new address. Then, wondering if she could sit through a movie (the plane left at eight) she found that *Motherlode*, one of Dan Prader's old pictures was playing in an art house on Cienega: on an impulse she called Jill and told her about it.

"If you'd like to go, Mother, I could pick you up and we could have tea afterward. Would that be all right?"

It seemed a pleasant idea. Seeing the picture would pass the afternoon and tea, later, fulfill a purpose she had been turning over in her mind for some time.

She was delighted when Jill accepted.

Nancy had visited the house on Lefferts Drive less than half a dozen times. She had gone there first to pay a duty call, immediately after her marriage: neither Jill nor Dan had been at the wedding. Nancy had arrived on a rainy afternoon in November, stepping firmly, in high-heeled alligator shoes, over the drift of unraked leaves in the yard. Jill met her in a clean housedress, a bandanna around her head, and with evident pride showed her over the gnomish house and its untended environs; she brewed a pot of strong black tea and chattered away as happily as if a new daughter-in-law came to call on her every day. They stood together in the room Harold had slept in as a boy, tenantless now except for a shelf of little objects whittled out of pine—animals, weapons and such—which Dan had made for his son in the old days.

"Oh, we lived in other places, but this was the best. That chair you're sitting in, Harold held onto it the first step he took. And I wouldn't let Dan sell it . . . he wanted to, blame fool. Oil wells, orange groves, God knows what he bought and sold, but not this place. I put my foot down. Never a day did it go unrented till we moved back. Here it was, waiting . . ." she finished triumphantly, her eyes darting at Nancy's bracelets, the handbag that matched her shoes, her odd-colored lipstick. The widow of a famous man, she thought, maybe that's the kind of woman Harold needs. She will teach him the ways of the great world.

And Nancy taking stock of the other woman in her turn, thought, yes, she's the kind who would know the money wouldn't last. Only a woman like this would live in grand houses but keep a small one rented and repaired against the day when it would save her life. And as Jill chattered on, filling in the patchwork quilt of family history, Nancy visualized Harold taking his first steps, learning his alphabet, coasting down the sidewalk in his red wagon. It was hard to imagine him as a little kid, perhaps because of the odd, angry boyishness which made it equally difficult to picture his eventual maturity. I wonder what went wrong here, Nancy thought, what turned him against his father. Or didn't that begin till later?

This train of thought almost betrayed her into a grave social error. From Harold's references to Dan she had pictured the latter as a reckless self-centered man whom no one could get on with and whose marriage, like his career, had been a failure; she had concluded (although he had not stated this) that his mother shared his feelings of rebellion.

(145)

Nothing, she found, could have been further from the truth. She had been approaching this discovery when Jill suddenly broke off her reminiscences.

"Lord now, you wouldn't be wanting to hear all this old-time stuff."

"But I do," Nancy said quickly. "I think it's fascinating. Everything about Harold is interesting to me. I want to keep . . ."

She had been about to say "keep from making mistakes with him," but had stopped herself, realizing the implication would be that she wanted to do better in marriage than Jill had done.

Jill leaned forward. With a knowing look, she prodded her caller in the midriff with her forefinger.

"Don't tell me," she cried, "I know what it is—the worry of all brides. You want to keep Harold home. That's it, isn't it?" she insisted with another stubby, rapid prod. "I know, sweetheart. Didn't I sit in this very room by the hour, worrying over the same thing with Dan? Many, many's the time I sat here, with dinner drying on the stove and me turning on all the lights for company. Maybe he'd call, maybe he wouldn't. That's the ways of a man and there isn't a damn thing you can do about it."

"I suppose not," Nancy said, confused.

"But I'll tell you one thing," Jill went on, heedless of the interruption, "Harold's not the man for catting after women. He's a good boy, he never run wild much. Just you show a patient face when you have to and he'll come round."

"Oh, I'm not worried about that," Nancy said defensively. "That's really not it, Mother. I was just about to say . . ."

"Save your breath, honey," Jill said. "I can read your thoughts as clear as if I saw them written out. You want a word of advice, is that it? A tip from an old person who's been through the mill? Well, I'll give it to you. Just you be there when he needs you and I tell you what, you'll be as happy a woman as I've been all these years. Can I tell you more than that?"

Later, as Nancy rose to leave, Jill again looked her over carefully, prodding her several times at close range, as if to test the resilience of her flesh. "You should have a baby, dear. That's important, too, and don't you ever forget it."

"Why, I—intend to," Nancy said. This was true, but only in a vague way: she and Harold, in discussing the subject, had agreed it was a matter to be deferred till his career was better established.

Jill winked as if they now shared a great secret. "Have a flock of them," she said. "I failed Dan. I could never have but one." She stared at Nancy, squealed with laughter, then put out her small, square, none-too-clean right hand and pressed it firmly on the abdomen of the beautiful, stylish girl.

"You'd have a swell baby, I think."

Nancy's first impulse had been to draw back. She was afraid Jill's hand would soil her dress. Feeling that the half-arrested movement had been apparent to Jill, she forced a dutiful, daughterly smile.

"Well, if I do I hope it's just like Harold."

Jill snorted. She pulled her hand away, the warmth of which seemed to have burned a pattern through Nancy's I. Magnin girdle.

"You don't, Mother?"

Now Jill spoke her credo. She waved aside her own troubles, the ups and downs, the unfaithfulness and all the rest. She paid her tribute to a lifetime of hard living.

"I hope it's just like Harold's dad . . ."

23

Possibly the basic right which Harold had removed from her, Nancy thought, was her right to a separate identity. If she couldn't take a role, take a trip, think for herself—if she were reduced to being an appendage of another person's career, no matter how glittering, she had been wiped out. She had to put up resistance at some point, before it was too late. But where? She'd knuckled under on the issue of acting; now if she gave up going to New York she would suffer a defeat from which she might not recover. The holiday, as she had called it to herself, had lost much of its attraction for her: she would rather have found some excuse to join Harold in Mexico. She gave this alternative some thought and then, rejecting it, wrote Harold a letter in which she tried to clarify her thoughts about her marriage.

> . . . *we seem suddenly to have found out that we look at most things differently, we don't even talk to each other without quarreling. You've lived and breathed Hollywood ever since you were a baby; I haven't. I'm an outsider and I always will be. Maybe that's the real trouble: that we're entirely different kinds of people* . . .

Putting things down in black and white had been a relief,

in a sense, but the letter, as she progressed with it, became sterner than she'd meant it to—almost a good-by.

> . . . sometimes I wonder if you understand how different. People like me can work in pictures, but we can't be a part of them, the way you can. You live in a different world than we do, you think differently and your emotions are different. You are always talking about "heart," but with you "heart" is an attitude rather than an expression for real emotion. What about my emotions? I may make-believe sometimes; I guess all real love has a little make-believe in it, but that doesn't mean I want life to be laid out with chalk marks like a love scene on a sound stage. I know how easily those marks rub out; I don't think a marriage or a life laid out that way has much chance of succeeding . . .

She posted the letter on her way to her lunch with Freddy Rogiot at Romanoff's, their first public appearance together. Choosing Romanoff's had sounded harmless enough when Freddy first suggested it but during lunch, looking at the familiar faces in the booths around them, Nancy could hardly eat, fearful that some columnist would make a "seen together" item out of the harmless date. It wasn't till dessert that she lost her self-consciousness and began to talk about the things that would be fun to do in New York. It would be better, she insisted when they parted, if Freddy didn't take her to the airport: it would not look well, after such a public lunch, for them to arrive together. She would meet him there a little before take-off time, at eight the following evening. Thus, after sleeping rather late, she was left with only the afternoon to get through.

Probably there was no sense even mentioning the trip to

Jill, it might disturb her. Not only might, it would. But did you ever know what was in the mind of a person like Jill? Never. A woman who, according to Harold, had been mistreated, betrayed and exploited by her husband for years but who regarded herself as the happiest of people and her marriage as a triumph—such a woman was a mystery and would always remain one. She was a character. Granted. Also a little Charles Addamsy. Well, granted. But she had something. Oh, yes, she did.

"... tip from an old person who's been through the mill ..."

That had been her phrase, that rainy day—it seemed so long ago now.

What was the tip? Nancy had forgotten. Something about having babies. Well, that, too, would have been typical, or ... maybe it was something else, something Jill had not made clear or even said. Something that might be the solution of everything. And God, how she, Nancy, needed a solution. Now was the time for it. Time for all good men to come to the aid of the party, the sentence she'd typed hundreds of times in secretarial school, trying to learn to be a steno before she'd become lucky and landed the job with John Powers. That had been a job, too; life might have been a lot simpler if she'd never left it.

Driving Harold's MG toward Lefferts Drive, Nancy thought with a pang of nostalgia of those days before Harold, and even before Christian, when she and four other girls who were models and two who were airline stewardesses lived in half a brick house on Bank Street, New York. Six boys lived in the other half and the boys' side had a tub whereas the girls' side only had a shower which meant that in order to take a tub bath a girl, in appropriate bathrobe, with towel in hand, had to pass from the front door of the left half of the house to the front door of the right half of the house . . .

A Good Humor truck, lurching off Fountain Drive, almost collided with her, and Nancy gasped, swerving the MG out of danger. It would be just her luck to smash one of Harold's fenders: he would never forgive her. Then, in the middle of imagining the scene between herself and Harold with regard to the fender, Nancy remembered that there was a chance, just a faint one but still a chance, that she might never see Harold again. Or not as his wife. And at this thought, tears, unreasonable and ridiculous, rose to her eyes: outside Jill's gate when she had stopped the car, unsmashed, she wiped her face carefully and got out very slowly and walked up the path to the front door, noting that now there were no unraked leaves but that the patch of lawn was dry and weedy. Jill, in a blue silk suit that looked home-made, was standing in the open front door; Nancy went toward her with a smile. Perhaps, sure enough, Jill knew the answer; they would sit and talk after the movie, there would be plenty of time, and Jill would tell her a way to make everything come out all right.

24

Jill trembled as the title *MOTHERLODE* and then the words, *"Starring Dan Prader and Betty Compton,"* came on the screen. Basking in the light of other days, her mouth

(151)

slightly open, as if she could hear better that way, Jill waited for the sound of his first words.

I hope it doesn't disappoint her, Nancy thought, she's so wrapped up in it, but probably it couldn't disappoint her; this must be like living part of her life over again.

Suddenly, as if conscious of being watched, Jill twisted to one side, seizing Nancy's arm.

"Look—he's coming out now!"

And in truth, the door of the set (a cabin) was at that moment opening. Dan appeared, shading his eyes; he peered down a mountain trail along which, in a cut to the reverse angle, a woman on horseback could be seen approaching. As she rode into the shot he helped her down. They embraced briefly.

"*Honey,*" Miss Compton said, "*they shot Big John.*"

"*The devils!*" Dan said. "*They'll be here next.*"

"*I'm afraid. I'm afraid for us!*" Miss Compton said.

Dan turned his head slightly and the camera, moving in, outlined his profile against the sky.

"*We've got to hold the claim!*"

Nancy, who had never seen her father-in-law in the flesh, studied him with interest. So this was the man, or a shadow of him, who had created such strange tensions, influencing Harold (and through Harold her own life) so potently.

How big he was! She had expected this but also expected that he would be crude and callous, somehow, and that these qualities would be apparent. This was not so. There was harmony about him, in the way he moved and spoke—a fascination, like a natural force, that made you watch him, listen to him.

Yes, she could understand how he had become a famous star. What struck her as odd, now that she could appraise

(152)

him, was not that he had succeeded but that he had not retained his success. It must have taken not one or two foolish actions but many of them, years of them, to bring him down. As for Harold, she could understand better now how hard it must have been to deal with such a father. She pushed her personal thoughts aside, trying to pay attention to the story, creakily unfolding; in this, however, she was distracted by Jill.

Her mother-in-law was putting on a show of her own. When Dan fought for his woman in a barroom she jerked her fists to strike his blows, twisted her head in pain when he was struck: when the agents of a powerful mining company conspired to steal his claim she warned him with cries which caused spectators near her to turn around.

"Watch out, now! Careful, Danny-boy!"

Only once did she stop looking; this was when Dan, having emerged a victor from the barroom fight, took Miss Compton in his arms and repeatedly kissed her. Jill blocked out this scene by placing her hands over her eyes. She had never been able to stand seeing him kiss another woman on the screen.

The picture was reaching its climax. The half-breed leader of the claim jumpers laid an ambush for Dan; the two fought with fists and knives, rolling slowly toward a precipice. Nancy saw that Jill's legs were twisting as she tried to keep Dan from slipping over the edge. The rest of the audience, which had been well-behaved so far, failed to take the scene seriously; giggles broke out in several places, increasing and spreading during the next sequence—one in which Miss Compton searched for Dan in a snowstorm.

At first Jill did not notice the audience reaction, but a feeling crept through her that all was not right.

(153)

"What is it? What's wrong with them?" she whispered to Nancy.

"Nothing, Mother. Just some kids. The others all love it."

"Kids . . ."

Jill raised herself slightly, glaring around at the audience. No, it was not the kids, others were laughing too; the infection had spread all through the theater. Nor were people laughing like an audience at a comedy when the laughter is proper and becomes a bond. These fools laughed in dabs and spurts and chuckles, each person superior and isolated, alone with his or her little patch of mockery.

Dated though the picture was, it should not have provoked all this: Nancy realized with deep annoyance that the appeal of such revivals as *Motherlode*, presented on a double bill with equally old but more artistic pictures, was to give the audience the joy of ridicule.

Jill, now in a frenzy, had stopped looking at the screen. She stood up, throwing out one arm in an oratorical gesture.

"Shame! For shame!"

Nancy pulled at her dress.

"Mother Prader! Don't!"

"I will. I know my rights," Jill said harshly. "I won't have a work of art insulted."

"Quiet, please," someone commanded.

"I will not be quiet. You and those like you are the ones who should be quiet," Jill said loudly. A girl usher with a flashlight hurried down the aisle; she flashed the light this way and that. Nancy put her hands on Jill's waist, feeling the sharp ends of the pelvic bones under her dress; she forced her back into her seat. Jill sat quiet, breathing hard but cowed for a moment while the usher, flashlight in hand,

(154)

stood at the end of the aisle, evidently not sure who had caused the disturbance.

Miss Compton had found Dan, half-conscious, in a snowdrift.

"Honey," she cried, *"what happened?"*

Dan raised himself on his elbow.

"I killed him," he said weakly. *"It was the only way."*

"Tum-te-tum-tum."

A bass voice hummed the music theme from *Dragnet,* and the audience laughed again, this time all together.

"The facts, ma'am—we want the facts," a kid piped.

"Oh, you fools," Jill shouted in the darkness.

The usher (a female) had spied her now, sidled down the row of seats.

"Madam, you'll have to be quiet."

"I'll have to be quiet," Jill cried, incensed. "And what about them—what about what *they're* doing?"

"Ssh! Please!" the usher said. "You were making a disturbance before. If you won't be quiet, I will have to call the manager."

"Call him and see if I care," Jill said in a loud voice. "Just call him, I'll have you discharged . . ."

"Very well, then—"

The girl aimed the beam of her light rudely into Jill's face. Then she snapped it off and went away, perhaps to carry out her threat.

"Call the police if you want to," Jill muttered, though the girl was out of earshot. "I'll tell them what's going on here."

"Mother," Nancy pleaded, "let's go."

"Why? We paid money to see the show. I want to see it, if these fools will let me."

A small island of vacancy had formed round her in the audience, those seated nearby having moved to other places.

"Please, Mother Prader. We can come back some other time."

"I will not . . ." Jill said, but allowed herself to be led out. In the lobby, near the ticket box, the usher was addressing a stout man with glasses.

"I've warned her but she refuses to . . ."

Jill turned from Nancy. She wheeled, addressing the pair with contempt.

"All right, I'm going," she said, "if that's what you want. But I want my money back. Either I get it or I go to the police. Which will it be?"

The usher stepped back but the man with glasses said politely, "I'm sorry, madam, we do not make refunds."

"All right for you, then," Jill said threateningly. "That's my husband they're insulting in there with their screeches and their jokes. What do you think of that?"

The manager, indifferent till then, looked at Jill now as if he had some doubts about her sanity.

"Please, Mother," Nancy said. Putting an arm around Jill she led her out onto the street. Jill was so angry that her teeth were chattering.

"I'd like to kill them all," she said. "My God, what got into them?"

"They're used to a different kind of picture, that's all, Mother."

"Different! They don't know good from bad, that's what it is. I've still got reviews home, I'll show them to you . . . Raves, every one of them."

"I'm sure, I'm sure, Mother," Nancy said, leading her along. She was distressed that her idea of seeing the movie

(156)

had turned out so badly; she had never conceived of this possibility.

"Shall we have a cup of tea somewhere? That might make you feel better. Or a drink . . . How about that?"

Jill shook her head. Her cheeks looked drawn, she seemed tired beyond words. "Home, let's just go home."

25

On the way back to Lefferts Drive, Jill became quieter. She sat hunched over in a daze of exhaustion, thinking of happier times—of the première of this same picture when there had been more people just in the première grandstand outside Grauman's than inside that place today. She remembered how she and Dan and Harold had attended in their white buckskin suits and how Harold had refused to wave to the crowd.

When she'd brewed and drunk some tea, her vitality revived; she began to play the hostess. After all, it had been nice of Harold's wife to come. It had been kind of her to take the trouble about the movie and all.

"I'm so sorry," she said, "for the fuss I made."

Suddenly she put her head back; the wild banshee wail of her laugh rose in the steam of the teapot. "The blame fool manager with the glasses—the way he looked at me. The poor blame fool, how could he know? . . . Will you have something to eat? When Dan gets back we'll have a steak that thick—" she measured with her fingers, "and the trimmings. Eating right, he says, is what has kept him young . . ."

Nancy looked at her with a quick, new gift of understanding. Jill's torment in the theater had shown her much she had not guessed about her mother-in-law.

"I think you miss him a great deal . . ."

"Not me, dear," Jill said stoutly. "It's heaven when he's gone. Only I get to thinking sometimes, wondering what he's . . ."

Nancy pushed her teacup aside. She leaned across the table.

"Mother Prader, you must understand me. Don't take offense at this. But . . . I know Dan is doing a stunt in Harold's picture. Harold mentioned it and . . . if you're worried, if you'd like to go there to be with him. . . ." Jill's wild glance, her hand fumbling a stray lock of hair almost stopped Nancy but she finished. "Well, I just mean I'd be glad to . . ."

Jill said slowly, "You'd give me the money?"

"Your son's money, Mother," Nancy said. "I'm sure he'd . . ."

"God . . ."

Jill rose. She rolled her eyes like a mad woman, then walked up and down the little kitchen, switching her buttocks at each turn.

Nancy, watching the performance, remained at the table.

"Can she really be mentally ill?" she thought.

Jill stood still in the middle of the floor. The light from the hanging bulb cast pools of shadow on her gaunt, small face.

"I'd thought of asking you. I had! And now . . ."

"It's nothing, Mother. I'm only too glad to."

"Glad! But I've got to tell you. It's the dandiprats he runs with, every time he's out of my sight. The whores with their false faces and false titties, too, the kind you pump up with a little rubber hose. They make that kind, they tell me. That's what goes through my mind, and . . ."

She paused, gasping. She had planned to tell, to make a clean breast as she had to a few others: Mrs. Arden, Mr. Dakropolis, those who had been witnesses or had helped with the problem. She had wanted to give out the whole tale of the miserable life she had with him, how he spent every cent he earned, sometimes before he got it, and the way he chippied —but now that she started speaking, all these grievances were forgotten and in their place entirely different words poured out, the real words which till then Jill had kept hidden even from herself.

". . . being apart from him. You get used to . . . and as I say we've never been apart. Hardly in near thirty years. He might get hurt and that's the truth. Killed even. A man, Snitch Macklin, was killed working with him once, putting their horses off a high one. If anything . . . well, if it did happen, I wouldn't want them others handling him, strangers . . . Nobody ever did one this high, though—it's risky, risky . . ."

"Of course, Mother."

Jill sat down with deliberation. She took the check Nancy had written as if it were something very fragile.

"Oh, I thank you. I do thank you for this." She raised her head, her glance composed again, dry, birdlike. It had suddenly occurred to her that there was in all this a secret explanation. She guessed what it was.

"You're going too? Is that it?"

"I'm taking a trip, but not to Todos Santos."

Nancy made her voice very casual. She lit a cigarette. She felt for some airy and sophisticated phrase, such as Springfield Folger might have used, she thought, needing the phrase desperately, if she was to cover her own uncertainties of the past weeks, her appointment with Freddy Rogiot this very evening at the airport—these matters and, still more, her almost painful reaction to Jill's emotion.

"I guess I'm not as lucky as you. Dan needs you, at least you're sure of that. But Harold . . ."

Jill poked her forefinger into the pot to see if the tea was hot or cold. "If you think Harold doesn't need you I guess you just plumb don't understand Harold."

"Well, Mother, I suppose . . . I don't think I can explain, but . . ."

Jill, bowed over the pot, looked at her with foreboding. So that was it! Trouble in the home.

"He rushes by," Nancy said. "He leaves me so alone."

She picked at a crumb on the oilcloth table cover, her face smooth, young, hard-set.

But now was the time, now, if ever, to probe for the truth Jill might tell her and that she had never tried to learn.

"It's fine that he's successful. I like that. I wouldn't stop him. But I don't seem to have babies, though you told me once I should. We go around to parties. I don't know. We had so much fun out of this and that, so different from the way with my first husband. Christian was older, you know, a lot older. Harold was . . . I just can't tell you how I felt about him. Everything. Just everything I'd ever thought of feeling for a man till we were married and then—bang. He stood me in a corner. It's as if he didn't need me or need anyone, he just wants me around for set-dressing. Maybe all very successful men are like that, he's still so young. Maybe it's just him, the way he is. Or it might be mixed up with the way he hates his father . . . He talked to a psychiatrist about that once but I guess he never did find out the answer . . ."

Nancy, now having picked the crumb to pieces, brushed the pieces onto a napkin; she placed the napkin on the table and was still. Jill poured the cooling tea. She had not gathered much from Nancy's speech; even the term "psychiatrist" was vague to her. But one phrase struck her solidly and found resistance and it was to this that she replied.

"Harold doesn't hate his father. That's where you're wrong."

Nancy hesitated. She did not like to contradict. Perhaps Jill had invented this in order to comfort herself for the break in her family.

"But, Mother . . ."

"You don't believe me, do you?"

"I'm sure you must have a reason for what you say. But Harold has always told me . . ."

"Never mind what he's told you. This is the truth as sure as I'm sitting here. Ever since he was a little tyke he's loved and worshiped him."

There was a cruel thing Nancy could say. She did not want to say it if Jill needed this dream she had made up for herself, the lie about the affection between son and father. Then she thought, I must say it or there will have been no point to any of this.

"Then why did Harold drop his father's name? Why doesn't he ever see him? You see, it isn't that I don't want to believe you, but . . ."

Jill shook her head. Her shoulders were hunched, pressed down by hurtful bygone things. But her mouth set stubbornly.

(161)

"He loves him. They misunderstood each other. That's all . . ."

"Then perhaps . . ."

"I'm not saying Dan's an easy one," Jill said, ploughing on into the tunnel of the past. "He and Harold, well! We disagreed about the boy. I told him he was wrong. But Harold in his heart has never faltered. He's a loving one. You should know that if anybody does . . ."

Now she peered hopefully at Nancy, wanting some confirmation from her. Nancy could not give it. Yes, she had once thought that Harold was a loving one but the very love she needed and hoped for he had not given, though he had professed it; how then believe he could love someone else for whom he professed hate?

But she could not deny him to his mother.

"Yes, yes. He has great love in him, I know. He's been . . . wonderful to me."

She looked at her watch, startled to see that it was after six. If she were to catch the plane at eight she must go at once. She had planned to allow herself three hours to go back to the house, bathe, change her clothes, get her bags. Then perhaps a snack at the airport. Yes, go now, at once. The talk was in a danger area anyway; if she stayed she would only say something to hurt this woman for whom she had recently acquired so much pity and admiration.

Jill was sitting primly at the little table, smiling at her.

"Ai, now! I knew it but it's good to hear you say it. Only why didn't you have babies, like I told you to the time you came, remember?" She put out her hand and her laugh, revived by the hope Nancy had given her, screeched in the quiet house.

"That's what you need," she said. "Have them, honey. It
(162)

will be all right. It doesn't hurt. Heck, now," she went on, wondering if the hurt was what had frightened Nancy from this natural project. "If they'd of hurt I'd never of had Harold. I'm afraid to prick my finger with a pin, and that's the truth."

Nancy rose. Getting on the baby topic was one thing she wouldn't do.

"Perhaps if we'd had them," she allowed herself to say, "things might have been different. Now there may not be any time."

It was as close as she could come in words to the admission that her marriage might be about to end. But she must go quickly now before Jill's pecking glances and her poking finger probed and jabbed the meaning out of it and she began to ask more questions.

She said to change the subject, "If you're going to fly, there's a good plane at ten o'clock. You might be able to make that, it's the one Harold took. Is that how Dan went?"

"Him?" Jill cried. She'd been holding out her hand to say good-by but now she pulled it back in surprise. "Not him. He's in enough crazy danger all the time, I wouldn't let him fly. Not me. That man went by the train."

26

The four bags, overnight case, wardrobe case, makeup box, hatbox, all new Samsonite that Harold had given her for the honeymoon, were ready in the hall and Nancy ready with them, bathed and changed, very smart, very much the woman of the world in her gray traveling suit and dark mink stole. She had done the last things. She had locked the windows, put the MG in the garage, taken Bobo to the boarding kennel, phoned for a cab. Now all she had to do was step outside and, when the cabman had carried the bags out, lock the door behind her. Then all the days that had added up to emptiness would be inside and she, as the lock clicked, outside, free—herself again.

It was then, before the cab slid down the driveway, that she knew what she would have to do.

"We'll have to hurry," she said to the driver.

On Sepulveda Boulevard, there was a delay. Cops were routing traffic round an accident: an ambulance had backed in toward a smashed car. Beside the car, a gray-haired woman was trying to get into the ambulance. She was uninjured. Possibly she wanted to travel with some other person, already placed inside; she was arguing furiously with the driver. The latter, refusing her request, climbed onto his seat; the ambulance started off. The woman, still trying, ran after it a few steps, beating on the door with her fists. Nancy looked away. She did not like seeing such things: the accident itself seemed like an omen and the gray-haired woman, though she hadn't looked a bit like Jill, reminded her of Jill. Jill would have been the kind to beat on doors with her fists or, better, force a way inside, if anyone she loved were there. Once more Nancy renewed her determination: she must and she would take this one last chance, gamble that what Jill had told her about Harold was true. For it was Harold, not Dan, who stood in the greatest danger in the making of the picture: it was Harold who had assumed responsibility. Like Dan, but even more than Dan, Harold was gambling his future on a successful outcome: if Jill were right and anything, under these circumstances, happened to his father, he, Harold, would be destroyed. Also this situation, bad as it was, had brought about another: if their marriage still had any chance, Todos Santos was where she would find out about it.

Fred Rogiot was walking up and down near the taxi ramp; as the cab pulled in he came forward quickly with his curious hitching limp and said, "I thought you'd never come. The plane leaves in five minutes." And she said, "We were delayed by an accident. I'll go inside."

It would be better inside. You couldn't yell words of destruction at a man with cab horns blowing in your ears. But that limp of Freddy's; he would never be able to manage the bags without a porter, she thought, wondering whether Freddy would have appealed to her so much if he had been able to walk like other men: what did she want to do, grow out of his groin like a new leg? She looked around to see if he was coming and perceived him in the distance, struggling with the bags; he dropped one and stumbled over it; she thought he

(165)

might fall but before she could move in his direction a porter reached him—just in time.

"Looks as if we'd made it," Freddy said. He smiled at her fuzzily, mopping his forehead with a silk handkerchief.

"I'm not going."

"What on earth do you mean?"

"I can't explain now, Freddy," she said. "I can't go, that's all. I'll phone you in New York. Now you really must hurry."

The despatcher was calling the flight for the last time and a belated passenger carrying a violin case rushed past them toward the gate.

"This is insane."

"I know," she said, "but there's something I must do. I'll explain it all to you, only not now; there's no time. Please cancel this," she said to the flight clerk, laying her ticket on the counter, "I've had a change in plans."

Not waiting for the man's answer she took Freddy's arm, propelling him toward the gate; she walked along the ramp in step with him, apologizing.

"I feel horrible to disappoint you, but you must understand."

"I don't," he said. "I'm goddamned if I do. I thought at least we'd have the trip together. I thought we'd . . ."

"Freddy," she said firmly, "you're an angel. I like you more than anyone I know. Please don't spoil our last moments together. I'll write you tonight and explain everything."

They had reached the end; the plane, enormous at such close range, towered in the dusk; the flight crew was about to remove the gangway.

"Wait," Nancy shouted past the ticket taker, "there's another passenger . . ."

"Good-bye, then," Freddy said coldly.

He handed out his boarding slip and passed through, turning once to wave, his face pale and set; the steps were being held for him and the moment he had mounted them they were pulled back and the door of the plane slammed and fastened. As the aircraft cumbersomely wheeled, then moved with gathering speed toward its take-off position Nancy, watching, felt a deep sense of relief. She did not wait to see the take-off but went back to the desk.

"Can you ticket me to Todos Santos, Mexico?"

The clerk's face assumed the look of crafty patience.

"I'm afraid we can't exchange your space on Flight 20, ma'am. The aircraft has departed and . . ."

"All right, then; never mind. I'll buy another ticket. Or don't you fly people to Mexico?"

The clerk, still evidently feeling she was not right in the head, looked up her destination in a rate book. "We can connect you with a Mexican plane in Tia Juana," he said dubiously. "You replane again in Mexico City for Todos Santos." After an apparent struggle with his company training in courtesy he added, "If you're sure you want to go."

"When do I get there?"

The clerk again referred to his book.

"The direct flight takes five hours to Mexico City: from Tia Juana there are several stops. We have no current information on the flight from Mexico City to Todos Santos."

Already her letter to Harold had been on its way ten hours. But mail flights were often slower than passenger flights: there might still be time. Leaving the clerk to write up her ticket she went to the Western Union desk and sent Harold a straight wire.

ON MY WAY TO JOIN YOU. IF YOU RECEIVE LETTER
FROM ME MEANTIME BEG YOU NOT TO OPEN IT.
LOVE.

NANCY.

Feeling suddenly hungry and almost lighthearted, she went
up to the buffet and had two daiquiris. Pretty soon she would
know, she would know everything. And for the moment, there
was nothing to do but have another daiquiri and wait to see
whether Jill Prader was also catching the ten o'clock flight that
would connect with a plane in Tia Juana.

27

Living day by day with a woman you loved was like a trip
through a familiar countryside: you knew the sights without having to look at them—the roofs of towns, the position
of certain houses, the comforting hills with their encircling
fields or patches of woodland. Thus you had security until
some quarrel performed for this happy land the service of an
earthquake or a forest fire and when you looked next time the
old scenery was wiped away and in its place, born overnight,
appeared a landscape like Siberia.

Harold had known, when this happened, that his marriage
was in trouble. The big change had begun after his argument
with Nancy about acting: it had increased swiftly day by day.
The glacier age had been inaugurated with the chat about her

trip to New York. Well, all right. It had been stupid, all of it
—his own conduct as well as hers, but calling a quarrel stupid
did not keep you from knowing when it was serious. If he had
needed more proof, it was obvious from the fact that in the
twelve days the Duart Company had been on location he had
not had a word from her till now.

He stood in his sweat-darkened clothes in the lobby of the
small hotel with its bullfight posters and potted ferns, looking
at the telegram which the desk clerk, Policarpo Sanchez, had
handed him when he walked in. Sent the night before, it had
been delayed in transmission by the unknown but potent fac-
tors which delayed such matters in Mexico; it must have been
in his key box all day while he worked with the company on
the cliffs above the sea.

So she had written him a letter.

He wasn't supposed to read it. Was that good or bad?

"There was a call too, sir—operator nine two in Los Angeles. You wish that I get this operator for you?"

"Yes, please. I'll take it up in the room. And will you see
if you can locate Mr. Sowells for me? Tell him I'd like to
speak to him."

"Very good, sir."

Policarpo Sanchez' English was excellent and he liked to
show it off. Policarpo was a good man, an efficient man: there
were all too few such men on the staff of the Hotel Europa in
Todos Santos.

Harold turned from the desk, looking over the crowd in the
lobby once more for his assistant. Without Roy, he could not
decide whether or not to shoot the cliff stuff in the morning.
Usually stunts involving major hazards were left for the last
day so that the possible loss or injury of the person involved
would not retard operations; today, however, a bulletin fore-

casting unsettled weather for Saturday, when the stunt was tentatively scheduled, had come through from Mexico City.

Roy was supposed to be available to discuss things like this. And where was he?

Annoyance made Harold fretful. He wanted, more than anything, to get out of his dirty clothes, to have a bath, a drink, a meal, some sleep. It had been a tough day—a very tough one: he was not sure whether getting word from Nancy at last made it tougher or easier, he could not sufficiently clear his mind of current work problems to guess at the state of mind behind her cryptic telegram. What a day! To start with, a rainstorm had delayed them over an hour—not the usual Mexican four P.M. thunder shower but a real whiplasher which got everybody soaking, followed by gray skies that turned the gold reflectors a lifeless yellow and set Cameraman Shelby Deane to inquiring sarcastically whether they were supposed to be shooting day for night; he had, he said, a filter for that, but not one that would make night look like day.

It had all been strained enough, with nerves stretched tight and even the crew turning surly when, to top it off, Rab had quarreled with Miranda: he could throw her off any time he wanted, underplaying when she was high or punching his lines when she was trying for control, leaving her there with egg on her face. What had happened today was much more than a difference in timing or the natural friction between person-alities: he had really shown spite, not seeming to care whether or not the tension thus developed injured his own scenes—a recklessness unusual in so experienced an actor. At three o'clock, with the excuse that her corset had given her indi-gestion, she had retired to her trailer and had tears. Harold had gone in to comfort her and coax her back to work but ended by sending her back to the hotel.

Should he call her room and invite her to dinner? But no, he thought, if I do that I'll have to take her part against Rab, it's not the right move. Probably the best thing to do was send up a bottle of champagne; maybe she'd drink it all and get such a hangover that tomorrow she wouldn't care what gave.

A stretchout pulled up to the hotel entrance and a slender man wearing a hunting jacket got out carrying a camera case and a musette bag. He swayed as he walked, as if he felt ill: possibly he had just come from the plane after a rough trip. Harold wondered who he could be, catching sight at that moment of Linc Hyman's dark head in the crowd. Linc was the department legger in charge of unit publicity, a solemn, saturnine kid whose mournful face and long gangling body were both animated by a puppyish anxiety to please.

"I suppose you heard what happened."

Linc grinned.

"Everybody's yakking about it?"

"Well, sure. What else have they got to yak about? Did you lose much shooting time?"

"No, but if this goes on tomorrow we'll lose time. I still don't know what started it."

"I could find out, boss," Linc said eagerly. "I could talk to Miranda and—"

"Stay away from her. I want her to simmer down. The only person you might find out from is the Rab, our phony Irishman."

"Now, boss, Rab's been Irish ever since he went with the Nat Goldstone Agency. You shouldn't say those things."

Policarpo spoke across the desk to Harold.

"Beverly Hills, Señor. Holding on the line."

"I'll take it upstairs."

Harold patted Linc's shoulder. Linc was so anxious to begin

his mission he was wriggling all over; even his skin had a kind of wobble to it.

"I'll talk to you later."

Blocked from the elevator by a bunch of kids waiting for autographs, he turned to the stairs. It wasn't likely, of course, that Nancy would telephone, after first writing and then wiring; still, you couldn't tell. During the last ten days he'd rehearsed all of her possible calls to him: the forgiving, the angry, the tentative . . . How are you, I was thinking of you . . . the good-by forever, I've decided that it's best we . . . He'd heard them in his restless sleep; he'd listened to them on the set when the actors were speaking different lines, in other voices, while the seas were breaking in front of the camera or horses running through the mesquite. The only trouble was that if the call came, no matter which one it was, his reply could be foreseen, only one was possible. I love you, I miss you. What are we quarreling about?

The telephone was ringing as he unlocked his room.

"Don't go 'way, dear. I have Mr. Zeidman for you."

So it was Miss Frobisch! So who had expected Nancy?

There was a series of ear-splitting clicks, then the Mexican long-distance operator intercepted.

"Bueno, Señor Heston. Momentito . . ."

There were more clicks; Zeidman's high-pitched voice became audible, charged with a kind of worried paternalism.

"Harold, how be you?"

"Fine, Zeid. Just fine."

"What kind of a day did you have?"

"Great, Zeid, great."

"How many setups?"

"Seventeen. We got the love scene outside the cabin and picked up the rest of the chase."

"Swell, baby. That's wonderful. How do you feel, kiddy?"

"Well, you know. A little tired—but just great. I think we shot some great film."

"You happy with it, baby?"

"I am, Zeid, and I think you will be. Of course, we'll know better when you and E.T. have seen the dailies."

"That's what we want to see."

"Film will be shipped tonight, Zeid."

"Swell. Say, Harold, one thing. Any problems? Any friction?"

"Nothing more than the usual nerves. It was hot out there."

"Miranda's all right? She isn't giving you any trouble, is she?"

"Not that gal. She's a trouper. They don't make them any better."

"Swell, baby. She likes everything then?"

"Everything except her corset. Says it hurts her bottom."

The circuit began to buzz at this point; Zeidman thought Harold had said "horse" instead of "corset"; the word had to be spelled for him.

"Well, doll," the producer finished, "glad it's going so well. Keep that crazy Irishman in line and give Dobbsy my love. 'Bye, now. I'll call you tomorrow . . ."

Harold hung up slowly. He felt he had given a good account of himself but he was sweating. He lit a cigarette, wondering which member of his staff had told Zeidman about the Rab-Miranda trouble. The stoolie must have been on long distance the moment the day's shooting ended—perhaps even earlier.

Linc Hyman stuck his head around the door: Harold motioned him in.

"They know?"

Harold nodded. Linc puckered his lips.

"Well, that didn't take long. Who do you think passed the word?"

"Doesn't matter. There's one in every company."

Linc looked thoughtful.

"They'll be watching us a little closer now, though, won't they? Figuring on trouble . . ."

"They always figure on trouble," Harold said. He did not add "—especially with a new director." The Eye was on you constantly and very literally, hooked to the retina of some ambitious, favor-currying lackey. The Eye could not be avoided, it had to be accepted as an occupational hazard like the heat, the clash of nerves, the daily ten-hour race against the sun. Harold felt tired to the middle of his bones. He mixed himself a drink from the whisky on the dresser, took a swallow or two, then lay down on the bed.

"I thought you were going to talk to Rab."

"I didn't have to."

"What do you mean?"

"The bartender had the whole story. He gave it to me while I primed myself to tackle Rab. You want it in one word?"

"Carry on."

"Jealousy."

"Whose?"

"Rab's, natch. He was spanking Miranda for two-timing with another guy."

"You're kidding—"

"Scout's honor."

"Who's the guy?"

"Dan Prader."

Linc had had it on his tongue to say "your father" but thought better of it. Though the father-son relationship was

(174)

known throughout the company, it was not considered etiquette to mention it in front of the director.

Harold sat up. He finished his drink, wanting another right away. Next to rain, pestilence, or a general strike, the worst thing that could happen to a film company on location was a quarrel between the principal players. Only a person with Dan's talent for doing harm would make, instinctively, the move for bringing about such a feud.

"I suppose I should have figured on that one," he said grimly.

"I guess nobody figured it," Linc said. "Just one of those things. They were down in the bar last night. Rab and Miranda. At least, that's what my friend said. They had a squabble and Rab left, so Dan bought the lady a few drinks and they went on from there."

Harold grunted. He was too annoyed to make articulate comment. No doubt Dan had only been having fun, but his own kind of fun: there had been a purpose behind it, as always with Dan's doings—the purpose being to enlarge Dan, gratify his ego, use other people, no matter how, just to be using them, perhaps. These reflections churned in Harold's mind as he remarked with bitter emphasis, "The stupidest thing I ever did was get that bastard a job in this picture."

He had quite forgotten, in his irritation, that Dan had been assigned to *Leatherlegs* before he himself was—also that (unless his own phone call to Von Kramm could be considered decisive, not a completely necessary deduction) he had had only a remote connection with the fact of his father's employment.

Roy, entering in time to hear the last remark, closed the door carefully behind him. He set down a sheaf of papers on the dresser.

"I'm sorry to hear that, boss, because he's going to cost us some more money."

Harold stared at him.

"What do you mean?"

"I just got the weather report. It looks like tomorrow is the day. Which being so, we got to build the take-off chute so he can use it in the morning—"

"But the chute was supposed to be all ready a couple of days ago. I talked to you about it."

"That was before he picked a new spot for it."

Harold slowly got up. He walked over to the mirror and stared at his own face, as if by checking his appearance he could modify the information he had just received.

"And since when," he said in a choking voice, "does a ram-rod put a company on golden time?"

"He has a right to rig his own stunts," Roy said. His heavy shoulders hunched forward defensively. "That's how it's always been. That's how it has to be. He's the guy who's going over the edge."

"Nobody's questioning that. He can rig them—but we can pick where he does them. That spot was picked by the location department before we ever got down here; he'd seen the stills."

"Well, sir," Roy said, "he picked another cliff, that's all. He went out there and looked at the spot we'd okayed and he didn't like it. I don't know. You'd have to ask him yourself . . ."

"I will ask him, I'll goddamn well ask him. I'd also like to know why nobody took the trouble to check with me."

Roy's relaxed air was now deserting him.

"He ordered—er, asked for the change yesterday. The boys

were just starting the chute on the lower cliff, so I couldn't see any objection to . . ."

"You mean the one he picked is higher?"

Roy seemed to feel that he'd already conveyed this information.

"Sure, it's higher. Thirty or forty feet higher at least, but the camera setups are better. It will make better film. So I didn't figure that you'd . . ."

"Roy," Harold said, "you figured quite a few things and you didn't figure right. I wish in the future you'd quit trying to be a mind reader and stick to operational procedure."

Sowells' face sucked in at the cheeks but his eyes and voice remained steady.

"You don't have to eat me out. This stunt wasn't scheduled till next week: it seemed reasonable to move the chute as long as he wanted it moved and there was time."

"But there wasn't time, was there?"

"I couldn't know then the weather would go shifty on us."

"We'd agreed on something; you changed it."

"Dan changed it. Any time a guy who's getting paid for one stunt will do a tougher one for the same dough you have to go along with him."

Harold turned away. In his bafflement he was almost ready to accuse Roy of conspiring to create this difficulty. Could Roy be the stool who was reporting company troubles to the Front Office by long distance? Certainly he was gunning for a job as director: he'd been wanting that for many years. And how better to polish apples than by this cute little trick about the chute? If the stunt turned out well he could claim credit for setting it up on the higher cliff; if it turned out badly he could phone and—

But no. That was going too far.

The source of trouble wasn't Roy but Dan. Coming on top of the business with Miranda this matter of the chute was intolerable.

Any possible capacity which Harold might have had for viewing Dan's activities with humor had collapsed before the pressure of the problems in hand and his own baffled, mounting rage. Even the strain of his relationship with Nancy, putting his own nerves on edge, was tied in with it all: this, too, far back in his life, had somehow been fostered, pre-shaped by Dan.

"Maybe the guys won't have to work the whole night," Roy was saying hopefully. "Maybe only till two or three A.M. It might not come to such a lot of money, not enough to make them sore Up Front . . ."

Harold said, "I'm not authorizing them to work a goddamn minute. If you have them move the chute you do it on your own responsibility."

He crossed to the dresser, picking up the requisitions Roy had put there; he tore the packet up and tossed the pieces into the waste basket. All of his fatigue, confusion and anxiety had fallen together into a familiar, recognizable pattern: hatred of his father. None of the problems confronting him was separately insuperable: each could be dealt with but Dan could not be dealt with. Ever since he, Harold, had put on long pants Dan had been waiting, huge and inimical, to defeat him. This was Dan's master-stroke: the blocking of his own first chance for an important success. He felt cornered, deprived of will and even of the power to rebel just as he had felt in his boyhood when he had tried endlessly and hopelessly to win his father's approval. Dan had withheld approval then; now he wanted the whole world to withhold approval. He had

(178)

created extra costs, upset the actors . . . What next? Harold remembered Abe Limbagh saying ". . . surgical removal of the relationship . . ."

Well, a professional removal was also possible; not only that, it was the only course now open.

Turning from Roy, Harold spread out his arms, the first two fingers of each hand reaching out and downward: he did not realize he was doing this, nor remember that in this position, with his fingers in the slots of the wire fence, he had stood waiting for his father as a boy, looking down the drive up which the huge pale car would come.

"Look, Roy—and you too, Linc," he said. "Try and locate Dan Prader, wherever he is. Locate him and send him up here to me. I want to talk to him."

28

The electric fans on the ceiling of the Tlaxcantonga Club turned slowly, stirring the gray banks of tobacco smoke in the bar and gambling rooms. The Tlaxcantonga Club was Todos Santos' best place of entertainment: besides the gambling and the bar there was a small dance floor where an orchestra played and the Tres Caballeros, two men and a girl in *charro* costumes, sang the music of the country. The Tres Caballeros were singing now. All the chili-bean numbers sounded the same to Miranda but she nodded and smiled at the Tres Caballeros after each number.

Dicen que está llorando la molinera
porque ya sus amores van a la guerra

Miranda didn't know what the words meant but they gave her a pleasant, melting feeling that was appropriate to the dimness, the smells of the liquor and smoke and the drowsy movement of the slowly turning fans. Miranda had the type of pelvic structure which looked well on a bar stool and she was very decorative, sitting there in her tight skirt and the lowcut peasant blouse through which her skin shone with a light of its own. She sat quietly and happily, drinking tequila with salt and lime the way Dan had showed her; to keep her happiness firmly and smoothly within her she paid no attention to the argument which had been going on since Roy Sowells and Linc Hyman had joined them in the bar.

"I did my best, I'm telling you," Roy said, "but he has resistance. He has plenty of resistance."

"He has for a fact," Linc Hyman put in. "You better go and talk to him. It's the only way."

"Why can't he talk to me in the daytime?" Dan said. "This is my own time. I'm relaxing now. Hey, mesero," he said, addressing the bartender by the only term he knew for people who gave service for food and drink in Mexico, "otra tequila for the lady, for me Orange Crush. You guys want anything?"

His tone, though decent, was not cordial, nor did Linc or Roy regard the invitation as serious.

"No, thanks," Roy said, speaking for both. As the bartender placed the drinks in front of Dan and Miranda, he reverted to the former topic.

"If I was putting that nag in the drink tomorrow I'd want a chute. Only it ain't built and we got to build it. It's seven o'clock now and the guys are at dinner; it's going to be tough

(180)

enough to round them up and get them out there. I'm counting on an okay, mind you, or I wouldn't have the Mexicans standing by, but they get overtime too, don't forget."

"Overtime," Dan said in his large rasping voice. "I'm tired of hearing about overtime. You'd think this was a jutemill or something, the way you guys are talking. Whose money are we spending, yours or Duart's? Are they going broke or something that they can't afford a . . ."

"Dan, listen to . . ."

". . . goddamn chute."

". . . reason."

"If it was me, Dan," Linc suddenly cut in, "I'd go and talk to him. You want the chute."

"Who says I'm not going to talk to him?" Dan demanded angrily. "I got a right to finish my drink first, haven't I? And Miss Dobbs has a right to finish her drink. Wouldn't you say so, honey?" he concluded, raising his large arm and cuddling it in the notch of his companion's waist.

"I sure would," Miranda said with feeling. "I sure as shooting would."

She tilted against Dan, looking up at him tenderly. He looked so wonderful in his big hat and splendid clothes among the small dim people in the bar: the perfect figure of a man. She wished Roy and Linc would go away and leave her alone with the solemnly turning fans and the melting music and her inner consciousness of something new and wonderful that had just happened.

It had happened tonight, she didn't know the exact moment: perhaps when they were starting out to dinner and Dan had been so wonderful, throwing handfuls of money to the ragged kids around the car. Or perhaps later, when he danced with her, or when he picked her up as if she were a doll and set her

(181)

on the bar stool. What she'd needed all her life, she had decided, was a man who had some style, not a rat with a frigidaire brain like Lucky Mansfield or an egotist like Rab.

It had happened, anyway. The moment did not matter. The point was that she was in love, more in love than she had ever been. Her mind drifted away from the present as she thought of how good she would be for a man like Dan Prader.

With him she would be fulfilled. She would overcome that certain trouble that had so disturbed her recently—the feeling that she could not belong wholly to any man. She would work and slave for him like a woman in a thatched hut —like Nina, for instance, in *Sod*; she would cook his food and wash his clothes; if need be she would go on the streets for him like the Chinese broad when she had to have her eyes slanted with tape every day for *Sal of Singapore*. All the unknown selves within her which had come out only when she could act them she would be in real truth for him. Why couldn't the guys leave the two of them alone so that she would enjoy this little bit of happiness, the first true spark of real true happiness that had ever come to her? Yet here again she must be humble, must stay in the mood of the new role and accept, she felt, whatever pain went with it. She put up her hand and pulled Dan's chin around so that she could look up past his big nose—the only feature of him which, if she were going to be quite honest with herself, she would have changed; could plastic surgery do anything for a man's nose, if it was that big?

"If you have to go, dear," she said, "I'll be here. I'll be right here waiting for you till you come back."

He looked back at her with the strangest, tensest look she had ever seen in him and she thought, he's afraid, but what of? What could make a guy like this afraid?

But Dan immediately hid the fear planted like a worm in the brain behind the massive, undestroyable features. He got off the bar stool, putting down a note to pay for the drinks.

"Okay, you stay here. Linc and Roy—" He spoke with command, disposing of the palace guard, "—you fellows take care of her. I'll be back in fifteen, twenty minutes."

He straightened to his full height, larger than lifesize in the smoky room, imposing and noble as some figure of folklore.

"The tab's on me, remember, mesero," he said, pointing his finger at the bartender. Then he turned and strode out of the room.

"Please play something. Play something new," Miranda said to the Tres Caballeros. But the Caballeros must have thought that she was asking for an encore; they began again the same old tune, the tune of tonight, forever linked in her mind (however tired she might be of it) to the birth of this, her greatest love. And as the Caballeros sang she hummed softly, moving her head in time to the music, her smooth lips moist and sensuously pouting.

29

In front of the Tlaxcantonga, surrounded by the usual mob of big-eyed, bird-boned Mexican kids, waited Miranda's lavender Cadillac, chauffeur-driven from Los Angeles so that its owner might be spared the humiliation of riding in company stretchouts. The chauffeur, slumped behind the wheel, straightened up when he saw Dan, but to his surprise the latter motioned that he would not need the car. At any other time, transportation by Cadillac would have been exactly to Dan's taste; he had never quite got over the feeling that such cars were still, or in a short time would be, always available to him. But at this moment he did not want to ride; the Tlaxcantonga was only a few blocks from the hotel; walking this distance would give him time to adjust himself to what lay ahead.

So far, in the making of the picture he'd had luck. He'd rigged and ramrodded the required work easily and he knew he had done it well; also, since the company had been shooting two units and Roy Sowells had directed the second unit, which had photographed most of the horse work, he had been able to stay out of Harold's way. Not that he foresaw trouble. Not at all. Harold had been friendly to plug him for the job in the first place and he had not acted differently since; when they'd met on the set on the first day they'd shaken hands and since then, at any chance meeting, friendly words had been spoken, friendly looks exchanged. He hadn't expected Harold to pop off with "Dad" or any stuff like that in front of the company; that wasn't in the cards. On the other hand he wasn't playing secrets, so if he said "Son" that was all right, too.

A man his age could say "Son" to most anyone, he guessed. It was an expression he often used. It just sort of eased things along.

Dan struck out along the uneven adobe sidewalk, his big hat pushed far back on his head as was his habit when he was thinking. He had hoped to be able to get through the whole assignment, and especially the last day, without arguments. Some directors, where stunts were concerned, were thickheaded; you couldn't get anything done unless you argued.

Others let you go your own way. It was your ass in the sling, not theirs; when you asked for something they gave it to you. He remembered one stunt in the comedy, *Fireman, Come A-Runnin'* where he'd had to jump out of a third-floor window and land on the ground—for laughs. He'd rigged the stunt by digging a pit and filling it with boxed Kotex, then a tarp over the Kotex and dirt sprinkled over the tarp. The Kotex had cost plenty but his fall had been painless and the stunt had been the best thing in the picture. And now, with a picture on ten times as big a budget, they were beefing about overtime to build a lousy chute!

To hell with it.

What was picture business coming to? If they were getting that cheap it was better not to work. You could always sit in a bar somewhere and watch TV.

Like most men used to heeled boots Dan walked with small steps, his back straight and his stomach pulled in. He'd meant to take his time but now, too soon, the lights of the Europa showed at the end of the dark street. From the tightness inside him—the same tightness and dryness which he felt before any difficult stunt—he knew he was approaching a decisive moment. Slowing his steps, he tried to talk himself out of this conviction.

The chute, now . . . well, the chute was necessary. He'd made that clear right from the first. Naturally, it would have been better to have a platform too, as he'd explained to Roy when he first saw the stills; a platform could dump the horse onto the chute with legs stretched out in diving position; when you rode him on you never knew if he would get in that position or not.

Either you landed on top of the horse, alive, or underneath him, dead. All right. They hadn't given him the platform, so

(185)

the chute, at least, was a must; as for the choice of cliffs to jump from, he could sit down with Harold and prove to him that the high one was better than the low one. No bulge at the bottom, no rocks, deep water. And besides, it would make better film. Even a patient in a mental hospital could see that much. Why wouldn't a smart guy like Harold see it? Sure, he could sit down with Harold, man to man, and they would straighten the matter out. It had been a long time since he and the boy had sat down this way; it would be a good thing for both of them . . .

But with this came another thought: when had they ever sat down together, either when Harold was a kid or when he was grown? There should have been a time for it: perhaps both had been waiting for such a time but it had never come. Worries had come instead, making the right time harder to find for the talk that would fix everything, the few words that were needed . . . and so the years had passed and bitterness crept in, hope had been lost and the boy . . . well, the boy hadn't made it easier, taking another name and all; he'd gone underground as it were, and so . . .

How could they talk now, how could it be done? This was the truth—and it was this that had come to him in a flash when Roy had first told him that Harold wished to see him. It was this that had made him long not to go at all and had put fear in his heart.

Nevertheless, one thing was different now. There was a picture to be made. Hot or cold, they had to make it; they were both in it and they had to dig their way out or one would be as badly off as the other. This logic was itself a kind of hope and with his sole reliance on it, standing in the hotel corridor, Dan raised his hand and knocked on Harold's door and a voice said "Come in."

(186)

30

Dan did as he was told.

"Shut it," the same voice said. It still did not sound like
Harold's voice nor did Dan, for a moment, see his son. Then,
as he backed up against the door to make it close, keeping his
hat on as a man might on entering a place where he did not
intend to stay long, he perceived Harold sitting in an arm-
chair, slumped down so that the high arms almost hid his face.
He had a glass of whiskey in his hand and he was staring
straight at the door, a good-looking, mean-looking guy, his
narrow bullet-shaped head pushed forward from his thin
shoulders. His glance shifted from the door to his father. Dan
looked coldly back, seeing the smartness and power of Harold
and also, as a kind of revelation, that there was something
sick and bullying about him, some quality which made him,
Dan, despair for the outcome of this meeting.

"Roy said you wanted to talk to me."

Harold's voice rose from the depths of the chair. It had
again that strained, wild edge to it, a sound which Dan had
heard only once before, the time Harold dismissed him from
the *Blade of Castile* set.

"Roy's wrong. I don't want to talk. I want to tell you something. So you'll know it came from me and no one else."

Dan waited. So it would be this, just as he'd feared—something bad, something like *Blade of Castile*. But if that were it he wanted it soon. He could not stand the waiting.

"Speak your piece."

Harold stood up.

He said, slowly and clearly, "I'm closing you out. You're through as an employee of this company."

Dan rubbed a hand over his face. More than ever now he felt the need to sit down but not seeing any other chair except a small stiff one which seemed too close to Harold, he crossed slowly to the bed and sat down on that. Once seated, the purport of what Harold had said struck him more fully and he did a stupid thing—he laughed, not with any intention of annoying Harold, though it was immediately apparent that his act had this effect, but out of shock, just as an audience at a mystery film howls when a skeleton's hand seizes the heroine's throat.

Harold's eyes, reddened from sun glare and from drinking, flicked from side to side.

"You'll find out it isn't so goddamn funny. I mean what I say."

Dan saw the damage his laugh had done—that is, if anything in a situation already hopeless could be considered to do damage.

"You can't do it, son," he said in a low voice.

"You'll goddamn well find out I can. And don't tell me you've got a contract. I don't give a damn about it. The studio may pay you off; personally, I think your actions have given them grounds for not paying anything, if they want to take that position."

Dan moistened his lips.

"I don't know just what actions you might be referring to."

(188)

There was silence for a moment. Harold slowly emptied his glass and set it on the floor beside him. Then, with a sort of gasp, he hoisted himself up in the chair.

"You don't, eh? You have no idea, is that it? You think it's been easy, having you around here! Got no idea, I suppose, that you've caused any trouble. Oh, my God . . ."

"If I have, son, I'm sure I . . ."

"Know how many setups we lost today? Six at least, all on account of you. Rab upstaging Miranda. Bah! You didn't know about that, I suppose, got no idea what caused it. Well, you wouldn't have. But this about the golden time . . ."

"I didn't ask for golden time. I . . ."

"Never mind. It's out, anyway; we'll just do without the chute, the same way we'll do without you. How do you like that?"

Dan's eyes seemed to grow closer together—a sure sign that he was losing patience.

He said in level tones, "I'm not putting that horse off the edge without a chute, and that's for sure."

Harold reached for the bottle; he poured himself a drink without looking at the amount, then drained it off. The liquor and his self-stimulated rage helped to dull the feeling that his plan to throw Dan off the picture would not work.

"I just got through telling you that you—"

"Quit it, Harold," Dan rasped. "Be your age. You can't get anybody else to ride a horse off that cliff, even off the low one. And I've read the script. You've got to leave the stunt in. The whole climax depends on it. So who's kidding who?"

"What would you say if I told you I'd just called Zeid and he'd agreed to it?"

"I'd say you were full of shit."

(189)

He could tell from Harold's tone that he was lying about Zeidman. The kid was floundering—full of hate but not knowing just what to do about it.

"—besides," Dan went on, "what would be the sense of it? The stunt's a natural, and I can do it. It's good for you and it's good for me . . ."

"Nothing you could ever do would be good for me. I think we've both known that for a long time."

Harold was trying hard to hold on to his temper, but it seemed he'd lost, or was about to lose, his ability to think clearly, and this too angered him. Surgical removal—that would mean to have it over fast. He had to get Dan out of here or there would be no telling what might happen.

"If the new cliff is what you're mad about, let me tell you something: the high one makes better film."

"So would a thousand-foot cliff, if we could find one. That's not the reason you want to use it."

"Then you tell me the reason."

"I think," Harold said in a choking voice, "that you would like to hurt me in the motion picture business. You never wanted me in it in the first place. You'd do anything you could to hurt me or ruin me if you could."

"Even breaking my own neck?"

"Especially breaking your goddamn neck. There's something about you that's not like other people, you never did care whether school kept or not. That's what made you good at stunt work in the first place. Well, you can't get away with it . . ."

"I don't figure to get killed, son," Dan said steadily. "I never have. That's why I'm alive. This is a swell break and I want to make the most of it."

"That cutting job at Columbia was a swell break for me too,

only you didn't want me to take it. You were afraid I'd live to top you some day and I have. Just keep that in mind—" his voice rose "—and this. You're not going to get killed in a picture I'm directing."

"That's for sure," Dan said. "You don't have to take it on trust. I'll give you a guarantee."

"Trust!"

The word seemed to infuriate Harold.

"You're a hell of a one to talk about trust . . ."

Wild thoughts about the olden days, those thoughts which he had been pushing back since the beginning, were now almost overpowering.

"I trusted you once, see. That's how dumb I was. Yes, when I was a dumb, skinny, mother-ridden punk, living back of that big steel fence . . ."

He broke off, looked for his glass, failed to find it, and drank out of the bottle.

"Never mind . . ."

Dan felt obliged to defend himself about this fence.

"Your mother and I tried to do our best. The fence . . . Well, I guess you were lonely. That was bad, I know."

"Lonely . . . that wasn't the point. I thought you were the greatest guy that ever walked on two legs. That's how dumb I was in those days . . ."

Matters long buried out of sight fought to take possession of Harold's voice.

"What the hell does the fence matter? The point was . . . I don't know. I bragged to the other kids about you. I had pictures of you doing stunts. I showed them to the other kids in school so they'd believe in you too. I've still got those goddamn pictures. Why I never burned them I don't know . . ."

First the fence! Now the pictures . . . What harm was

there in any of this? Yet, helplessly, Dan felt defensive when such things were mentioned.

"You used to ask for the pictures," he said. "It wasn't as if we, as if I . . ."

He had started to say, ". . . forced them on you," but this speech too was unnecessary; so close were he and Harold in their anger that they could understand each other like old friends.

"Scared! Yes, that's what you were. Because you might have to be ashamed of me . . . I could have liked baseball and all that, but not the way you pounded it into me. You always made me feel I couldn't live up to what you wanted. You couldn't stand having an undersized runt of a kid like me, you wanted one that would be as tough as you were. I tried and tried. Mom thought you were a great guy too, and that only made me try harder. Finally, I got sick. The sickness I had was *you*. I went around like a vegetable. Just a nothing, a blot . . . It would have been a relief just to turn into something chemical in the earth, like vegetables do . . . Well, goddamn it, I got over that. I went out and did one thing for myself . . ."

"Harold, son . . ."

"So, I didn't die! I started growing up. If I wanted to grow I had to do it myself. All right, I said, screw him. If he fights me, I'll fight him back. That time you spoke so mean to Mom, arguing against my taking that Columbia job, the one chance I might ever get—that did it. I hated you then. I took the damn job anyway. Oh, Jesus Christ, how proud I was the day I got my first check . . . but what's the use—"

Dan said, "We were proud too—your Mom and I. We knew you'd go on and up. She—"

"Mom, maybe—not you!" Harold said wearily. "But—

(192)

well, it doesn't matter now . . . Too late . . ." he finished
vaguely.

"It's not too late when—"

"It is, though . . . Once I was on top, I thought I'd tell
you all this, maybe then I could stop being mad at you—but
when I saw you on the *Blade* set, it all came back. I wanted to
make you feel . . . but that doesn't matter either. All I know
is you've tried to cross me up ever since I came on this picture.
I'm just fixing it so you can't do that any more."

31

Dan nodded. He saw more clearly now what this was all
about. The trouble with Miranda, the overtime costs for the
chute were just excuses for a showdown. They were the cards
Harold was playing to prove once more, as he had with *Blade
of Castile*, that he was top man now.

Harold still seemed to feel that they were in a contest of
some sort. That was his main mistake. If there had ever been
a contest it was over now and Harold had won it: that would
have been a cinch to prove to anyone who wasn't half worn out
and three-quarters drunk and imagining, as Harold did, that
he was a bedeviled kid instead of a grown man. The way to
prove it? Just call Harold's bluff and walk off the picture.
That would be the way, all right, and for a moment Dan was
tempted to take it. He would still get his money: that was

written down in black and white; also, he would be escaping from the very risk that Harold thought he didn't care about —the risk of not being alive this time tomorrow night.

Only a guy who didn't care, himself, whether he lived or died would suspect someone else of feeling the same way. The job was not "clean"—a word which in Dan's vocabulary meant properly prepared for. He felt easy with a job only when he was able to think about it a long time in advance and weigh up its risks and the best means of keeping them under control.

That was how you divided the men from the boobs. The boobs got killed. You didn't last long in stunt work, if all you knew was how to cross yourself and take a slug of whiskey.

"You can't win now," Harold was saying in effect, but that was just where he was wrong. He could win now, just by accepting the dismissal Harold had handed him. Harold might not even know the trouble the studio had been put to in finding a stuntman: Harold had come on the picture late and by that time everything had been arranged. Unless he missed his guess, E. T. Zeld would want to be told why Harold had fired him. Phones would begin ringing then, all right. Harold would be in a bind for sure and he, Dan, would be on his way home, with money in his pocket.

So the temptation pulled at him and he talked back at it, saying to himself, there's something on the kid's mind beyond all this. That's why he isn't thinking straight, maybe why he's drinking too. I'd never heard he was a drinker; he couldn't be one and get ahead like he was. This picture, now—it could be a turning-point for him like the one I had when I told Quib Monahan where to get off; from that time I was going downhill faster than I will be in that chute tomorrow if he gets it built for me. And thinking of the chute and the cliff, Dan again addressed a speech to himself. You've been in bad spots before, you got out of them all right. What's the matter with you? Do you believe in that crut of a filthy superstition about death in the motion picture business coming in threes, and that you are the third?

He reached over and took the bottle out of Harold's hand and set it on the floor.

"All right," he said, "I'm fired. You're letting me off the hook. Well, I've got news for you—I'm goddamn glad to be off . . ."

"Okay," Harold said. Now his eyes slowly moved up until they met Dan's and Dan saw the uncertainty that was in them back of the drunkenness and the fading anger.

"I'll tell you one thing, though," Dan said, "then you can forget I said it. I've had a lot of luck in my life, both kinds, good and bad, but having a kid to top me was the best, while it lasted. I'm halfway sorry, now, you didn't make it stick."

Dan picked up the bottle. Defying his practice of lifelong abstinence, he took a swig out of it and handed it back to Harold. Then he put on his hat and went to the door.

"So long, partner," he said, "I'll see you around some-time."

Without looking back he opened the door and went out into the dimly lit, rather sour-smelling corridor of the Hotel Europa. He started to walk down the corridor toward the lobby, at first very slowly, then more rapidly. So valuable did time seem to him now that, once in the street, he proceeded almost at a run, heading for the Tlaxcantonga, hardly noticing the taxi which was Todos Santos' equivalent of an airport bus and which swept around the corner just in front of him with several passengers aboard.

"What did he have to say?"

Roy Sowells leaned across the table, breathing the cactus-smelling fumes of tequila into Dan's face.

"He fired me."

Miranda giggled, then looked horrified. Linc Hyman, who had been dozing, snapped awake.

"What's he going to do about the stunt?"

"Told me he was going to write it out of the picture."

"Are you kidding?"

"That's what he said. I go by what people say."

Roy rubbed his hand over his face.

"Congratulations."

"For what?"

"For getting yourself an out. You got a contract—perfect. So you'll be paid anyway. You're smarter than I figured . . ."

Miranda put her hand on Dan's. "What's he talking about, honeybun? You didn't want to get fired, did you?"

"No, I didn't," Dan said truthfully.

Roy looked across the table at Dan, his eyes creased up with fury.

"Boy, did I pull a brodie when I got you on this picture."

"Why don't you tell that to Harold?"

"I don't have to. He knows it. The only thing he don't know is, without you we don't get the job done." Roy pushed back his chair. "Well, if you people will excuse me, I'm going out someplace privately and get stoned."

Linc also rose.

"Good night, all," he said. He bowed in a half formal, half insulting way first to Miranda, then to Dan.

Dan grinned at him.

"You figure I was looking for an out too, Linc?"

Linc wobbled on his long legs, looking confusedly from Dan to Roy.

"I don't know, Dan. Jesus! I just don't know."

"Okay," Dan said, "I get the pitch. Both you guys could be right, I *could* be looking for an out—and if I was this could be it. Only it so happens, I'm not."

"You mean," Roy said skeptically, "you'll come back in the picture, if he asks you to?"

"All I mean," Dan said, "is—he's top man. Sell him that. Maybe he's got a little tiny notion that he's done the wrong thing. Only—never let on he can't get the picture made without me. If you did that, he'd never take me back. I raised this guy—remember? Sure, we've had troubles—but I know him. He's got something on his mind that I *don't* know about —something that's got nothing to do with getting the picture made. He's half canned and blowing off steam for a pile-up of old grudges. Let me be the goat, see? Tell him how whipped I am, how bad I feel . . . maybe he'll change his mind."

"And if he does?" Roy said slowly, a light of comprehension and of something like respect now lightening his beefy, stonehard face.

"And if he does," Dan said, slipping his arm around Miranda's waist, "just let me know. I'll be right here awhile. And if you send those guys out there to build the chute, maybe I'll see you in the a.m."

32

It was almost eight o'clock when Roy Sowells' call came through from the hotel. Dan, slowly returning to the table, looked so serious that Miranda, although no seeress, knew what the call had been about. She had begun to resent actively this interference of professional matters on an evening which had begun as such a glorious adventure. She cuddled up to Dan and, when he failed to respond at once, she ordered more tequila: when she had licked a dab of salt, drunk the strong spirits and bitten her lime, she put salt on Dan's hand and licked that off too.

"Are you really going to jump that horse off that mountain tomorrow?"

"It's not a mountain."

"What is it, then?"

"Just a kind of a high spot."

"They said it will be the highest jump ever made with a horse."

"I haven't made it yet," Dan said cautiously.

"I know, and I wish you wouldn't. You'll never know how much I wish you wouldn't. I was sort of glad when Harold fired you. Do you mind?"

"Why should I mind?" Dan asked vacantly. He was thinking of the construction crew on their way out to the cliff Roy had said—but in Dan's mind's eye already out there, working with the big arcs lighting the sky and the generator roaring, building the chute as if it were a gallows.

Well, he'd asked for it. Now he had it.

"Because I knew you wanted to do it. And I just wanted you to be safe for me."

"I'll be safe. So let's not fight about it." Dan raised two fingers. "Otra tequila for the lady. Otra Orange Crush for me."

"You're so damn proud of that kid of yours and you fight with him so."

"Let's forget about it, huh, baby?"

"All right," Miranda said. "Only I'll tell you a secret. A big, awful secret. I just wish I'd had a kid, even if I fought with him. I wish, I wish, I wish . . ."

"I'm going to eat some dinner," Dan said, "how about you?"

"We're going to eat the best damn dinner that's ever been eaten in this goddamn town," Miranda said. "And then we're going to drink some more. *You're* going to drink too, you bastard. Not that lousy orange junk, *that* rots your stomach. We're going to eat and drink and then you're going to make love to me. Is that all right?"

"I don't know what's wrong with it," Dan said.

He could not, at the moment, have added anything to the schedule just outlined. Not anything except—possibly just one item: Jill would have been better than Miranda. His nerves hungered for Jill, his comfort in bad times, his luck-piece, as it were, for such jobs as this ahead. Maybe he'd call her later. Maybe . . . but barring Jill, who was not available, he wanted the most attractive woman who was. The question of technical "loyalty" never entered his head. With

Miranda's well-curved and amply perfumed body close to him Dan was able to keep from wondering what Roy had said to Harold to change his mind, or what time the guys would finish with the chute.

The food came and proved satisfactory: it might not be Ciro's, as Miranda pointed out, but a steak was a steak and with enough chile on it, you should worry if it was a little tough. Drinks, which continued through the meal, came faster afterward; Dan for the second time that evening tasted alcohol —he had a half of his companion's tenth tequila. Miranda was now rapidly approaching a mood in which complete privacy was indicated.

"I love Mexico," she said fervently. "It's alive. Hollywood is dead, Danny-boy. It's dead and it stinks."

"You know it," Dan said. He signaled to the waiter for their check.

"It stinks," Miranda said. "And it's cold, cold as Forest Lawn. That's why I'm drinking this tequila, to get the chill out of my bones. The Hollywood Freeze. You know what I mean?"

Dan, busy paying the waiter, indicated that he did.

"It's a lousy situation," he said. "What do you say we go, baby?"

"I'll tell you when I'm ready to go, sweetie," Miranda said, "and I'm not ready yet. I'm telling you I'm still cold . . . Put your arm around me, Danny-boy. You're warm and you're a talent. Maybe that's the reason Hollywood died, because the no-talents took over. They run things now, they do it with committees. Did you know that?"

"I'd heard something about it," Dan replied. Miranda seemed very intense and he looked at her worriedly. If he did not get her out she would soon lose, he was afraid, all in-clination to go to bed with him.

"It used to be, if you joined anything, you turned out to be a Communist. Now if you're not on a committee you're not a talent. People don't even laugh any more. Do you re-member in the old days, how they laughed? Sometimes a company would quit work for a day just to laugh at one gag."

"Laughing costs too much now, I guess," Dan said.

He pushed back his chair, preparing to rise.

Miranda said, "Let's stay one more minute, one little minute and drink one more tequila. Because I'm so worried."

"Nothing to worry about."

"I don't mean *that*. I mean me."

With a wave of his hand, Dan discouraged the Caballeros who were about to begin a new song. He raised Miranda gently to her feet.

"What I mean is," she said, "I look sexy. I know the way I look. But mostly I don't feel a thing. It's the Freeze, like I told you. I only loved one man in my life. He was my agent, Johnny Kochek. I suppose you never heard of him."

"Was he well known?" Dan inquired. He felt better now that she had started for the door.

"He was not," Miranda said. "I was the only decent client he ever had and I double-crossed him and signed with Charlie Feldman. Johnny was four feet and a half high. He had a bad heart. He died in my arms, and ever since then I've had the Freeze."

Miranda was crying. The tears, rimmed with mascara, made stripes under her large, beautiful eyes.

"That was a lousy break."

"That's not what I'm talking about . . ."

The chauffeur was opening the door of the lavender Cadillac. Dan helped her in. She settled back on the upholstery, putting her head on his chest.

"I just don't want you to be disappointed, that's all."

The car started with a soft flowing motion which lapped both passengers in a sense of joys to come.

"How could anyone be disappointed in you, baby?" Dan said gallantly.

Miranda's body jerked, but he could not tell whether the spasm was caused by a sob or a suppressed giggle.

"It's on account of the Freeze . . ."

It was clear that she needed some encouragement; in an effort to supply it, and also to reassure himself, Dan kissed her. They embraced again, more briefly, outside the hotel, after which Miranda dismissed her driver with one succinct word:

"Scram!"

"Thank you, madame. Good night, madame," the driver said. He got back into the car and drove away.

For several minutes, in the cool, spicy air, Miranda and Dan stood embraced; when they proceeded into the hotel they did so at a slow pace, she pressed to his side, he stalking along with dignity, glaring from under the great hat. There was something about their entrance reminiscent of the costume pictures in which both, from time to time, had worked—an atmosphere not of today but borrowed, as it were, from the legends of a golden, riotous past. They had passed, without glancing at them, the stiff chairs under the fern plants in the lobby, had almost reached the desk when, in an amazing change of pace, Miranda's body shot forward; next second she was sprawled on the marble floor in front of the elevator. It was immediately clear that her propulsion into this position had not been caused by any collapse on her part but by the action of a person who had approached from behind and who (a split second later) leaped on the fallen actress and began to pummel her unmercifully.

33

There was no mistaking that small, violent figure—just as there was no accounting for its presence here in Mexico. Dan, deeply shocked, stood like a tower of jelly, staring at the wild scene on the floor. Could this be happening? How had she got here?

"Jill—"

He grabbed at her but she rolled out of reach, both hands yoked in Miranda's lacy peasant blouse, which tore from neck to navel. Both women were screaming words which the clerk, Policarpo Sanchez, with his knowledge of English, knew were unbecoming in guests of the Europa. Undeterred, he jumped over the desk and got into the contest, seizing Miranda's leg.

"Jill, honey—"

But Jill's rage, following a pattern set up in such situations through the years, bypassed him, focusing on the guilty female.

"Whore! Home wrecker! I'll show you . . ."

Though outweighed, the surprise attack had given Jill the advantage: she pressed it fiercely, getting one hand loose from the blouse to claw Miranda's face and jerk out a handful of luxuriant dyed hair. What devil brought her round, always at just the worst time, Dan wondered: he circled the rolling, struggling women, looking for a handhold, wondering whether there could be anything in her damned claim of intuition.

". . . *policía* . . ."

The dangerous word, spoken by a dignified elderly Mexican, frightened Dan more than the battle in progress.

"God, no. No cops . . ."

"*Ai, chihuahua . . .*"

Sanchez backed off, watching interestedly. The tide of battle was turning. This time Jill's opponent was no frightened weakling like Josie, the dental technician; this was a woman who had slugged her own way up in the world. One of her slippers had come off and as she rolled over once more her hand fell on it. A slipper with a four-inch tapered heel is, in the hands of a sufficiently aroused woman, a deadly weapon; Miranda struck with it only once, a glancing blow but enough to stun Jill. Miranda pulled the slipper back to strike again, but in this moment Sanchez, with rare presence of mind, threw the contents of a flower vase, blossoms and all, into her face; the lady gasped, then screamed; she turned from Jill, making a quick try at kicking Sanchez in the groin. Dan picked up Jill. He hoisted her on his shoulder and dived for the elevator; by the time he reached the third, his own floor, Jill had revived sufficiently to pull his hair and kick.

"Let go of me . . ."

"Baby . . ."

"You and that . . . I'll kill her . . . I'll . . ."

"Take it easy, honey . . ."

The effort of keeping Jill across his back was difficult; Dan staggered as he strode along the hall. Hearing the noise,

(204)

a Mexican couple, Sr. y Sra. Morales, guests of the hotel, opened their door slightly; at the sight of the immense man reeling past with a protesting, redhaired woman held in air the Moraleses slammed the door again and bolted it. Señora Morales leaned against it while her husband telephoned to report what he had seen.

Downstairs, Policarpo Sanchez had been using the last of his strength to keep Miranda from following Jill; he took Señor Morales' call somewhat out of breath.

". . . It is nothing. Hear me: they are people of the cinema northamerican . . ."

Jill had stopped struggling the moment Dan closed the door. She and Dan stood face to face as slowly, almost fearfully, he set her down on her own legs. In such situations she was always adamant, sure of herself, resorting to violence only when absolutely necessary—he for his part guiltily contrite, anxious to give an account of himself by lying but at the same time aware that lying was no use. You could never tell how things would work out with Jill when she was in such moods . . . but she was formidable always, and he tender and, if not too battered, fearful, curiously pitying. That Jill, she was something. You had to watch her, she could get mad all over again in a flash and seize a weapon, a pair of scissors or anything, like that time she had thrown the kettle.

He towered over her, his face blank and miserable but at the same time glowing with health, polished by sun and wind so that it had a high gloss to it like a barbershop shoeshine. She straightened her clothes, watching him out of the corners of her eyes.

"Well . . . and what have you got to say?"

"I never—"

"Great. Go on. I love that start . . ."

"I never touched her, Jill. I swear . . ."

"You never . . . Ah, you goat."

He had taken the wrong tack as usual. If he had brazened it out he might have had a chance, though a remote one: this way, his lies and penitence and above all his longing for her left him mixed up and defenseless.

"I'll tell you how it was . . ."

"Do you think I came three thousand miles to lis—"

"We were just . . ."

"—ten to your lies . . . But go on. Don't let me stop you. She's just a lonesome little virgin, huh? Probably she's broke too, on five thousand a week, so you had to buy her dinner. Then you had a few drinks and . . . God . . ."

Her eyes rolled as her rage came back in its inevitable final spurt; he knew what she was looking for—a knife, a gun, something to throw . . . but he was ready. It was a good thing he knew her ways. This time the flurry was brief, Dan holding her off quietly while he twisted out of range of kicks and let her blows fall on his huge, tough body unnoticed.

"I don't mind your screwing, but I can't stand your damn lying . . . So . . . so-o . . . she trapped you, I suppose, she roped you into it . . ."

No human being could sustain this pitch of rage for long. Her fury changed to melancholy at his neglect of her.

"There I am, sitting home alone. And when I go out, where do I go? To see one of your stinking pictures, so damn lonesome for you I could hardly stand it, while you . . ."

"She's nothing to me. You know that . . ."

"Nothing . . . She's been with everyone in Hollywood. Why should you be an exception? . . . Well, I'm sorry I interrupted. If that's how you feel go on, go to her."

"You know I'm not going to her . . ."

(206)

"You're right you're not going to her."

Jill was rapidly, and as if absent-mindedly, taking off her clothes. Even after such scenes, and sometimes most sharply then, Dan's old hunger for her came back; he seized her, trying to kiss her mouth, which she twisted away. She ran toward the closet, he grabbing her from behind, holding her to him.

"If I'm so homely, take your paws off me."

"You're the tops. You know that . . ."

"Sure! It's great to have the tops at home, so you can run after whores on the outside . . ."

The pattern of their thirty-year-old marriage, endeared to both by long habit, grotesque, fierce and healing, reestablished itself in their nerves.

"I never ran after her. She asked me to have a drink and . . ."

"Take your hands off me . . . She's young and I'm old. That's it, and don't deny it."

"You're worth ten of her."

"Because I'm here and she's downstairs."

"Because you're better-looking. You're a better lay . . ."

"How do you know I'm better if you didn't . . ."

"Because I can tell . . ."

"But I'm your wife. All right. Wives are dull."

Sex was not only the best way to pacify Jill, it was the only way when she was on a rampage. All thought of other women left him as she turned at last, not permitting him to touch her but moving in front of him, nude and glistening, weaving her old, familiar dance of desire.

"What are you looking at, if I'm so bad you have to run after whores?"

"You're the best . . ."

"But I'm not good enough. I'm only a wife, a redhaired runt . . . All right, look then. I ought to dye it, I suppose . . ."

"Baby . . ."

". . . Go get yourself some glamourpuss that has it curled at Westmore's. And perfumed too, I suppose . . . Well, I'm no glamourpuss, so don't bother with me . . ." Kicking her slippers off she now at last permitted him to touch her: Dan seized her hungrily, lifted her against him while he kissed her on the mouth and stroked her belly; after a moment in which she held herself rigidly still, as if listening to some far-off sound, perhaps music, she began to return his caresses.

"All right, all right . . . but just remember, it's the last time . . ."

"Honey, if I ever look at another woman as long as I live, may God strike me . . ."

"Ooh, where have I heard those words before . . . Don't SAY IT. God might . . ."

"Sweetheart . . ."

". . . be listening. All right . . ."

"Doll . . ."

"All right, all right," she said. "I told you, but . . . wait till I take my stockings off, can't you?"

34

Approximately a half-hour earlier, Nancy Heston, accompanied by a bellboy carrying her four admirable pieces of luggage, had arrived at her husband's room, the number of which she had obtained at the desk. The bellboy knocked, then knocked again and, receiving no answer, tried the door-knob.

"*Está abierta,*" he said, smiling at her with the joy which all Mexicans take in situations suggesting possible intrigue.

Nancy did not need to fall back on her high-school Spanish to understand the sense of this, but since the intrigue angle had also occurred to her she decided not to make immediate use of the situation, at least not without some warning.

"Just a minute," she said. Changing places with the boy, it was she who now opened the door a few inches; she spoke softly into the darkness beyond.

"Harold?"

There was no answer; she opened the door a little further, but she did not speak again. There was no need to. He was definitely there; she could hear him breathing, him or some-body: she spoke again, announcing herself as a wife should, she felt, when arriving unexpectedly at her husband's quarters.

"It's me, Harold—it's Nancy."

Still he did not answer, though now she could see his dark

(209)

head on the pillow; gaining confidence, she moved closer. From a yard away she smelled the liquor on his breath and bent a little closer to make sure. He was sleeping like the dead, he must have gone to bed drunk—yet this was not like him: only once or twice in the whole course of their marriage had she seen him take too much and then only in a celebrant, happy sort of way.

Turning back to the bellboy she pantomimed for him to bring the bags in and be quiet about it; when this had been done she tipped him and sent him out. She had seen where the bathroom was and, after considerable groping, found the light there and turned it on; still Harold did not move. What in the world had made him go on a bender, now when he had so much responsibility and must have been so busy? It was puzzling—just as it was to contemplate what his reaction would be when he woke and found her there. Would he be glad or sorry? It had not occurred to her till then that he'd be anything but glad, but she had not foreseen this sleeping or the drinking that must have preceded it. The air in the room was so stuffy she opened the window, then prepared for bed.

Better to have him sleep and wake to find her there; they could talk in the morning. Yes, that would be far, far better, the only way really, except for one question, the question which the sleeping and the proof of his recent behavior made more formidable.

Had he received her letter? Or had the wire, as she hoped, arrived first? . . . And from this immediately rose a correlated question, even more important: if the wire had come first and the letter second, had he obeyed her instructions not to read the letter? She wondered what she would have done in his place. She gave this some thought, standing beside his bed, the light from the open bathroom door making her eyes look crafty, catlike. No, she decided, she would not have obeyed, she would have read the letter—any woman would, but men were different; men had their own weird standards about things like that, they might feel honor-bound to do as they'd been asked. That was the way they were—a trait which did not, in her opinion, supply proof that they were more honest or reliable but only that they were different, perhaps without the intelligence to be as curious and hence as tempted as a woman would have been.

No, men had their deep and shallow ways, the only trick about recognizing these being that a woman's corresponding ways were only corresponding and in no way similar. Here was Harold surprising her by having drunk himself unconscious: suddenly she felt, for no reason she could accurately name, sorry about this. He and his strict regime, his leaving of parties at eleven, his systematic exercise and all the rest of it, doing this with the biggest opportunity of his career now in the balance, its outcome hinged on his being at his best—it really was strange. He stirred in his sleep and she stepped back quickly so that if he opened his eyes he would not see her; it was important somehow that he should not . . . but he didn't open them, only moved his head enough so the light now fell into his face. He looked much younger when he was asleep; she'd noticed this before, perhaps because Christian, in the last days especially, had looked in sleep as if he were already dead.

Christian vs. Harold.

She wondered when, if ever, she would get over this habit of matching one man against the other in memory and observation, shuttling perpetually between present and past. It was not possible or even fair, fair to another person, to live in two time segments simultaneously; it had not been fair to Harold, that she knew. Probably he should have married someone who only had one time level available to live in, some cute debutante from Santa Monica who had been to UCLA and majored in physical education.

He looked younger, yes, but he also looked helpless. This was something new. There were dark smears under his eyes, below his thick lashes; she had the idea that he'd grown thinner. Every human was a pool of mystery . . . herself and Harold, Christian alone at last, deserted by his women, his agents and his audiences.

And Dan . . .

And Jill . . .

She coldcreamed her face. Harold's weariness was pitiful, his drunkenness even more so. Jill had been so right; he'd needed her or needed something, someone; he was not the way he'd been; he was not cocky, hurrying, cold, successful; he was beat, he was worn out.

Suddenly Nancy shivered. Someone had knocked on the door, then knocked again; standing in her nightgown in her husband's room she felt, perhaps because he did not know that she was here, as if she were some interloper, a chance woman whom the house detective, with controlled peremptory scorn, would ask to leave.

"Just a minute," she said, barely audibly. She groped for a robe, found one at last and opened the door, not before the idiot had knocked again. It was the bellboy and he had something on a tray: an airmail, special delivery letter, addressed to Harold in her own handwriting.

35

Light crawled into the sky. It crept upward from the bottom of the world, causing solid objects to seem darker and heavier; things on the earth took on individual shapes, then shades, and finally colors. Long before this stage of the new day's coming had been reached, however, it was possible, on top of the cliff, to make out the chute, a trough of raw pine wood indented in the earth, slashing diagonally across the cliff's surface to the edge of its huge outcropping lip.

The carpenters had finished the chute an hour before dawn and after their going there was silence on the cliff. Land and sea quivered in the spell of the widening gray light; from below could be heard the thud of the waves as they lashed at the base of the cliff; mixed with this sound, after a while, came a faraway drone of gasoline engines. The drone became a roar; from the direction of town a caravan of trucks appeared, rolling out onto the cliff top. There were trucks which carried lights, reflectors, scrims and cables, a camera truck, a truck containing wardrobe and another truck filled with equipment to be used solely in applying makeup to human faces; there was a commissary truck, a latrine truck, a hospital truck, and a truck containing horses; following the trucks were passenger cars carrying the crew. The drivers lined their vehicles across the rear portion of the cliff and the men, in silence, and with sleepy, wooden-looking faces, got out and began going about their business.

Harold was one of the first to arrive. With Roy Sowells he inspected the camera sites: a platform on top of the cliff to shoot Dan's takeoff and another, some distance down the side, to pick up his descent and "pan" with it. A third shot of the jump (from below) would be made from a boat with a hand-held Eyemo camera. A special cameraman had been flown in from Hollywood to operate this camera; Cameraman Shelby Deane introduced him to Harold. The man's name was Casey Sharpe; he was the baldish, slender fellow whom Harold had seen getting out of one of the stretchouts the evening before, and as they shook hands he noticed, as he had during his previous glimpse of him, that Sharpe looked ill.

"Have you had much experience with Eyemos?"

Harold asked the question less to obtain information than to have a chance to observe the new man; the Eyemo operator had a vital part in the day's operations and it was important to know he was fit for the job.

"Yes, sir. Eleven pictures. I'm always on call for Eyemo work. Got started in it during wartime."

"That so? I did some Eyemo work myself around that time—"

They chatted for two or three minutes, exchanging notes on their service experiences: Harold then gave instructions on the manner in which he wanted the scene photographed. Sharpe answered briskly and seemed intelligent and eager to work. Possibly, Harold thought, his appearance was not indicative of poor health; picture business sometimes produced such faces. Harold knew men who looked like walking death but had not missed a day from their jobs in twenty years.

(214)

"Better tape the box so it'll be waterproof in case you drop it overboard. This is one piece of film we don't want to lose."

Shelby Deane answered for Sharpe.

"Don't worry. I fixed that myself."

"Swell. But the next thing is—don't drop it . . ."

"I think I can promise that I won't, sir," Sharpe said levelly. Again his voice inspired confidence, but as he raised a lighter to his cigarette Harold saw that his hand was shaking; he had an instinct—he regretted later that he had not obeyed it—to send Sharpe to the first-aid truck for a checkover. At the moment, however, he had other things to think about; he shook hands and watched the Eyemo man climb into the company jeep for a ride down the winding trail, bulldozed some days before between the higher and lower cliffs. At the bottom of this trail was the patch of beach from which the camera boat would be launched through the surf.

In a few minutes everything would be ready. Roy Sowells had instructed the company in the signals to be used—one shot to start the three cameras rolling, two shots to alert them for action and send Dan and his horse toward the chute. The first and second camera operators and a member of the boat crew had blank cartridge pistols with which to fire three—the emergency signal—in case there was any trouble.

"Want me to call a coffee break, boss?"

The question was merely Roy's way of intimating that he was ready for action.

"Just a minute."

Harold looked for the tenth, or perhaps the twentieth time that morning, at a place he did not want to look at—the place between the special-effects truck and the horse trailer where Dan sat alone. He sat on a prop box, his shoulders

hunched and his hat pulled over his eyes, whittling a stick:
he was very skillful with a jackknife and often, Harold remembered, in his childhood, would come home after work
with some smoothly whittled and entrancing object in his
pocket—a jaybird, a pistol, a whistle, a dagger: Jill had saved
a number of such things, kept them, he knew, in his old
room in the Lefferts Drive house. Not that such presents were
ever revealed at once; that was not Dan's way, it would spoil
the fun. He would walk into the house, kiss his wife, then
look at his small son in a certain manner which caused
Harold to jump up and down.

"What pocket is it in?"

Dan would turn away, his voice gruff and his manner
abstracted.

"Who says it's in a pocket?"

At this Harold would become more excited than ever.

"In your hand then, you're hiding it in your hand."

"Hand, hand—" Dan would appear to be confused.

"Which hand?"

"That one, that one—"

And as Dan skillfully passed the object in question from
one hand to another, Harold would grab at each in turn, then
try to climb higher, his small arms just long enough to en-
circle one of Dan's huge legs while Jill, losing patience with
the game, would exclaim, "Gee, Dan, don't make him any
sillier than he is. If you have anything for him, for God's
sake give it to him . . ."

Until now, this very moment on the cliff, with so much to
be decided in the next few seconds, Harold had had no idea
of when or why Dan did his whittling. He had done it at work,
that was all anyone had known for sure. But now, watching
the slow-handed, large, remote and walled-off man, whittling

(216)

something or other there off by himself, he wondered. "Was that what it was? Did he always whittle before doing a stunt?" If this was so, then all the treasured things—the miniature windmills, the Chinese boxes, the Indian heads, the planes— had been charms, totems Dan had manufactured to distract himself from some approaching moment of deadly danger.

"You okay?"

He had asked the question once that morning, sure that the answer he received was the same he would get if he asked it a hundred times.

"You bet, son. Feel swell."

"Want to look over the camera setups?"

Dan had shaken his head, his eyes on the pine stick and the slow nibbling blade of his claspknife.

"Nope. Leave that to you. Just holler when you're ready."

So there had been nothing to do. Nothing except leave him there, somber and alone in the sun, with the reflectors tangling their harsh beams in front of him, whittling to keep out thoughts of danger.

The slim, controlled shavings that flicked from Dan's knife-blade were stitches knitting up the past and present.

At least we're in business, he thought, and that's something. What about that now, he thought, do I owe that to Dan? I'll be damned if I want to owe him anything, and still . . .

It hadn't been his idea to take Dan back on the picture. He'd been sitting, drunk and supperless, in his hotel room when Roy found him. Roy could be tough. Not that Harold had taken as the truth everything Roy said, but he had made one point and made it well: if Dan had wanted to get out of his commitment, the act of firing him had been a goofy move.

It had laid the cards right in Dan's hands.

". . . All right, so what," Harold had said, "I fired him. So let it stick . . ."

"Great," Roy said. "You think I can phone Central Casting to fly someone up here for this spot? Listen, I want to level with you: without this guy we're in trouble."

"Trouble he made," Harold said defensively, but he felt shaky. He'd depended on Roy. Now, having got rid of Dan, it looked as if he were losing Roy too.

"This time you made it."

"Maybe. But I'm not backing down, either," Harold said almost shrilly. He stopped, realizing that he had exposed to Roy the real core of his thinking.

Roy hunkered on his heels beside Harold's chair.

"Want to know something? He figured you'd feel that way. Said to tell you he was beat, whipped . . . Do you get it? Hell, if you're settling a personal grudge—settle it later. He *wants* to get back."

"Why?"

Roy blinked. All drunks wanted to know whys. Yet to Harold, at that moment, the question seemed unanswerable so he repeated it.

"Why—if he's got such a good out, and he'll get paid anyway? Tell me that," he said with great craft, prodding solemnly. He'd cornered old Roy that time.

But Roy, much to his surprise, had an answer.

"Because he's a pro. He's got a job to do. You got one and I got one or we'll *all* be canned. Do we take him back and shoot the jump, or do we fold up this company and head for home?"

In the end, reluctantly, he'd told Roy to use his own judgment, knowing what Roy would do, but still, in a fashion, putting the responsibility for changing his mind on someone

(218)

else. Roy was another horny-handed bastard like Dan: both of them were in cahoots, most likely, but it didn't matter too much now.

Get the picture made. Settle the grudge later.

That made some kind of sense.

He remembered refusing to let Roy help him get to bed but had no memory of how he got there. He'd been sleeping like a dead one when the rest of it happened: even now, in broad daylight, he had trouble believing it . . . but until the day he was a dead one sure enough, he knew nothing would beat the feeling he'd had when he woke toward morning and found Nancy there, not in the next twin bed but in his own, pressed up against him. The only bad part of this, if any part could be said to be bad, which it couldn't, was that he hadn't wakened earlier: aside from one hasty yet somehow vastly satisfying act of love they hadn't had time to be together or say anything to each other; that would be later.

Having Nancy with him made things different with regard to Dan, too: maybe you could just think clearer with one worry less to nag you. It seemed now as if he and Dan, after last night, had less to settle.

And after today? Would they have less then, or more? There was always a chance, of course, Dan might not even be around to settle anything with. Should he go over to the arrogant, whittling son of a bitch and shake hands with him? Harold looked at his watch, realizing it was late for such a gesture.

Roy was picking his teeth. This was a bad sign. It meant the company was losing time and usually could be counted on to follow the question about the coffee break.

"Give them positions . . ."

The stock order applied to the acting personnel rather than

the crew, the latter usually being in positions anyway. However, though only one person would be in front of the cameras this morning, the order had to be given. It was expected.

Roy picked up his megaphone, equipped with a battery loud speaker.

"All right. Positions, everybody . . . You better get mounted, Dan . . ."

36

Dan got up. He brushed the shavings off his clothes, folded his knife and put it in his pocket. He set his hat straight on his head and walked toward the horse trailer. The horse he was to ride, a stockily-built young bay, was standing here, saddled and bridled; Art Dollarhyde was holding it on a tie-rope while a special-effects man rubbed soapsuds on its hide to make it look as if it had been running. The horse seemed strong and well broke; it stood quietly with its head down, not moving as the special-effects man worked it over. By its sloping shoulders and the way it was muscled in the flanks it looked as if it might be a mountain horse; if so, that was good. Horses trained in the California mountains were generally at ease in high places, far superior in this respect to the flatlands horses of the southwest cow country. Dan examined the bit—a plain bar bit which Dollarhyde had covered with a piece of hose. He had removed the curb strap and set the reins in the rings closest to the bit instead of those at the ends of the cheek pieces, where pull would have exerted leverage.

Even if the bay's mouth was sensitive you could lean into it a little with a rig like that: you could set yourself against it, helping the horse to keep his head at the right angle when he was in the chute.

"Does it look okay to you, Dan?"

Dollarhyde's voice was easy but he was watching Dan closely for some sign of approval. He had given a lot of thought to the bridle rig and was hungry for a word of commendation. In the old days he had saddled many horses for Dan: he felt from the fact that Dan had given him no instructions this time, and had not even tried the horse, that he was on his mettle.

"Appears to be," was all Dan said.

The special-effects man stepped to one side. He dropped his sponge back into the bucket of suds.

"Good luck, Dan," he said.

Dan did not reply. If there was anything he did not like it was for some jerk to wish him luck before a stunt. He took hold of the horn and mounted in a quick flowing motion, pulling himself up till his left foot was level with the stirrup on the near side before moving this foot forward into the stirrup itself. Dollarhyde slipped off the lead-rope and Dan squeezed the bay's sides lightly, moving him off at a walk, then in a slow easy lope. He liked the young horse's action, finding as he figure-eighted him that he went equally well on both right and left leads. He began to warm up as he worked the horse slowly on the sunny grass; the bay was willing and quiet and when he changed leads he did it with a powerful, smooth thrust, hardly perceptible to the rider. Feeling a happiness and oneness with the horse Dan was sorry, in a way, that the bay was so perfectly trained; some good hand, perhaps Art himself, had worked hundreds of hours to give this horse his manners and develop his intelligence. It seemed too bad that such a horse should be used expendably. Since his own fear was past, at least for now, and his recognition of death and acceptance of its possibilities still strong in him, it never occurred to him that he was using himself in the same fashion.

Quiet in the saddle, he turned the bay right and left, crooning to him in a kind of toneless singing which was his way with a new horse that he liked.

"We got a job to do, brother," he told the bay.

The little bay was all right. No man, when you came down to it, was all in one place like a good horse, mind and body working as one. A horse did what he was trained to do. No crap about him. No regrets or fears or superstitions. Men made up fairy tales to scare themselves. Two were dead. So there had to be a third. Stuff like that. Not so with a horse. He was either right or he was wrong, and this one was right.

"We're going to get ourselves a little ocean bath and then we'll get dry in the sun," Dan told the horse.

He kept looking over his shoulder as he rode, trying to see if Roy was raising his signal pistol. But the assistant, conferring with Shelby Deane at the number one camera, spoke through the megaphone.

"Hold it a couple of minutes, Dan . . ."

Script Girl Dolores Lansing, a plain-faced, full-bodied girl wearing khaki slacks and a man's o.d. shirt wrote in her book:

A.M. 10:11 Company given positions.
A.M. 10:14 Stuntman Prader mounted, to enter camera left.
A.M. 10:21 Delay called by Asst. R. Sowells.
(222)

Jill, turning her head where she sat beside Nancy in the stretchout, tried to see what was happening below the cliff. At the moment when Roy's iron-amplified voice had called Dan to get mounted, she had pulled an ivory-and-silver rosary out of her handbag and begun to pray, her lips moving with the words of the prayers but her mind darting elsewhere.

Hail Mary, full of grace, the Lord is with Thee, blessed art Thou among women and blessed is the fruit of Thy womb, Jesus . . . (Ai! If you could do and feel the right things instead of those acts and emotions that made trouble for you and brought sorrow to the Little Mother and Her son, Jesus: the fighting, the crazy jealousy, the fears. Where, where did those feelings come from that consumed the body and mocked the soul? Yet . . . you couldn't put them off entirely until you had made your peace and were done for.)

Holy Mary, Mother of God, pray for us sinners now and in the hour of our death. If only Dan had seen the priest, she thought. She had asked him in the past to do it before some dangerous act, but his answer was always the same: he wouldn't. He'd once explained how he felt: that only cowards turned to God in trouble, if they were not people who turned to him ordinarily. Just like him: the fool. It infuriated her to be left to do all the praying for the family.

Jill's eyes jerked open; she too had heard, at the same time as Nancy, the three shots from down below—the trouble signal.

"What are they doing?"

"I don't know. It's some trouble in the boat . . ."

Dan had heard the warning in time. He took up on the little bay and the horse, almost in the chute, swerved to the left and threw his hind legs under him, coming to a skid-stop like a roping horse when his rider has looped a calf and is getting off to tie.

He had been perfectly set for the stunt; stopping this way shook him up.

What could have gone wrong in the boat?

As he quieted the bay he could see the jeep coming up from the beach, raising a thick cloud of dust. The jeep came out on the level clifftop and headed for the first-aid trailer. Sam La Brasca was driving; a guy beside him was twisted around to steady a third person who lay on an improvised stretcher propped across the side seats behind. Doc Phillips ran out of the trailer and he and Sam and the other guy carried the man inside. Roy also went in; he reappeared in a moment and went back to the parallel.

"Casey Sharpe passed out; sunstroke or something."

Shelby Deane began to swear. Harold glared furiously at Roy. He remembered how he'd noticed that the Eyemo man looked ill: God, why hadn't he had him checked, as he'd thought of doing?

"That's a lousy break."

Harold's face screwed up with thought. He was considering a drastic decision—but no other seemed possible.

"Couldn't Shell operate the Eyemo?" Roy suggested.

Under ASC regulations, a first cameraman could operate any piece of camera equipment on a job, Harold knew. He also knew that under emergency conditions, a director himself could take over a camera if he were qualified.

"He can't operate this one. I need Shell up here."

"Then who—"

"Me. Tell Dan to dismount and relax. We'll need about ten minutes to get the boat out there again and get lined up. I'll fire a shot when I'm ready . . ."

37

Dan had dismounted. He stood leaning against the horse with which he had formed such a firm bond; he had the taste of fear in his mouth, disgust in his heart, and a shivering weakness in every part of him. In addition to all this, he felt cold: heedless of the fact that he was staining his clothes with the special-effects lather and the genuine, activity-born sweat on the bay's withers, he tried to pull warmth from the bay's warm, breathing body while the chunky horse, in his turn, stood quite still as if to help, swinging his head round to see what his rider was doing or about to do. They had become a unit now, whatever was afoot they would do it together, to the best of their ability.

In her canvas chair, Dolores Lansing placed her book in her lap and wrote:

A.M. 11:21 Eyemo Cameraman Sharpe ill, replaced by director.
A.M. 11:42 Action resumed.

Another shot from Roy's gun. Dan swung the bay around: at a smooth canter he drew near the opening of the chute, concealed with earth and grass so that it would not show in the cameras. The bay's hoofs hit the planks of the chute: he went in and stretched, setting himself naturally in an almost perfect diving position. To Dan, the ground was tearing past in a haze of reflector glare and dizziness and the earth opening ahead of him into nothing: he went out into space, falling through a huge arc of air, looking upside down at the edge of the cliff behind and above him and at the sky and all the lovely dangerous and spinning earth which he had liked so much and which he was now leaving.

In the boat, Harold stood against a thwart, his eye pressed into the finder of the heavy little Eyemo: in the finder Dan and the horse appeared in air at the edge of the cliff like a weird two-headed bird, coursing immensely outward and downward; the bird-man-horse did not stay in one piece or fall in the place which calculation had indicated. Instead, the man-horse passed completely over the boat where it divided into two parts, man and horse, the two divided components striking the water with immense impact; each throwing up its separate, shocking plume of spray. The horse reappeared immediately, head and neck shooting up clear, then settling back to a small dark triangle as the bay swam strongly toward the shore.

"God! Where is he?"

Even while his eyes searched the water for Dan, Harold thought once more of the film: the jump, he knew, was perfect, the separation of man and horse having come too late to show. Only—to be safe himself Dan should have stayed mounted.

Sam La Brasca struggled with the pull rope to get the boat's outboard motor going. Harold's clothes were heavy on him as he dived, came up, dived again, found Dan at last and hooked an elbow under his chin, bringing him to the surface. Sam had the motor going now. He brought the boat close enough for Harold to get a grip on the side, then killed the motor while he helped to pull Dan in.

Ashore, the two men left with the jeep were wading into the surf and the crew of the number two camera were running down the road toward them, also with the evident intention of offering help: the four of them dragged the boat up on the sand. Harold tried to force brandy into Dan's mouth, but it ran out of his slack lips; then, with Dan across a seat, head down, an amateurish attempt at artificial respiration was begun, Sam and Harold collaborating in this as the jeep climbed upwards. The flat space on top was rougher than the road; Harold sat on the floor, holding Dan's head to keep it from bouncing. The jeep, with Merv Perkins of the number two camera crew driving, charged straight for the hospital trailer. Doc Phillips had the door open: Sam and Harold, with Perkins helping, carried Dan inside. They did not shut the door; they would have had to shut it in Jill's face. She had run from the stretchout to the edge of the cliff, just before Dan jumped; when she saw him taken from the boat to the jeep, she knew where the men were taking him and started toward the trailer. The entire company, shocked by the outcome of the stunt, watched her frantic, wobbling run in silence. The sight of a woman running is odd at any time: somehow the motion of Jill's figure, her smallness in her dark clothes, or perhaps the fact that no one else on the clifftop was moving dramatized the seriousness of what had happened; she went into the trailer. Nancy Heston, who had started to follow her, changed her mind. Roy Sowells entered, crossing over from the number one camera. It was hard to figure out how one medium-sized trailer could hold so many people and keep a secret at the same time.

Dolores Lansing, who had been standing beside Jill at the cliff edge, went back to her chair. She wrote:

A.M. 11:24 Scene 241, 242 completed.
A.M. 11:24½ Stuntman Prader hurt.

She wrote these words very carefully, in a handwriting which, like the rest of her, was well formed, firm, and competent. Having completed this task, she put her pencil back in the loop made for it on the clip-binder of her work sheets. She dropped the work book into the canvas pocket on the side of her chair. Then she began to shake; the more she tried to keep her hands and lips and her whole body quiet the worse the shaking got. She had held script on about three dozen pictures, mostly of the indoor variety; she had never seen a dangerous stunt performed before or a man injured at work. A cup of coffee, she thought, might be good for the shakes, but all the coffee in the commissary truck had been drunk during the morning. She wondered whether anyone was going to call lunch, then realized at the same instant that she did not feel like eating any. Much to her own surprise—thinking about nothing except lunch—she put her head down on the arm of the chair lettered "SCRIPT" and broke into sobs.

38

"It's incredible," Miss Carnavon said, "incredible and brutal. If I hadn't seen it with my own eyes I wouldn't have believed it—leaving him there to die!"

The *Scope* representative had now stopped being a human tape-recorder; she had become a voice.

"Nobody's left him, ma'am," Linc Hyman said. "They're doing the best they can for him."

Miss Carnavon gave a sort of whinny.

"The horse, you fool, the poor horse. Wait till they hear about this in Mr. Zeld's office."

Linc, staring at her in amazement, thought, ". . . and we were wondering who the company stool pigeon was! I never knew they brought them in from publications . . ."

Miss Carnavon pointed at the sea where Dan's mount, turned sideways by a wave or confused about its bearings, had headed around and was swimming parallel to the beach.

"Men!" she exclaimed. She flipped her right arm out in an angry gesture. "Doing such things to an animal. For film! For a piece of celluloid! You're sadistic butchers—all of you —and I'll say so in print."

Linc Hyman kept quiet a minute, then he said hopefully, "Look—someone's gone out after him."

It turned out to be true. The loader of the number two

camera had stripped to his shorts and had gone out through the surf; he was making an effort to turn the horse landward.

"Good—then at least there's one human being here. I'll have to find out his name."

She turned to a gaffer standing near and yelled at him. "Do you know it—the name of that brave man down there? Does anybody know it? I suppose NOT—you all hate him, probably, because he knows how to be kind."

Hyman watched the horse's wedge-shaped black head moving in the water, hoping Miss Carnavon would not write something damaging to *Leatherlegs*. If she did, of course, he would be blamed! What a lousy break, having a horse-loving lesbian dame like this on the set when a tough stunt had to be done.

Mentally, he began composing the sort of release he would give out, with studio approval, if the worst came to the worst.

> *Daniel Prader, 51, former motion picture actor doubling for the Duart star, Rab O'Grady, on location at Cape Todos Santos, Mexico, was accidentally killed today when his mount fell with him.*

That might be a safe way to put it—better, anyway, than indicating his death was the result of a planned risk.

> *Prader, who had a long career in pictures, was the father of Harold Heston, Duart director. He is survived by a widow, Josephine Heston Prader. Funeral services will be . . .*

The death of any performer never helped a picture: the news of it, if still fresh, could give audiences the uncomfortable feeling that they were watching a ghost. So he would have to lay off the publicity—though in a way this was a pity.

(230)

What a story you could get out, if you could tell everything, go back into Dan's past, his early stunt days, the Ringo Kid series, his quarrels, his romances. Twenty-five years of the world's most fabulous business would be compressed in that story, twenty-five years which he, Linc Hyman, knew only by hearsay, crowded with the shapes and faces and antics of other ghosts as colorful as Dan. But even as he thought what kind of a story it would be a sense of futility possessed him. Who, outside the people in the industry, would understand it? From the corner of his eye he kept watching the trailer: now he saw Roy Sowells come out, look around and head toward him. Roy was not running but there was a look about him which telegraphed bad news. Forty feet from Linc he made a motion with his right thumb—the same motion an umpire makes when calling a man out at the plate. Linc felt sick. This must be it!

Roy said, "Harold wants to talk to you. Is it okay to leave her?"

With a jerk of his head, he indicated Miss Carnavon. She had paid no attention to them, still looking at the rescue of the horse.

Linc shrugged. What in hell did Miss Carnavon matter now? He followed Roy across the work area toward the first-aid trailer. Everybody in the company was watching them.

39

Dan Prader sat on the right-hand bunk, naked except for a cotton blanket. The blanket had partially slipped off, exposing his large hairy torso, scarred with the marks of spills and lumpy where some ribs, broken in a long-ago stunt and improperly set, had humped under the flesh. He had one arm around his wife, Jill; in the other hand he had a brandy bottle and was drinking out of it.

What was important and slightly incredible to Linc at that moment was that Dan was alive, he had made it. Feeling it was probably bad form to show surprise that a man was alive when he might have been dead, Linc stuck out his hand; the most logical thing to do just then was to congratulate Dan on having made it. There was something wrong, however, in the way Dan looked at him and the way the others looked, and Linc Hyman pulled his hand back again. There was something very wrong in the trailer: a celebration should have been starting, if not well on the way, and the bottle in Dan's fist not held there but passing from hand to hand and everyone talking and telling his version of how it had been and how he personally felt about it.

Dan's large creased face presided somberly over the silence in the trailer. His expression reflected the gloom Linc had taken to mean bad news as applied to Dan. Glancing into the

(232)

other bunk Linc understood what was the matter.

Casey Sharpe, the Eyemo cameraman, lay in this bunk. Casey Sharpe was the guy who was dead. His eyes were closed and his mouth slightly open, with bright new and ill-fitting false teeth rearing up in it. Casey Sharpe lay dead there and his nose—aristocratically thin, as dead men's noses always are—pointed to the ceiling. Casey Sharpe lay quiet, having already acquired the indifference and the air of weary authority which dead man have and which is the element of their superiority over the living.

Harold, who was closest to the trailer door, put his hand on Linc's shoulder.

"It wasn't sunstroke, the doc says, it was his heart. He was dying when they brought him in. It had nothing to do with his work. He just collapsed and died of a defective heart."

"Yes, sir," Linc said.

Doc Phillips now spoke up. This was his field and he felt obligated to get in the conversation.

"Coronary occlusion," he said. "Do you want to make a note of it?"

"I can remember," Linc said.

"All right," Harold said, "you handle it. Phone the studio. Contact the relatives direct or have the studio contact them. Find out what they want done with the body. If they want to have it shipped back, make the necessary arrangements. This may not be public relations but in a way it is and you're the only guy we can spare for it."

"I'll attend to it," Linc said. "Anything else?"

Dan, nude and massive, sat on the bunk looking at the floor. Then he looked at Casey Sharpe.

"The poor son of a bitch," he said. He took a swallow of brandy.

"I wish you'd stop drinking that stuff," Jill said. "You never drink it. What's come over you?"

She tried to grab the bottle from him. Dan wrestled her for it.

"The doc gave it to me, didn't he?" Dan said. "I guess I got a right to drink it, if it's medicinal."

"Medicinal, my foot," Jill said. She spun around to her son. "Harold, I don't want him drinking it. Make him stop—"

"Take it easy, Mom. He'll stop," Harold said, and Dan grinned at him.

"Like heck he will," Jill said. "What kind of a doctor are you," she said to Phillips, "giving him brandy? Why, it could make his heart quit on him like—"

Her glance traveled to Casey Sharpe. Phillips, not bothering to defend himself, pulled the sheet up over Casey's face.

"His heart won't quit, Mrs. Prader," the doc said. "I'll guarantee that."

"*You'll* guarantee it," Jill said viciously. "A lot you know. If you were any good you'd be working in a hospital or something. A real doctor would of saved that poor man's life."

Seeing an opportunity, she grabbed the bottle from Dan and took a swig herself.

Doctor Phillips looked hopelessly at Harold.

"Will you be wanting me right now?" he said stiffly. "Otherwise, I should phone town on the short-wave. We have to make disposition of—"

"Sure. You go right ahead, Doc."

The presence of the small mute corpse seemed to make Harold unusually polite.

Roy stepped between the doc and Harold. "The guys will be wanting to know about Dan. Couldn't he step out there now and ease their minds?"

(234)

Harold nodded. "Good idea. Doc, don't say anything out there about Casey Sharpe. As yet, that is."

"I understand," the doc said.

Dan got off the bunk; he held the blanket around his legs.

"Give me a pair of pants, somebody," he said.

The trailer spun around as he stood up; he staggered and sat down abruptly.

"Whee!" he said.

"You see, you see!" Jill said. "What did I tell you? You shouldn't be walking around. Make him lie down, can't you?" she said to the doctor.

"I am disqualifying myself from taking any further part in this matter," the doctor said with dignity.

"Wait a minute, Doc," Harold said. "I'm asking you this in the name of the company. Is he fit to go out there or isn't he?"

"He's fit to do any goddamn thing he wants," the doctor said. "He blacked out from the impact of the water. I don't think he suffered a concussion. I've advised him to go back to the hotel and go to bed. If he wants to ignore that advice there's nothing I can do about it."

He opened the door and went out of the trailer.

"Where are my pants?" Dan asked.

"Do you want to catch cold, on top of all?" Jill said. "They're sopping wet."

"Well, they'll do for now," Dan said. "Come on, honey, and find them. I've got to get out there."

"Oh, you—" Jill said. She went out and got the pants where she had put them, in the kitchen of the trailer, her heart, as she helped him put them on, melting with love. Where, in all the world, was there a man like that? Who else would do what he had done and then put on wet pants and go out, just to show a bunch of guys he was alive? Thanks to Thee, O Virgin Mother, for Thy mercy and protection. My never-ending thanks and prayers to Thee for Thy great mercy . . . But, she thought, why did he have to come through with no hurt at all: it might have been better if he'd been hurt a little, so he wouldn't do these crazy things again. She went to stand at the window, watching as he walked out into the sunlight and the crew, with wild whoops, came charging from every direction, shaking his hand, pounding him on the back.

This will spoil him for sure, she thought: the ornery big bastard. He'll remember this day as long as he lives.

Harold, Roy and Linc sat at the trailer table, listening to Dan's ovation, which was still in progress outside. The Mexican spectators from the hill had joined in the fiesta: three of them had broken through the crowd around El Gringo and lifted him up, attempting to carry him off on their shoulders in the manner of triumph accorded successful matadors; even in his stripped-down condition, however, Dan was too heavy and the attempt had to be abandoned.

"I'd better break it up, boss," Roy said.

"Certainly, Roy," Harold said in the very polite way he had adopted. "But how?"

"I could call lunch," Roy said dubiously.

"Well, wait a minute. I have an idea. I want your opinion on it, and yours too, Linc. Do you think this—er—business about Casey Sharpe, poor guy, could be kept quiet? For this afternoon, I mean."

"I don't get it, boss," Roy said.

"Well—it's just that—death in a company always affects morale. We've been lucky so far, got the stunt in the can and all. I don't want to lose three or four hours' work if I can help it."

(236)

He stopped, looking expectantly from Roy to Linc.

"Do you mind a suggestion, boss?" Linc said.

"Why no, no, Linc," Harold said. "That's just what I want —suggestions."

"Well, sir," Linc said slowly, "since you ask me, I'd say that the—the news about Casey wouldn't have a depressing effect. Of course, in a way it would, but he's dead. There's no way around that. And there's been so much talk about the superstition of three-in-a-row that—well, in a way, this will clear the air."

"I think I see what you mean," Harold said. "In other words, this finishes up the trio. End of cycle."

"That's it exactly," Linc said. "Of course, lots of the guys don't pay any attention to that kind of crap and never will. But there are others that do. And—"

Harold swung round to Roy.

"Do you agree with that?"

Roy looked thoughtful, then shrugged.

"Maybe. I don't think we'll lose any time, if they know or not. They're all hopped up now about Dan coming through. They'll work. Now can I call lunch?"

Harold looked at his watch. It did not do, even in such circumstances as this, to forget the schedule and he was not going to forget it. This was the first time that a death had occurred in a picture he had been directing; he felt he had handled the situation satisfactorily. Possibly, from an emotional point of view, the correct thing would have been to stop shooting for the day, but who would have benefited? Certainly not Casey Sharpe, and not himself: not even the crew who, out of maudlin sympathy, would have got drunk in town and been unfit for anything tomorrow. No, he was satisfied with his decision to keep working—and let some stool pigeon report *that* to the

Front Office. Zeidman, he was sure, would back him up if there was any criticism. And what was there to criticize? His job was to get the picture made and he was doing his job.

"Yeah," he said to Roy, "you better call it."

40

The commissary crew set up the meal on the serving tables but for once there wasn't the usual rush to line up: half the guys were still grouped around Dan, celebrating with him. Anything he said got a laugh if he wanted it to—as when, if someone asked him how he felt, he would say with great heartiness "Swell! . . ." then clap a hand to his back and stagger, pantomiming anguish.

Harold stood a little apart, watching: Well, they'd done the job. This was, in terms of their profession, a big job, a real one—and a triumph for both of them; he didn't like to think, now, of what would have happened if Dan had quit last night, the way he could have. Which was real, then—the way he, Harold, had felt about Dan last night, hating and fearing him, wanting to run away from him or, better, knock him to pieces, or the way he felt now, loaded with pride and yes, damn it, affection? He watched Dan swaggering and clowning, drinking in his new-found glory, milking it the way he milked everything, as if reality were not enough so that he had to have something bigger, better than reality. Big Hero, big phony . . .

(238)

Maybe the hate and the fear had been phony too, though come to think of it, Harold thought, they were spurs that he'd used to drive himself up and on that he didn't need any longer . . . Maybe we are all phonies; this crazy business is what makes us that way; we get so we can't tell what's real from what isn't, the disease I always told Nancy she had. When we manage somehow to do one strong, true thing we keep exaggerating it and selling it and messing with it until we stop believing in it ourselves. I believe in him, though; it took a long time but I believe now, and that belief's not going to change.

He pushed through the ring of guys around Dan.

"You big silly son-of-a-gun, are you ready to eat?" he said, and Dan grinned and said, "Well, I don't know why not."

"By God, listen to him," Sam La Brasca said. "Now he wants to eat—and an hour ago he acted like a corpse."

"Some corpse," Harold said, feeling the slight uncomfortable lull that followed Sam's words, Sam and the others instantly remembering that there was a real corpse with the company, not too far off.

He turned to Dan and put his hand out.

"Something I forgot to say, Dad . . . Thanks. You did a great job."

Dan gripped the offered hand, first lightly, then in a manner calculated to break every bone in it.

"No kidding. Do you think the film will be all right?"

"It will be the greatest. No way it can miss."

"Son, I—" Dan began. He put his arms around Harold and embraced him and the two pounded each other on the shoulder blades like a couple of Mexicans while the crew beamed. This father and son reunion might be an act, but if so it was the kind they liked.

"Let's go and eat," Dan said.

On Duart locations there was always one table set up with real napkins and good silverware for the stars and director and important guests, if any. Harold had intended having Dan and Jill served there but Jill had other ideas: she had filled four plates and put them on the grassy slope back of the commissary truck and there, with the rest of the company moving over to their neighborhood as the grubline moved past the serving table, the family banqueted in state. Here also, as they sat down, Harold said, "Dad, I want you to meet my wife, Nancy."

"Pleased to meet you," Dan said.

"Well, it's about time," Nancy said. "How do you do, Mr. Prader? I'm so proud to be in your family."

"I'm kind of proud myself," Dan said and then, big ham as usual, went over and kissed her.

Jill dabbed at her eyes. I'm getting old, she thought, if I bawl at little things like this. Then she looked carefully at each of the three faces closest to her and blew her nose. We're a family, she thought—a family at last. And she added, in her thoughts, thank you, little Virgin, for this too, for it is the best of all.

After lunch Jill went back to the hotel but Dan was enjoying himself too much to leave. He made several rides with the second unit under Roy's direction—Harold having gone in town to shoot some street stuff with Miranda and Rab. When he got some time off he went to the trailer and got out the bay horse, checking him for injuries: he felt pretty friendly to the bay horse and for something to do he rubbed him down with liniment, even though Dollarhyde had already done this once. "We made it, partner—we got out of that one," he told the bay, rubbing the liniment into him with his hands, especially around the pastern joints where he might have strained himself setting his body in the chute. It was getting toward five; soon, he knew, Roy would fold up the unit; he had made a mental note to talk to Roy about his check. If Duart issued the check for the stunt on payday, which was Monday, Jill would probably try to grab it: he must tell Roy not to let her have it, no matter what story she told. Not that he himself would waste it: most of it was going in the bank. But, hell: a little money in your pocket was all right. Not that he'd bet a horse or blow it on a dame, but there were a few more things at Gebbie's he still wanted. After that—who knew? Naturally, he'd drop in at *The Cinch* or *Bellyful:* there was nothing wrong with either spot, so let Jill scream her head off. Going to a place like that was not only a pleasure, it was an investment: you could shoot the breeze a while and get the word on what was going on. Have a few laughs. A man owed it to himself and what the hell, one thing led to another, and first thing you knew you had a hot tip on some studio call and then— socko!—you walked into another job.

41

Nancy lay on the hotel bed, watching the edge of the late afternoon sun on the sill below the drawn venetian blinds. The room was reasonably cool and Nancy felt the coolness flowing pleasantly against her from the sheets of the bed: she

sipped the drink Harold had made for her and listened to him
singing in the shower.

> *. . . dreaming of a star*
> *The nightingale tells his fairytale . . .*

Harold's vocal style in bathrooms was a Palmolive approxi-
mation of Nat King Cole: usually he sang "All the Things
You Are." She had never heard him do "Stardust" before;
in fact he had always said he hated the tune. I won't say
anything about it, though, she thought: whatever has happened to him now is good. It's not the time to kid him. She
reached over and set down her drink on the bed-table, twisting so as to see herself in the wall mirror opposite, her loins
pressed down into the bed and her head and shoulders
raised and pulled sideways; though the position was difficult she held it for almost a minute, giving her body that
intense attention which she brought to bear on no other subject. She was not dissatisfied with what she saw: she had lost
a little weight, not much but just enough those last days in
Los Angeles when she was so disturbed about her flirtation
with Freddy and everything. This was to the good, she felt, she
must not put it on again. And she was really still quite brown!
If there was one thing she liked and that looked well it was
to be brown all over, not with pieces of white on the most interesting parts of you like skin painted to look like clothes:
it was quite wonderful to have a place to sunbathe properly
and she thought with affection and anticipation of the house in
Bel-Air, closed but cared for, watered by the visiting gar-
dener, guarded at night by the Burns patrol, awaiting her return . . . the house and the hedged-off green box of the sun-
yard behind it.

Harold had turned off the shower. In a moment he came out
(242)

of the bathroom, still drying himself, making wet footprints on the rug. Inconsiderately he planted himself in front of the mirror to brush his hair: Nancy, with a sigh, settled back against the pillows.

He grinned at her from the mirror.

"That ocean is salty. I had salt all over me in cakes when I went to change my clothes—and no place to shower."

"I almost died when you went in after him."

"Somebody had to. It was me or Sam La Brasca and I was nearest, that's all."

"It was wonderful just the same," Nancy said.

Maybe that's what made the change in him, she thought— pulling Dan out. Maybe that evened up some old score between them.

"I'm glad it was you," she said sincerely.

He turned to look at her. He had fastened the towel around his waist like a sarong.

"So am I. He was great, wasn't he?"

"Simply great. I'm dying to see the rushes. I do hope they turn out well."

Wrong thing to say: with Harold, you had to conclude in advance they would turn out well, not just hope so.

"You can't very well go wrong, with three cameras," he said with a slight haughtiness. He made himself a drink and came over to the bed. She wriggled over to make room for him.

"What were you thinking about?" he asked.

"When?"

"Just now, when you came out. You were looking pretty solemn."

"Nothing."

"You wouldn't look like that if it was nothing . . ."

"I don't know. I was thinking it would be good to be home again. I want to sunbathe. And—everything . . ."

There was a slight pause; then he said, "You wouldn't have got much sunbathing in New York."

Nancy let the silence remain. She was not yet sure she wanted to talk about this.

"I'm afraid New York was a stupid idea," she said at length. You'll never know how stupid, she thought. She thought of the letter, which had grown out of this idea but had been even stupider, wondering again at her luck in having the bellboy deliver it to her. She had not trusted the torn pieces to the wastebasket; she had flushed them down the toilet.

"I never did know what put you up to it."

"It doesn't matter, does it?"

"Well, no. But still I'd like . . ."

She sat up, turning to face him.

"Harold," she said with much earnestness, "I don't think we . . . I think we'd be happier if we didn't probe and poke at each other all the time."

"Who's probing?"

"You. When you came out and asked me what I was thinking."

"You used to ask me what I was thinking about and I never minded," he said.

She sipped her drink, already regretting her slight outburst.

"I know I did," she said, "and I'm just liable to again. It was a stupid idea and I'm glad I gave it up. But you . . ."

"Go ahead."

"You just don't seem to understand how restless I felt sometimes, and . . ."

"Wait a minute. Sure, that's pretty obvious. Only—you

said, 'felt,' past tense—meaning you're not now?"

Suddenly she felt she could expose her secret thoughts to him—could do so fearlessly, as in their courting days, without feeling he would use the knowledge later as a weapon against her.

"I don't know. Maybe we grew up. Or you did, anyhow, I felt that today. We might make mistakes again, but we won't make the same ones over again."

And it is true, she said to herself. Christian couldn't have done what Harold did today. Christian had a hundred and fifty different selves inside him but he couldn't have taken a hundred and fifty people on a location, with all the pressures Harold had, and not go to pieces. Thinking about Christian made her defensive. On the trip from Los Angeles, she had prepared an elaborate defense of herself and Freddy, just in case Harold had heard about that lunch in Romanoff's: she had even considered making accusations against herself so that the defense could be used. Now to her surprise, Freddy was ignored and a new charge substituted, also by herself—this time the true one.

"You were always a little jealous of Christian. That was hard on both of us."

"Don't you think I had a right to be?"

Harold spoke softly, his tone revealing much that she had never fully understood: the agony of his long thoughts, his slow, bitter conclusion about all this.

She said, "I didn't want to be an actress because of Christian but because of me. I was alone, you left me alone. Christian was nothing compared to you. If he had been I would have done what those widows do in India, committed whatever they call it, burning themselves up."

"How do I know what they call it? Am I Indian?"

"Then why do you go around dressed like one?" she said, pulling the towel off his waist. "Now you look better."

"Suttee . . ."

"What?"

"The name for it—suttee."

"That's a name," she said. "But not the name for anything I'm interested in . . ."

"You're crazy."

"Am I? Are you sure I am?"

She caught sight of herself in the mirror, feeling the pleasure of her senses in what she was doing increased by having herself as spectator.

Harold caught her at this.

"Stop watching yourself," he said. "I'll tell you if the scene is okay."

"Oh, God," Nancy said, turning on her elbow, "why did I ever marry a director?"

42

It was seven P.M. Nancy and Harold lay in each other's arms; Dan, with Jill beside him, held court in the bar; Miranda was applying makeup to a black eye before going down to dinner—her first public appearance since her trouble with Jill. In his room on the top floor Rab O'Grady was doing setting up exercises while from down the hall came the pounding of a typewriter where Roy Sowells was getting out the next day's call-sheets. Dolores Lansing lay on her bed, her face pressed into the pillow and her muscular but handsome legs sprawled out; the toes stretched downward like a ballet dancer's. She felt more tired than she had after any day's work she could remember. To calm her nerves and regain inward poise she told herself, as she had many times before, that what happened on location any given day was that day's business, and should be forgotten when the day was over. But when would she have sense and strength enough to take this attitude? Some day, maybe, but not right now. Certainly not right now.

Downstairs, in the hotel's one public phone booth, Linc Hyman was trying to reach a Long Beach, California, number which the studio had told him was the number of Casey Sharpe's mother; the call was taking quite a while to put through but Linc did not mind the delay, it gave him more chance to think of what to say. He had had the same trouble in World War II, when as Captain Lincoln Hyman, H & S Co. 28 Inf., he had had to write the relatives of men killed in his command.

There just wasn't much that you could say. You couldn't tell a woman, sixty-eight or seventy years old, that there was a superstition in film business that when two men died in the industry there was likely to be a third death soon afterwards, and that the death this time just happened to be her son's. Such an explanation would hardly be much comfort to her: even if she understood she would probably tell you it was plain gobbledygook, which of course it was.

Night fell on the cliffs above the sea; the tough grass, filling with moisture, straightened where the wheels of the vehicles had mashed it down. All equipment used that day, including the wood from Dan's chute, had been removed when the company left. Soon there would be little proof that human beings had ever been there, except a piece of film showing a man and horse jumping from the cliffs into the sea—even this in a fashion would always be questionable, man and horse in the film being only shadows or dream-shapes and hence not proof of anything in the real world.

ABOUT THE AUTHOR

BEFORE TAKING UP *permanent residence in California some twenty years ago, Niven Busch worked in New York City, where he was Associate Editor of* Time *and a staff writer for* The New Yorker.

He lives on a combined cattle and fruit ranch near Hollister and takes maximum advantage of California's opportunities for outdoor living, with special emphasis on hunting, fishing, golf and swimming.

In the past, he has written two kinds of books: on the one hand, novels that aspired only to entertain (and did so with enormous success); on the other hand, a body of more serious and memorable work. To the latter category—which includes They Dream of Home, Day of the Conquerors *and* The Hate Merchant—*he adds* The Actor.